THE DUKE'S PROPOSAL FOR THE GOVERNESS

Eleanor Webster

MILLS & BOON

First published in Great Britain 2023
by Mills & Boon, an imprint of HarperCollins*Publishers* Ltd,
1 London Bridge Street, London, SE1 9GF

www.harpercollins.co.uk

HarperCollins*Publishers*, Macken House, 39/40 Mayor Street Upper, Dublin 1, D01 C9W8, Ireland

The Duke's Proposal for the Governess © 2023 Eleanor Webster

ISBN: 978-0-263-30537-1

09/23

This book is produced from independently certified FSC™ paper to ensure responsible forest management.
For more information visit: www.harpercollins.co.uk/green.

Printed and Bound in the UK using 100% Renewable Electricity at CPI Group (UK) Ltd, Croydon, CR0 4YY

Canada,
g footwear.
including a nasty
oved that her creative
through the written word.
pursuing a doctoral degree in
ogy, and holds an undergraduate degree in
ory and creative writing. She loves to use her
riting to explore her fascination with the past.

To family.

To my daughters, father and husband who provided
love, patience, encouragement and frequent meals
to sustain me during this undertaking.

To my father-in-law and mother-in-law,
who are my greatest fans.

To our family pets, who enhance our lives
with a pure and unconditional love.

To Milton, the hedgehog.

And lastly to Basil the dog.

This mischievous canine provided company
and inspiration throughout the creation
of this manuscript.

Prologue

'Mrs Harrington is desiring an audience,' Benton intoned from the library's threshold.

Lord Lansdowne, Duke of Elmsend, looked up at this unwarranted interruption. 'An audience? I am not the bloody Pope. And who the devil is Mrs Herring-whatever?'

'Mrs Harrington,' Benton repeated. 'A relative of your late mother's.'

'Indigent, I presume?'

'I couldn't say, my lord.'

'How many indigent relatives can one woman have?' he grumbled.

'I couldn't say, my lord.'

'And what can she possibly want with me? And don't say you couldn't say. Where did you put her?'

'In the drawing room, my lord.'

'Tell her I am indisposed.'

'Indeed, alcohol does give one a bad head,' Benton said, with that slight tsk of his tongue, well remembered from schoolboy scrapes and all too familiar of late.

Randolph looked up to the ceiling. Thankfully it was pleasantly blank. His mother had had an unfortunate predilection for cupids. Few rooms remained unscathed. 'Fine. I will see her if only to stop you from looking baleful because some long lost cousin is disappointed.'

'Your mother was a very kind woman, my lord. She believed in family, my lord.'

'Except her family seems unusually large,' Randolph said. 'And indigent.'

The bonnet fascinated.

Really such a bright thing should not be allowed within the presence of an individual indisposed. Truthfully it more closely resembled an orchard than any form of headgear. Or a vineyard. Or even a greengrocer. Perhaps Mrs Harrington aimed to be a greengrocer catering exotic fruits. Did greengrocers sell exotic fruits? Dolph was not well versed in greengrocers.

'Lord Lansdowne!' Mrs Harrington's trumpeting tones quite startled him from his reverie.

'Mrs Harrington,' he said, making his bow before seating himself opposite a middle-aged woman, her stout form encased in dark mourning, a sharp contrast to the bonnet.

'I am so delighted to meet you,' she continued. 'Likely your dear mother mentioned me to you. I am your cousin. From Harrogate.'

'Indeed,' he said. It was, after all, entirely possible. His mother had had a large family. Besides, agreement seemed considerably less effortful than contradiction. Truthfully, he'd paid limited attention to his mother's rambling discourse. He sighed. *Odd how something once irksome becomes touched with nostalgia when no longer possible.*

He pushed the thought away, shifting his gaze back to his company. 'So how may I assist or were you wishing merely to renew our kinship?' he asked, languidly stretching his long legs towards the fire.

Mrs Harrington shifted with a rustle of cloth as she leaned forward, still talking in tones too loud for the situation. He wondered if the absent Mr Harrington was deaf. 'Yes, well, you see, your mother was always so kind as to send us a Christmas greeting and a little something for my dear Lucinda. Such a kind woman. And so very sad about your father and brother. Indeed, we expressed our condolences. And she wrote back. Even in her time of grief. Anyhow, it all rather made us hope that, upon our arrival, in London that…that…well…she might be…be kind enough to introduce us and lend us…consequence…'

He stiffened. He hated the quick stab of pain. He

hated this vulnerability. 'Indeed, her death does rather curb that notion.'

'I was so distressed.' Mrs Harrington pressed her hands together. 'But by the time I heard the sad tidings, I had already arranged to let our house. Besides, I'd packed up everything. Anyhow, I came up with the notion that we should come to London and hope for the best.'

'The best?'

Mrs Harrington's broad, pleasant face flushed. 'Yes, well, you see, Mr Harrington is recently deceased but I set aside a small amount for my dear Lucinda's dowry. It is no great sum, but sufficient if we get the right introductions. So we hoped that we might prevail upon our kinship—'

Dolph blinked, his thick head making sense of this convoluted information with difficulty. 'You didn't think perhaps my sister might prove more able in this regard?'

'She has been consistently away,' his guest said.

She would. His sister did not believe in putting herself out for others, particularly those of a lower social status. 'Convenient,' he said. 'And how exactly are you related to my mother?'

'Her uncle was a second cousin to my mother. Or is it third? Or perhaps it was her—'

He waved a silencing hand. It did not matter. His mother had helped her every relation, no matter how distant the connection. She seemed incapable of turning away family as though her father's fiscal fortune made her indebted for ever to those still struggling.

His own father had despised the practice. But then his father had despised his mother. She'd had neither a title, land nor social graces. Indeed, the occasional flat Yorkshire vowel still habitually slid into her words.

But she was rich. And he was not.

Dolph drummed his fingers against the arm of the chair. The drumming made his head hurt. He stopped.

'I'm sure you would be entranced if you were to meet my daughter. She is quite lovely,' Mrs Harrington said, speaking more quickly as she warmed to her topic. 'Well brought up. Her artwork is delightful. And she speaks French. Such a musical language, I always think. Indeed, her governess was quite fluent.'

The innocuous words felt like the heavy scent of lavender, which still lingered in his mother's sitting room, hovering about her writing desk and in the cushions of the settee. His mother would talk like this when he'd first inherited the title. She'd describe some eligible young lady, eulogizing about a fine countenance, pleasant smile or an improbable musical talent.

He'd disliked those conversations as much as he disliked being the heir.

He stood, the movement abrupt. 'You must excuse me.'

'Yes, of course.' Hot colour flushed into the woman's cheeks and neck.

He was being rude. He hated bad manners. They demonstrated a lack of control and an unkindness too much like his father's.

He made his bow. 'It was delightful to meet you. Do leave Benton your card. I will, naturally, call on you later in the week.'

'We would be entranced—'

He rang the bell, craving the silent emptiness that he both sought and hated.

Chapter One

The brisk knocking made Abby jump. The Harringtons had seen few visitors since arriving in London and the timing was most inconvenient, given that everyone else was out.

Pushing aside her sewing with some reluctance, Abby crossed the small entrance way and swung open the door.

A gentleman stood on the threshold. The sheer size of him startled. It was not only his height, made more considerable by his Hessian boots, but also his breadth. The great cloak magnified this dimension so that he dominated the foyer—though, truthfully, this was no great feat given its minute proportions.

'Good d—' Abby spluttered before her words were interrupted by the thunder of Basil's paws. A second later, the dog's bulk struck her from behind so that she was catapulted against the visitor. For a suspended moment in time, she found herself flush to the great coat, inhaling a smoky, masculine scent. Instinctively, she raised her hand to his shoulder.

'Basil!' she gulped, pulling herself away and half falling down the steps. 'Stop him!'

She lunged forward as Basil reached the bottom step, in a headlong rush towards the street.

With surprisingly swift agility for one so large, the gentleman turned, stepping down the stairs and simultaneously grabbing the frayed rope. Basil jerked to an abrupt halt.

'Yours, I believe?' The gentleman handed over the rope.

'Thank you.' She took it, stepping back into the front entrance and pulling the animal close so that he now almost sat on her slippers. 'You must be Lord Lansdowne.'

'I am.'

'You had best come in,' she said.

Truthfully, she was not entirely happy to see him. More precisely, she was irritated. After a week, Mrs Harrington had all but given up any notion that Lord Lansdowne would visit or help with Lucy's debut, and Abby thought it better that way. Her father had wasted too much time in flights of fancy, hanging on to futile dreams.

Abby was determinedly practical.

She stepped further into the small entrance way, pulling at the obstreperous animal, who now seemed unwilling to shift his considerable bulk, leaning heavily against her legs. Lord Lansdowne followed. His presence gave her an odd feeling. His size seemed to completely fill the narrow hall, making it feel airless.

Although this, she reminded herself, was scientifically impossible. The hall, while small, was not of the dimension where one individual would completely fill the space. Indeed, it was more likely that she was experiencing this odd sensation because he was an unlikely visitor at number thirty-one.

To be sure, she did not know what sort of person would be a typical guest at number thirty-one. To date, the Harrington household had received no one.

'Shall I close the door?' Lord Lansdowne enquired, stepping into the hall.

'Yes, of course,' she said as she retreated, almost tripping over Basil.

'Go!' she admonished the unrepentant animal. 'You know perfectly well you should be in Iggy's bedchamber.'

Basil wagged his tail and, surprisingly, chose to obey, loping back up the stairs, his feet a retreating scrabble against the wood.

With that situation resolved, she turned back to take the visitor into the parlour. 'Mrs Harrington is out but you are welcome to wait.'

At its threshold she paused, glancing back at their

guest. Everything about the man seemed in stark contrast to the rented house. The tall collar of his shirt and expertly folded necktie spoke of an entitled sophistication, making the dull furnishing and paint all the more obvious.

His expression was politely bland as though determinedly oblivious to the chipped paint on the newel post, the threadbare rug or the myriad of other telltale signs which each spoke of financial distress.

His very politeness irked. He would say all the right things but do little. That was the way of gentlemen. She'd seen it in her father's parish, where the local landowners, the Ashleighs, would agree amicably to all manner of improvements for their tenants and then do precisely nothing.

Moreover, Lord Lansdowne was no minor landowner but a gentleman of the first order, a member of the ton.

He was exactly as Mrs Harrington had described.

Exactly what she had anticipated.

And feared.

'Lord Lansdowne, may I pose a question?'

He raised an eyebrow. His hair was dark, and the combination of an angular jaw and sharp cheekbones gave him a strong, uncompromising aspect.

She squared her shoulders. 'May I ask the purpose of your visit?'

* * *

Good heavens, polite society would make mince-meat out of her without a vast and immediate improvement of manners. Dolph studied Miss Harrington but found she was not much improved with this closer examination. Her style appeared limited and where her mother had enjoyed flamboyancy, this female appeared quite the opposite. She wore a plain grey dress with her brown hair unfashionably scraped back from a high forehead. Her brows were dark, straight and framing blue eyes, currently peering at him with disconcerting directness.

'That question would seem somewhat impertinent,' he said. The female required a set-down.

'My father would have advised against it,' she agreed equably.

'A gentleman of sense.'

'Not really. Quite the opposite. He merely believed in social niceties. I prefer blunt speech,' she said, her gaze still unwavering. Her eyes, he had to admit, were quite striking. They were large, framed by long lashes and of an intense blue, azure perhaps, which gave them a mesmeric quality, as though one might sink into their depths.

Her hair, while neither fashionable nor flattering, was thick and of a deep chestnut hue. Her face was heart shaped, her neck long and elegant, and her skin had that English-rose clarity.

Certainly, she was not beautiful in the typical sense and yet there was something about her.

'I am afraid,' he said, pulling his attention back to the conversation, 'that I have not been blunt for the better part of a decade. May we be seated or must one stand for such candour?'

He noted the slight stiffening of her shoulders but she complied, swinging open the door and moving forward with a brisk and purposeful step. Dolph shrugged off his great cloak, hanging it on the stand before following her into a small, somewhat dingy room. A lacklustre fire burned in the hearth. The furniture looked to be of good quality, and an attempt had been made to brighten the place with a vase of flowers placed on a side table.

'Sit, please.' She indicated a small settee as she sat on an upright chair close to the hearth, smoothing her skirts while eying him with the obvious expectation of a response.

He sat also. 'My visit has no ulterior motive. Mrs Harrington paid a call and I am merely returning the courtesy.'

Her forehead puckered with concentration. 'I know but I worry that Mrs Harrington will perceive a promise in what, for you, is merely courtesy.'

'A promise?'

She paused, running her fingers across the cloth of her skirt so that it rustled. 'Mrs Harrington is the most dreadful optimist. She is positive that you will help with Miss Harrington's come-out and that Miss Harrington will make a quite splendid match and all their problems will evaporate with fairy-tale rapidity.'

He stared for a second, his usually impeccable manners quite forgotten 'You are not Miss Harrington?'

'Good gracious, no.' A smile lit up her face. There was something arresting about the transformation. Perhaps it was the mercurial change or the flash of self-deprecating humour. 'I am Miss Carstens, the governess.'

It made sense. Why had he thought that Miss Harrington would open her own door? Certainly, this woman did not have the manners of a well brought up young lady, although she seemed an equally unlikely governess. She had an authority quite opposite to the sad, dutiful creatures lurking within his sister's house, who disappeared into the flock wallpaper.

'I apologize. I had not realized that Miss Harrington required a governess.'

The smile widened. 'Oh, no, she doesn't. Indeed, Lu— Miss Harrington is extremely accomplished. I look after her brother. Ignatius.' Miss Carstens glanced heavenward as though that occupation required considerable patience.

'Ah, the dog's owner,' he surmised.

'Indeed, Basil adores him and vice versa. Ignatius is quite miffed that he could not take him to the museum.'

'I can see that, um, Basil might not be the best guest at a museum.'

She chuckled, a rich, warm, spontaneous sound, again at odds with her somewhat stern demeanour.

'Gracious, no. It is hard enough to ensure that Ignatius doesn't create disaster, never mind the dog. Indeed, I would have gone to help except—' She paused, and her gaze flickered to a work basket, a piece of cloth resting on its top. 'I was otherwise occupied.'

So Miss Carstens was footman, lady's maid as well as governess, which, he supposed, underscored their lack of funds, bringing them back to the original topic, Miss Harrington's debut. He shifted. He had no wish to discuss an employer's finances with a governess and yet, given the persistent set of her jaw and that direct, unswerving gaze Miss Carstens was unlikely to let the matter rest.

'So what would you have me say to the Harringtons upon their return?' he asked.

She was silent for a moment. 'I ask only that you be honest.'

He startled. The suggestion that he might lack honesty rankled and was certainly quite different from the flowery speeches typical of most females. 'You think I am in the habit of lying, Miss Carstens?' He used a tone which would have made even Benton quake. Benton seldom quaked.

'I am not sufficiently acquainted to know your habits,' she said, without a quiver. 'However, most gentlemen do not like social discomfort and stretch the truth to avoid it.'

She was disconcertingly correct, which also irked. 'You are well acquainted with gentlemen?' he asked, seeking to discompose.

'No, I am better acquainted with their tenants and prefer their blunt honesty. I found the most humble farmer more likely to follow through on their obligations than landlords with considerably more resources at their disposal.'

'Right,' he said, finding himself unusually nonplussed. 'So, given the disadvantage of my birth, have you any theories on what form this mendacity might take?'

To his surprise, she nodded briskly. 'You have a sister, Lady Stanhope. Mrs Harrington paid her several calls but she was unavailable. Which was rather convenient. I mean convenient for her but not for Mrs Harrington. Likely, you will make a vague suggestion that you could entice Lady Stanhope to include Miss Harrington with her own daughter's come-out.'

Randolph felt his jaw slacken as this had been entirely his plan. Indeed, he saw no reason why Madeleine should not be required to deal with their mother's indigent relatives.

'It does not seem entirely out of the question,' he said somewhat lamely.

'Except it will not do. Miss Harrington is too pretty. She is shy at first but, once comfortable, is engaging. No mother wishes to include an individual who might detract attention from their offspring.'

He gave a spontaneous bark of laughter. 'You really do believe in blunt speech.'

'It saves time.' A smile lightened her serious expression again, robbing these words of severity.

'You should laugh more often. You are quite comely.'

She bit her lip, flushing. Her confusion was both unexpected and disarming. 'Lord Lansdowne, I do not think such a comment appropriate.'

'I was merely practising,' he said.

'What?'

'Blunt speech.'

She flushed further, retorting, 'You were practising flummery, my lord.'

'Most women like flummery.'

'Then you must be making the acquaintance of quite the wrong type of woman.'

'Indubitably,' he said.

* * *

His heavy emphasis on this last word and the twist of his lips were discombobulating.

Indeed, Abby found herself again with that peculiar feeling of being bereft of air. She attempted to calm herself by focusing on the immediate surroundings, in particular a mark on the window currently highlighted by a ray of winter sunshine.

This did not prove helpful. Nor was she able to pay attention to the drab wallpaper. She found herself drawn instead to the sculpted nature of his mouth, the strength of his jawline, a single dimple on his left cheek, visible only when he smiled, and grey eyes slightly touched with green.

There was an intensity and intelligence to his gaze, she was thinking, just as a volley of barks disturbed the quiet, interrupting her rumination.

She exhaled with uncharacteristic relief. She knew herself to be usually unflappable. She had debated theology with her father, politics with Miss Brownlee and listened to all manner of ailments from parishioners—some rather personal in nature. But even Mr Edmunds's too frequent boils had not made her stomach feel so odd or her mind so skittish.

'That must be Mrs Harrington. Returned from the museum,' she said somewhat unnecessarily as Mrs Harrington and Lucy had both pushed open the door, entering with a rush of apologetic greetings.

'Good gracious, Lord Lansdowne! I am so delighted to see you and downcast that I was not here to greet you in person,' Mrs Harrington said, her expression both regretful but alight with almost schoolgirl excitement. 'Indeed, I would not have gone out, had I known you intended to visit. I am glad Miss Carstens was here, although I perceive that you have not offered His Lordship any refreshments? Good gracious, he will be parched. What will he thin—'

Her words were interrupted as Iggy and Basil blasted into the room. The latter circled the couch and, moved by apparently wild euphoria, grabbed a pillow, shaking it as he might a rat.

'Ignatius!' Mrs Harrington said, raising her voice to be audible above the racket of barks. 'For goodness' sake, do get that dreadful dog out of here. What will His Lordship think?'

'He isn't dreadful,' Iggy said, his face set in the mulish lines typical of a tired nine-year-old. 'He is very clever. He can catch rats and all sorts.'

Mrs Harrington frowned even more ferociously. 'We do not speak of such things.'

'Don't see why not. House is riddled with 'em! And outside, in the alley and in the dust—'

'Ig-na-tius!' Mrs Harrington repeated, heavy emphasis on every syllable.

Abby stood. She should intervene if only to save Mrs Harrington's vocal cords. 'I will take Basil to the kitchen. Mrs Fred might have returned and, hopefully, can find him something more satisfying than our furnishings.'

'Yes, and do organize tea, there's a love,' Mrs Harrington said with enthusiasm. 'There is nothing like looking at old bits and bobs to build up a thirst. And I am certain that Lord Lansdowne would love a cup of tea.'

Abby frowned, glancing towards this gentleman. 'Likely, he is too busy and just wishes a quick chat.'

However, far from taking the hint, that irritating man stretched his long legs towards the fire and, with an annoying quirk of his eyebrows, a wry twist of sculpted lips and a flash of that single dimple, turned back to Mrs Harrington. 'Not at all. Tea with relatives is always a delight.'

Abby marched towards the kitchen. She was aware of a breathlessness, which could not be explained by exertion. From behind, she heard the scuffle of Iggy's footsteps, muted by the laughter and merriment still audible from the parlour.

Bother.

The man was everything she disliked about the aristocracy. He had that nonchalant confidence and self-assurance, born with the innate knowledge that he was superior and need do nothing more meritorious than exist.

Miss Brownlee had hated that. Miss Brownlee had been her teacher and held unfashionable beliefs, daring to suggest that a person's worth might not depend on wealth, gender or nationality but merely because they were people, humans, individuals.

Miss Brownlee would have taken snuff from her tiny snuffbox and questioned why the Duke of Elmsend would bother with them. She firmly believed that those with power seldom bothered about those lacking power without an ulterior motive.

Moreover, there was something about Lord Lansdowne which reminded her of the Ashleighs: his easy manners, style and wit, which seemed less about humour and more about making light of everything.

'Do come along!' she said irritably.

Iggy had now stopped his slow scuffle only to hop, peg legged, along the passageway. 'I'm pretending that I lost my leg. Like a pirate. They often don't have legs.'

'Perhaps you could have a miraculous recovery before we get to the kitchen stairs?'

'Um…' Iggy frowned, before beaming with sudden enthusiasm. 'That is a wonderful idea. I could invent something that would work better than a crutch. Maybe it could move like a normal leg. With a joint and stuff. And I would make money. I am certain there are many people who would like new legs. Or better ones than their old ones. Mother said that our cousin's father or grandfather created something.'

'Grandfather. And nothing to do with legs. Weaving, I think. Lord Lansdowne's grandfather made a machine,' Abby said abstractedly, as they pushed through the baize door. Indeed, they still spoke of him in Harrogate with the transparent hope that his success might make their own more probable.

'Do you think Lord Lansdowne would know about it? Maybe he inherited a model or the design. Most inventors create models, you know.'

'I have no idea but please do not pester His Lordship with questions,' Abby said, stepping with some relief into the kitchen. She adored Iggy and Basil but both could be exhausting.

Although partially below ground, the kitchen was quite her favourite place in the house. It smelled of cake and spice. The fire crackled while late-afternoon sun shone through two high windows, casting an amber mosaic onto the floor.

Mrs Fred glanced up, her smile welcoming. Abby had known Mr and Mrs Fred for ever. During her mother's long illness, she would often hover within the warm, comforting confines of the Harrington kitchen with Lucy.

'You'll be wanting tea, I reckon,' Mrs Fred said now, turning towards Abby while simultaneously putting away the tea towel and reaching for a tray.

Mrs Fred firmly believed tea solved any domestic or national emergency. 'Fortuitously, I just made a sponge. I had that feeling I should bake today, don't you know? Seemed like my old aunt Mathilda was at my ear, urging me on, as it were. And here we have a fancy gentleman coming to call.'

'Humph!' Abby said as she picked up the copper kettle and marched into the scullery. 'If your old aunt Mathilda was planning a ghostly visitation, she'd have done better to scare the man into next week.'

'Oh, aye, and what's got you in a tizzy? You do not like the gentleman?'

'I do not know the gentleman,' Abby said. 'And have little interest in furthering the acquaintance. I greatly fear he will fill Mrs Harrington's ear with bafflegab. And she will spend money on dresses and flimflam and poor Lucy will be sat here without an invite. It would be better to go back to Harrogate. Mrs Harrington has many friends who would make them welcome, their money would stretch further and Lucy would feel less shy. The idea to come to London was daft enough when Lady Lansdowne was alive or would have merit if her daughter had an interest in our acquaintance. However, Lady Lansdowne is dead and Lady Stanhope determinedly away.'

'At least Lord Lansdowne returned Mrs Harrington's call.'

Abby rolled her eyes. 'The sister is more honest.'

Mrs Fred laughed. 'Or merely rude. You cannot judge every British peer based on the Ashleighs, who are, I admit, sadly deficient as landowners. However, we can't be judging the entire world by them.'

'I'm not. Only people of aristocratic birth,' Abby retorted as she took out the cups and saucers. Her father had been the eternal optimist. As a second son, he had chosen the church over the military, largely because he disliked killing and enjoyed oration. However, despite the weekly opportunity for bombastic oration, her father had not enjoyed other aspects of the role. Boredom led to behaviour ill becoming of a vicar, and her mother had spent too much of her short life trying to curtail his drinking, gambling and a love of fast horses.

'I just don't want Mrs Harrington or Lucy to get their hopes up,' she said.

Mrs Fred patted her shoulder. 'But a body has to hope.'

'If Father had spent less time "hoping" with Lord Ashleigh, it would have been better for all.'

Her father had always been convinced that the next hand, dice roll or race would provide financial redemption.

It never had.

'You know it wasn't entirely Lord Ashleigh's fault that your father met with an accident,' Mrs Fred said gently, jerking Abby's mind back from the past and into the familiar kitchen.

Abby swallowed, hiding that familiar stab of pain with a shrug. 'Lord Ashleigh shot the rifle that caused Jester to bolt. Indeed, the only time Lord Ashleigh showed even a smidgen of interest in the estate was when he wanted to host a hunting party or country weekend.'

Idly, she rubbed the rim of her cup so that it made a tiny whine under her finger. She grieved not only for her father but for her home, the tenants, the tiny schoolroom where she'd provided some basic instruction and those intangibles that Miss Brownlee used to talk about...purpose, belonging, independence and autonomy.

'Anyhow,' she said more briskly. 'My feeling about Lord Lansdowne has nothing to do with Lord Ashleigh, my father or his accident. I merely dislike the man. Besides, even if he were a veritable paragon, without a female sponsor, it makes more sense for Mrs Harrington and Lucy to go back to Harrogate. It would be the more prudent option.'

Mrs Fred shook her head. 'Sometimes, I think you were born with an old head on your shoulders.'

If this were so, it was through necessity, she thought. Her mother had died before she was even an adolescent.

'You don't need to worry about money,' Iggy announced, startling them both with his typical rapid-fire burst of speech. 'I am going to create a leg.'

'A what now?' Mrs Fred questioned with understandable surprise. 'Not in my kitchen you're not. And mind that dog. He looks to be sniffing after my lamb chops.'

Abby pulled Basil away.

'As for you, Miss Abigail,' Mrs Fred said, as she poured piping hot water onto the tea leaves, 'Mrs Harrington just wants to give Miss Lucy the best chance of happiness.'

'No doubt, except I question whether happiness will be found in a debtor's prison,' Abby muttered.

Miss Carstens reappeared, carrying a tray, with the boy trailing after her. Thankfully the dog was conspicuous by his absence. Dolph liked dogs well enough but Basil seemed particularly boisterous and not well suited to the drawing room.

Even before Miss Carstens sat down, Ignatius flung himself onto the settee, busying himself with the close examination of his knee and ankle, as though having a sudden fascination with his extremities.

'Iggy, you didn't want to have tea with Mrs Fred?' his mother asked, her tone hopeful.

'There's only one sponge cake,' the boy said, with indisputable logic.

Dolph had paid Ignatius little attention earlier but now turned his gaze on him. He could not be older than ten. His complexion was similar to that of his sister, fair and pale, but while she seemed quiet, bordering on dull, the boy dominated the room in a way unusual for any child.

As though aware of Dolph's observation, Ignatius turned, fixing his visitor with a scrutinizing gaze. 'They said London was interesting. I do not find it so.' He spoke in an abrupt, somewhat accusatory manner, his words clumped together in staccato bursts of speech.

'Really?' Dolph said. 'You must not have gone to the appropriate places? Most people find it quite fascinating.'

Iggy scrunched up his face. 'I went to the museum. It was too full of old things.'

'Museums generally are,' His Lordship said amicably.

'And not even interesting old things. Marble heads.'

'May I ask what sort of old things interest you?'

'I'm not really keen on old things. I like new things.'

'Indeed, and what sort of new things are you keen on?' Dolph questioned.

Iggy cocked his head towards him, eyes squinting as though unsure Dolph merited the effort of a serious response. 'Have you heard of Trevithick's Puffer?'

'Indeed,' Dolph said. 'Although I am not certain if it counts as "new" given that it is now defunct.'

Iggy let his foot drop to the floor with a slight thwack. 'You've heard of it?' he asked, new respect visible in his expression.

'A mechanized vehicle until its unfortunate demise.'

'True, 'cept it did not de-whatever. It blew up.'

'My mistake. Pray continue. Tell me all about this mechanical marvel.'

''xactly!' Ignatius said, with a wide grin. 'That is what Miss Carstens calls it. A marvel! It operated on steam like a gigantic teakettle.'

'You seem well informed.'

'Miss Carstens knows that stuff,' Ignatius said magnanimously, glancing towards Miss Carstens's rather firm features.

'Miss Carstens is full of surprises.'

'Yes, she is all right for a girl. And better than the tutor I had. I didn't like him. He didn't like me either, so he left. Miss Carstens let me make a butter churn using a water wheel. Only it flooded the dairy. Dora was surprised. And cross. She was the maid.'

'Ignatius,' Miss Carstens said, her tone echoing his mother's earlier admonishment.

'Well, she was! She said that you were encouraging my bad habits. And then Lucy said it wasn't ladylike and that you should teach me French, except I don't like French. I am more interested in pressurized steam.'

'Due to its more explosive nature, I presume,' Miss Carstens said drily.

'Have you heard of the Catch Me Who Can?' Iggy asked Dolph, ignoring this last comment.

'A locomotive on which one can ride which runs on a circular track in Bloomsbury at Torrington Square,' Dolph said and was rewarded again by a look of surprised respect.

'Miss Carstens said as how I could see it even if we do not have the money to ride on it,' Ignatius said. 'It costs a shilling.'

'Ignatius!' his mother said in a tone of acute suffering.

'Well, we don't. On account of Father leaving a lot of debts. But Miss Carstens said as how it would be a shame to come to London and not.'

'Miss Carstens, are you also interested in Trevithick?' Dolph asked, quickly interrupting his young host before he could further embarrass his mother.

She met his gaze, her surprisingly full lips twisting into a slight smile. He noted an expression in her rather fine eyes which suggested that she was not completely bereft of humour. 'No, James Watt's machine has more merit. It is less apt to blow up.'

Dolph felt his jaw slacken. He had meant to tease and was, instead, teased. 'We should go,' he said with an impulsivity unusual to him. 'I mean to Torrington Square. All of us.'

Ignatius gave a whoop and, for a brief instant, Miss Carstens leaned forward, an expression of eagerness flickering across her features. Then, with obvious effort, she checked herself.

'Ignatius, we do not want to inconvenience His Lordship,' she said.

'I never allow people to inconvenience me.' He stretched his long legs lazily towards the fire. 'My life's mission, so to speak.'

Her eyebrows pulled together. She was intriguing. A bluestocking, no doubt, but intriguing, nonetheless.

'It might prove overstimulating,' she said, glancing towards the excited boy with a tiny disapproving tsk as she pressed her full, well-shaped lips together.

'Ah, we definitely wouldn't wish you to become "overstimulated", Miss Carstens.'

'My concern is not for myself.' He noted a slight flushing along her cheekbones and it amused him that she had understood his double entendre.

'She worries about Lucy,' Ignatius explained, his tone heavy with disgust. 'She faints, you know. She fainted when I blew up the chicken coop.'

'Lud, country life sounds so exciting. I doubt our

city chicken coops ever explode,' Dolph said. 'Fortuitously, there are no chicken coops in Torrington Square so we should be safe. Indeed, it is quite fashionable. Only last week, the Regent himself went, I believe.'

This last statement had an immediate effect on Mrs Harrington. Previously, she had been focused exclusively on the teacups and sponge. Now, she straightened with a rustle of stiff sateen as she looked at him with an expression of obvious eagerness.

'Well, if the Prince Regent is impressed, perhaps we are being too cautious,' she said in her rather loud tones. 'Indeed, Miss Carstens, you have said that Ignatius has a lively mind and the best thing would be to keep him occupied and prevent boredom.'

'Oh, it would be just the thing for my relative's lively mind,' Dolph said.

'Thank you!' Ignatius said, his tone one of hero worship. 'Nobody understands the possible importance of Trevithick's machine. I would love to make something like Trevithick. If I don't make a leg. Which would also be interesting.'

'And potentially less likely to blow up,' Miss Carstens said.

Chapter Two

Two days later, Dolph honoured his impulsive offer
and headed to Wimpole Street in an unusually opti-
mistic mood. Indeed, he was just thinking that his
head did not hurt as much as was typical when his
vehicle pulled to a sudden, jarring stop.

He peered outside. An unconscionable racket was
coming from in front of the vehicle, shouting, barking and a general hullabaloo. A small but excitable
group had gathered, blocking the street ahead. At its
centre, he noted a large middle-aged lady, shaking
her parasol and in considerable distress.

Before he could take in further details, his view
was obstructed by the sudden appearance of his
groom's round, somewhat cherubic face at the carriage window. 'So sorry, my lord. Should I try to
disperse the group, my lord?'

'We may have encountered a force of nature beyond even your ability to control, Martin,' Dolph

said. 'I will get out and investigate the situation. Stay with the horses.'

Uncoiling his large frame, Dolph exited onto the street, carefully manoeuvring around the large, dirty puddle which threatened his Hessians. From this location he could stare over the shoulders of two burly onlookers.

The irate parasol lady stood beside a gentleman whose air of obsequious self-importance suggested a role as a minor bureaucrat. His only other notable feature, aside from rather lush side whiskers, was a rip in his waistcoat, incongruent with the rest of his meticulous appearance.

Opposite this duo and with her back to him, he noted a woman wresting a large animal, now caked in mud. Even though he could only see her rear, Dolph felt a tingle of recognition. This was intensified by her voice, clearly audible, if somewhat breathless from her exertion.

'Mrs Pollock, if you would stop waving the parasol, I am certain he would calm down! Likely he thinks it is a battering ram or something.'

'It is a parasol straight from Paris,' the middle-aged lady said.

'Well, he is a dog and hardly acquainted with French fashions!'

Dolph felt a ripple of mirth. Yes, the clipped tones were recognizable…the governess, Miss Carstens.

The lady shook the parasol again. 'I have put up with that animal digging at my roses, howling at the moon and causing all manner of mayhem for at least two weeks. It is more than a body can bear, which is why I called the magistrate. And now look how that dreadful creature has attacked the poor gentleman.'

She pointed dramatically towards the ripped waistcoat to emphasize her point.

'The "poor gentleman" attempted to sit on him. Besides, he is unused to the city and is homesick,' Miss Carstens said.

'Homesick? Homesick?' the lady expostulated, her voice rising an octave. 'His immediate execution will solve any homesickness!'

'Absolutely not! No! I will not allow it!' Miss Carstens straightened, allowing the animal greater movement, which he instantly used in an eager lunge towards the parasol.

'Fortunately, that is not your decision. That is for the magistrate to decide,' the other lady said, her tones haughty.

The magistrate stepped forward, patting his waistcoat and eyeing the dog with disapproval. 'I must agree with Mrs Pollock. It is a dangerous animal and should not be within city limits. I will arrange for its immediate destruction.'

At his words, the two burly individuals in front

of Dolph stepped forward, striding towards Miss Carstens and the dog with obvious intent.

Lord Lansdowne had been previously quite amused by the spectacle but now found himself moved to intervene, his fondness for animals surpassing his usual ennui. Besides, the boy, Ignatius, had that certain brand of oddness which likely made the company of animals preferable to people.

Dolph was about to say something when he was arrested by Miss Carstens's clear tones. 'I suggest that you do not hurt this animal until you have spoken to Lord Lansdowne!'

'Lord Lansdowne? Why would he care?' the magistrate asked.

Dolph was quite curious to hear the answer.

'It is his dog,' Miss Carstens said.

Dolph had not realized he had acquired an animal and felt certain he would have chosen one with better manners and less mud.

'Nonsense! His Lordship would not give house room to such a mutt and a distempered one at that,' Mrs Pollock said. She had a point.

Miss Carstens, however, gave a graceful shrug, or as graceful as could be managed with the dog still pulling with obvious intent to harm the parasol, if not the woman.

'Lord Lansdowne assured me that Basil is purebred. Indeed, quite exotic, a Belgian hunting dog and valuable. Mrs Harrington is Lord Lansdowne's cousin and we are obliging him by looking after the animal,' she said.

'Fiddlesticks. The entire household is irregular. Lord Lansdowne likely would have nothing to do with them and I doubt he has even met the creature.'

Dolph stepped forward.

At his movement, everyone's gaze turned to him with a precise synchronicity of motion. The magistrate opened and then closed his mouth. Mrs Pollock remained fortuitously bereft of speech while Miss Carstens's eyes widened.

Abby stared as Lord Lansdowne bowed, a sweeping, dramatic gesture.

'I am afraid I have not made your acquaintance,' he said to Mrs Pollock, who was thankfully no longer brandishing the parasol.

'This is Mrs Pollock,' Abby said, hastily recovering her wits and manners. 'Our neighbour. And the magistrate.'

'It is a pleasure to make your acquaintance, Mrs Pollock. I am Lord Lansdowne. You seem in some distress. May I be of any assistance?' Dolph smiled engagingly, a dark lock of hair falling into his eyes, out of place from his low bow.

'I...oh...' Mrs Pollock sputtered. 'I had not realized that this animal was yours and from Belgium.'

'My dear lady, I am afraid you are mistaken—'

Abby's hand tightened against the dog's rope. Her stomach twisted into a sickening knot. For some reason, she had believed Lord Lansdowne would support the story, if only to alleviate his own boredom.

'Lord Lans—' she began.

'He is from the Balkans,' Lord Lansdowne continued. 'Not Belgium. To be completely honest. And I have been recently advised that women admire honesty.'

She caught his gaze and saw the wry twist of his lips, a mix of smirk and smile. She had never encountered a member of the nobility with a sense of humour and now did not know whether to be irritated or disarmed, to laugh or take up the parasol against him.

Mrs Pollock, however, appeared entirely enraptured. 'My lord, you are too kind. And really, it is no great matter. I am likely making too much of such a small incident. A mountain out of a mole hill,' she said, tripping over her words in her eagerness to appease.

'Indeed, you have had great patience with my dog's shenanigans, and I can only beg your forgiveness that I have not instructed dear Bruno with better manners. Please do not punish him for my sins.'

A bit over the top, Abby thought. And Bruno? *Bruno?*

Bruno sounded like a disgraced Italian opera singer. Fortunately, Mrs Pollock was oblivious to any inconsistency, allowing Lord Lansdowne to bend over her hand while assuring him again that the matter was of no consequence.

'There is, however, the issue of my waistcoat,' the magistrate said, somewhat huffily, less disarmed by His Lordship.

'Absolutely.' Lord Lansdowne straightened. 'Please, allow me to compensate you for any damage to your property or your person. Give me your card and I will make the issue my first priority. Or the first priority for my secretary.'

Apparently mollified, the magistrate handed over his card, after retrieving it from his mistreated waistcoat. He then left, followed by the two burly dog catchers.

After a final farewell from His Lordship, Mrs Pollock also turned, retreating towards her house. The small crowd, surmising that there was nothing more to be seen, also dispersed and Abby found herself standing in the street beside His Lordship while Basil, exhausted by his near-death experience, sat docilely upon the cobbles.

'Thank goodness,' she whispered as the front door shut behind Mrs Pollock. 'And his name is Basil.'

Lord Lansdowne shrugged. 'Who names a dog after a spice? They don't even like spice. Besides, my error was likely due to a crisis of conscience in participating in such a bamboozle.'

'I am certain that your conscience is quite fine,' Abby retorted. 'However, I will concede that I sound ungrateful and I should thank you.'

'*Shoulds* are somewhat like castor oil for the digestion.' He smiled. The lock of hair still hung forward, grazing his eyebrows. That dishevelled lock gave him a younger demeanour, at odds with the tired worldliness that otherwise seemed to define his character.

'It is true *to dos* are seldom pleasant but I am sincere. I truly I thank you.'

'I was delighted to help. I always enjoy thwarting pompous bureaucrats, particularly those with side whiskers.'

Abby laughed. 'You actually do have a sense of humour.'

'I find it an absolute necessity. In fact, the episode has me intrigued. It suggests that you may be less circumspect than I had thought,' he said.

Circumspect!

Circumspect— She had never thought of herself as circumspect. Sensible or blunt maybe but *circumspect*? It seemed too close to dull. And, for some reason, she did not want Lord Lansdowne to think her dull.

Did the fact that she disliked tea parties, chit-chat

and impractical bonnets make her dull? After all, she and Miss Brownlee had written letters to Wilberforce and others espousing votes for women and decrying Britain's slave trade. Indeed, she'd even attended a meeting to debate such issues.

Such opinions were hardly *circumspect*, although she doubted whether they would be much favoured by Lord Lansdowne and his ilk.

Intelligent women with opinions were seldom admired by men with power. Writing pretty thank-you notes and invitations was applauded but trying to improve education or decrease injustice, not so much.

'B-a-s-i-l!' The long screech cut across the now quiet street, casting aside her introspection as Iggy bolted down the front stairs, throwing himself on Basil.

Mrs Harrington and Lucy followed more sedately.

'Lord Lansdowne,' Mrs Harrington said, her forehead puckered in worry. 'Good heavens, you must think that we are in perpetual chaos. Miss Carstens, I am so relieved you were able to negotiate the dog's release. I do not know how you managed as Mrs Pollock seemed so irate. Indeed, I am so thankful that Ignatius was in the kitchen and unaware of the situation. Otherwise I do not know what would have happened.

I'd have killed 'em. Hung, drawn and quartered,' Iggy stated with bloodthirsty pride.

'Good gracious, that is a somewhat violent solution,' Lord Lansdowne said.

Iggy nodded, still hugging Basil, who, unhappy with the tight squeeze, made grumbling noises into his whiskers. 'They were lucky Miss Carstens was there and not me.'

'Indeed,' Lord Lansdowne agreed.

'We have Lord Lansdowne to thank for today's happy resolution,' Abby said.

'Apparently Basil is an exotic breed for which I have a great fondness,' His Lordship announced.

'Really? But I rescued Basil from the pond when Mr Motham wanted to drown him,' Iggy said.

'Apparently, Mr Motham did not realize he had acquired a rare breed from… Belgium?' Lord Lansdowne said, humour lacing his tone.

'The Balkans.' Abby met his gaze and found herself smiling back in a shared appreciation of the farcical melodrama.

'You should definitely smile more often,' he said, then closed his mouth rather firmly as though his own words had surprised him.

She flushed and the very fact that she had now taken to blushing like a schoolgirl further irritated her so that she frowned with some ire at Ignatius. 'Please get up. You are almost sitting in a puddle. And we are causing a spectacle. Take Basil to Mrs Fred in the kitchen.

'But—' Iggy started.

'No argument. And perhaps you could apply your inventive mind to determining how to ensure that he does not escape again. He really cannot make a diet of other people's roses without consequence.'

'Indeed, as I am uncertain that even my charm could save him if he were to again imperil Mrs Pollock's flowers,' Lord Lansdowne said, with another wry smile.

The statement added further colour to Abby's cheeks, increasing her irritation.

She did not know what bothered her more, this ludicrously sudden blushing or the obvious truth that Basil could eat every rose in London and Lord Lansdowne would charm his way out of it.

It took at least another half hour before they were ready to leave. Abby sent Ignatius to his bedchamber to change while she accompanied Lucy to find a cold compress to calm her features, still flushed from the excitement and anxiety of the recent debacle.

Eventually, they were ready, and again trooped out of number thirty-one towards the crested carriage. Abby felt a peculiar sensation in her stomach, a fluttery feeling like a heat haze on a hot summer day. It was, she surmised, a reaction to the altercation with Mrs Pollock or the eggs at breakfast.

A footman opened the door and they clambered

into the coach. Ignatius sat against the window, pressing his face to the glass, unwilling to miss a moment. Mrs Harrington and Lucy sat opposite while Abby was squished between Ignatius and Lord Lansdowne.

The crush was uncomfortable—not physically uncomfortable, as the coach was spacious and well sprung, but disconcertingly uncomfortable. For an unfathomable reason she was aware of his long legs quite close to her own, the long lean fingers splayed against the cloth of his trousers and that, when he moved, she could discern the muscles of his thighs.

Moreover, she knew that thoughts about thighs or muscles were likely inappropriate and, more importantly, not typical for her.

Nor was it helpful that Iggy's constant bouncing made the cushions shift, which, combined with the carriage's movement, made her greatly fear she would be pushed against His Lordship.

'Ignatius, must you bob about so much? I am certain you will quite wear out His Lordship's springs,' Abby said with unusual irritation

'He is so excited,' his mother said both fondly and unnecessarily. 'I am myself. It is quite a fashionable event and thrilling. I am uncertain if I will feel strong enough to ride. Indeed, I rather fear I will faint.'

'Me too,' Miss Harrington, in her soft shy tones.

'Whether you choose to ride is entirely optional,' Lord Lansdowne said languidly.

'But you will be a ninnyhammer if you do not,' Ignatius added, dragging his attention from the scenery for sufficient time to glare with contempt at his sister.

Her father would have ridden, Abby thought. He had loved invention and anything new or tinged with the making of adventure. It was as though he was forever searching for an antidote to the tedium of his position.

Her mother would not have ridden, even when healthy. She would have worried that it was unconventional and might cause comment. Her mother had lived a life restricted by a need for propriety, as though, by following all social edicts, she could somehow compensate for her husband's love of cards.

Besides, she had had been more rooted within the practical, saying that sufficient accident and illness occurred without actively seeking either.

And Miss Brownlee… Abby smiled at her memory. Miss Brownlee would have ridden. She would have ridden not for the excitement but for the experience. Human ingenuity had fascinated her. She'd once said that if humans could cross vast oceans, there was no reason why they might not fly through the sky or frequent the moon.

'I think,' she said to no one in particular, 'I would regret choosing not to ride.'

Glancing sideways, Dolph noted that Miss Carstens had a wistful, almost dreamy expression. Dreaminess was something he had not anticipated. She seemed to have an eminently practical disposition.

'And why would you choose to ride, Miss Carstens?' he asked with genuine curiosity.

'It seems like the dawning of a new era. Heralding change.'

'Most people do not like change. You do?'

'If the change leads to improvement,' she said. 'Besides, it matters little whether I like it or not. It will happen.'

'Nothing is permanent except change.'

'Heraclitus,' Abby added immediately.

'You are well read. Your father was a scholar?'

'Yes, he had a fine library. I also had a friend, a teacher, who read a lot.'

'That was Miss Brownlee. She threw an apple at me,' Iggy announced.

'Like as not because you were scrambling up her apple tree,' his mother said. She added by way of explanation, 'Miss Brownlee was a lady of independent means and very intelligent but a little odd. She was too old to teach regularly at the school. However, she certainly helped the girls to become proficient in Latin, Greek and all manner of other subjects.'

'Miss Brownlee didn't teach me. She said she wouldn't have the patience. Maybe that was why she threw the apple. She also used to ride horses astride,' Iggy added.

'She rode astride because it is more sensible, comfortable and safer,' Miss Carstens explained. 'I liked that about her. She cared little about the opinions of others.'

'Then perhaps she was not human,' Dolph said softly, more to himself, because it seemed to him that every human cared what people thought.

Miss Carstens glanced at him. 'You think we are destined to care about the judgements of others?'

'We seek approval or belonging,' he said.

Their gazes met. He was struck again by the intelligence of her blue gaze and a feeling that she could see under the facade of the sophisticated gentleman, a sensation which made him feel oddly vulnerable.

He turned quickly to Iggy. 'So if this Miss Brownlee did not teach you, who did?'

'Miss Carstens now. Before that a tutor and the vicar. I did not like the tutor but the vicar was fine. He was not boring,' Iggy said. 'He was interested in all sorts of things. And horses. And galloping. Fast.'

'Ignatius! We don't speak of that,' Mrs Harrington said reprovingly.

'You see, he wasn't too successful in the galloping department. He met with an accident,' Miss Carstens said, the words abrupt and threaded with pain.

'I'm sorry,' Dolph said.

'It was some time ago.'

'Five months,' Ignatius said.

Miss Carstens flinched, while Miss Harrington kicked her brother, resulting in Iggy's sharp expostulation.

'I used to build things,' Dolph said, needing to distract the woman beside him. Or perhaps fearing that her grief might spark his own, like a contagion.

Iggy turned from the window. 'Like Trevithick?'

'Nothing so complicated. I attached cartwheels to a piece of wood and tried to balance.'

'What happened?' Iggy asked.

'I crashed into the cow shed. The cows did not milk properly for a week.'

And his brother, Barnaby, had tried and broken his arm. *There are moments in life*, Dolph thought, *which are branded into one's brain and which one cannot forget, despite the endless layering of distraction.*

He'd always remember his brother's shout of pain, his mother's fear and his father's anger.

'Was the dairy maid cross? Or your father?' Ignatius asked.

'Both.'

Never put your brother's life at risk. Ever. He is the heir.

Dolph remembered his father's words, somehow made louder by his size, as he'd towered above him, his silhouette black against the sun.

'Miss Carstens was cross when I almost blew up the chickens,' Iggy said, bringing Dolph's attention back to the present. 'She made me learn Latin declensions. Did your father make your learn declensions?'

'He advised that I memorize the peerage.'

And had fired Mr Jennings, saying that the tutor had been too lenient. Mr Jennings had left without saying goodbye. Dolph had been caned and sent to boarding school to become a gentleman, to learn manners, play sports and keep his hands clean.

Dolph glanced out at the passing scenery as they entered Bloomsbury. He'd never played that way again with his brother. They'd gone to the same school but Barnaby had seemed so much older, a perfect student, an athlete and head boy. They must have spent holidays together, he supposed, but it had not seemed the same. They had left behind the impulsive, impetuous joy and rough-and-tumble ways of childhood.

'The peerage doesn't seem very useful,' Iggy said.

'My father did not place high value on utility,'

Dolph said, glancing down at his soft, white, well-manicured hands.

They were not dirty.

Chapter Three

Clusters of people stood outside high fencing, now encircling Torrington Square. As the carriage pulled to a stop, Iggy half catapulted out, not even waiting for the groom to open the door. Indeed, his enthusiasm was such that Abby also scrambled down quickly, fearful that he might disappear into the crowd.

Fortunately, he did not. Instead, he stood quite still, as though overwhelmed or so fascinated by the noise and people that he needed time. Several other carriages stood outside the fencing. A queue had formed at the entrance and while they could see nothing from behind the wall, the clang of metal from within, mixed with excited shouts and a whistle, was clearly audible.

'May I purchase everyone a ticket?' Lord Lansdowne asked.

'Yes!' Ignatius said, nodding his head with vehemence.

Mrs Harrington and Lucy both shook their heads. 'Not to ride. I believe that seeing the spectacle will be sufficient for me. I have never been one for risk taking. I am more comfortable on terra firma,' Mrs Harrington explained.

'It runs on a track. It does not fly in the air,' Ignatius said, in a tone of some disgust, despite Abby's warning glare.

'I will also decline the ride. I believe the spectacle will be enough excitement,' Lucy said, the smelling salts already clutched within her hand.

'I will go, if only to keep an eye on Ignatius,' Abby said. Then she added, 'Although, truthfully, I am excited. I am no inventor myself but find the products of human ingenuity quite fascinating.'

It was the novelty, she supposed, that feeling that the world was changing and one was a part of this metamorphosis.

Lord Lansdowne strode towards the kiosk and they followed, gaining admittance to the enclosure.

As she entered, Abby gave a slight gasp, almost understanding Mrs Harrington's apprehension. It was so crowded that it was initially hard to see over the hats, bonnets and parasols. The smallness of the space made it feel more congested, giving the illusion that the number of spectators had multiplied.

By inching forward, Abby was able to catch a glimpse of the mechanism. It ran on a narrow, circular track, moving with surprising rapidity. It pulled a single carriage, and had a boiler and chimney, belching plumes of smoke. The hiss of the steam, the crowd's murmur and the clang of metal on metal added to the excitement.

As the apparatus moved forward, the rattle of the tracks mixed with the muttering of the crowd. They shifted forward to better observe, and yet with a hesitancy, ready to spring back at any moment.

Father would have revelled in such a scene. There would have been no hanging back for him. He loved invention. He loved novelty and progress, Besides, there was a bristling excitement to this scene which was contagious.

'It can go fifteen miles per hour. I do wish I could examine the mechanics,' Iggy said, as the machine pulled to a stop, white smoke puffing from a vertical cylinder.

'You will have to make do with the passenger experience,' Abby said firmly. 'I am sure that will be sufficiently exciting.'

'Indeed,' Mrs Harrington said. 'Just standing here is quite overwhelming. Thankfully I had the forethought to secure several vials of smelling salts about my person.'

'You are indeed well prepared,' Lord Lansdowne said. 'Miss Carstens, you feel you will be able to withstand the excitement.'

'I will manage.'

There was something in his tone and the glint of mischief that she both liked and did not like. It was a shared moment of humour, a feeling that he somehow understood her mushy rush of feelings even more than Lucy, whom she had known for ever.

But then she and Lucy were quite opposite, although the type of opposites which are often compatible. Mrs Harrington and her mother had been friends since childhood and welcomed Abby into their family circle both during her mother's illness and, more recently, her father's death.

'Be careful,' Lucy said, holding Abby's hand.

Abby had always loved the power of fire. When she was little, she would manhandle the bellows so that the kitchen fire grew big. She'd loved its roar, its heat and that feeling of vibrancy and excitement. She liked the causal effect, more air resulting in a larger fire. It was as though the excitement was meshed with a predictability which reassured.

She felt a similar excitement now as she watched the machine circle the track once more before coming to a halt, the steam hissing as the wheels clanged and then fell silent.

But there was something more. It was the knowledge that this was bigger than her excitement, fear or wonderment. This surpassed any of them, as individuals. It was about human ingenuity—

'Miss Carstens?' Lord Lansdowne stood with his hand outstretched.

She met his gaze and felt that odd, peculiar connection as though he had some understanding of her thoughts or shared them.

With an unfamiliar self-consciousness, she placed her hand in his. Instantly, she felt that awareness of her gloved hand within his own, as though the sensitivity of her skin had been peculiarly heightened, enabling her to feel the strength and warmth of his hand through the cloth.

She wanted to both snatch it away and, conversely, linger.

Ignatius, of course, had no tolerance for lingering. He needed no invitation, scrambling aboard and leaning precariously from the window to gain a better view of the mechanism.

'For goodness' sake do not fall.' Abby sat heavily, gripping the hem of his jacket so that she could pull him back.

Lord Lansdowne sat opposite.

With Iggy back in his seat, she glanced down at her hands, as though suddenly fascinated with her clasped palms. She felt peculiarly aware of His Lordship's proximity, his size, his physical presence and that peculiar intimacy that a shared experience can evoke.

The carriage doors closed.

There was a hiss of steam and a clunk of machinery. As though by common consent, the chatter from the crowd became muted with a hushed expectancy. Abby could feel the beat of her heart and the sensation that she could not properly breathe. Her mouth felt dry and tingles of excitement rippled on her skin. She looked towards the crowd and at Lucy and Mrs Harrington. The latter was almost hidden behind her favourite bonnet, a bundle of grapes dangling decorously from the brim.

The mechanism shifted. There was a grind of metal on metal, followed by a clang and a lurching forward movement.

Her heart, which had been residing within her ribcage, ascended into her throat. She had not expected to feel fear. Maybe it wasn't fear. Excitement and fear were close bedfellows.

Her breath quickened. The vehicle shifted forward, gaining speed. Lucy and Mrs Harrington gripped each other as though requiring this mutual support. Their pale faces blurred; even the bonnet became more muted until, eventually, they disappeared, as the mechanism rounded the bend.

Her heart thumped, its thunder mixed with the noise of the wheels.

Her father had described invention as touching the future. She felt this now, as though she stood on a precipice and, for this suspended moment, moved from what is and into what might be.

Lord Lansdowne turned to her. His face was full of an excited joy which she knew was reflected in her own. Her hand gripped the edge of the window. His rested beside her own—their fingers touching.

Even in her excitement she was oddly aware of the minute touch of their two fingers against the rail.

The machine jerked. The excitement shifted into fear. She grabbed his hand, the movement instinctual.

Their eyes met.

Every second seemed a separate entity, both disparate from her life and yet intricately and inevitably woven into its fabric. The ride felt both short and long.

When the machine stopped, with a final belch of smoke like it was some mythical monster, no one spoke. No one moved. Even Iggy sat still. Goosebumps prickled Abby's skin and the shushing of her heart still thundered in her ears.

'Thank you,' she said.

'That was remarkable.' Lord Lansdowne's voice was soft, husky as though he was still partially bereft of speech.

'It was.'

They still held hands. She could feel the heat of his fingers through her gloves and found their gazes locked. His eyes were grey and flecked with green. His note was straight, aquiline and his jawline strong.

Time stilled, binding them into this single moment.

Tendrils had loosened from her neat bun, just visible from under her bonnet. Her eyes were large and blue and her lips were parted. She bit her lip in a nervous excitement. They were so close that he could see the moisture on her lips, the three tiny freckles on her nose, like grains of brown sugar, and her long, dark lashes flush against pink cheeks.

Everything, even this marvellous machine, had dwarfed into insignificance. He was aware of her hand, against his own, the tang of smoke in the air, the whisper of excitement within the crowd.

'I was anticipating greater speed,' Ignatius announced, his imperious tones breaking the silence.

Miss Carstens startled. She jerked back, pulling her hand away. Dolph felt a mix of gratitude and regret.

'Can we go again?' Ignatius asked.

'No, no,' Miss Carstens said, her voice slightly breathless.

'How fast do you think it was? It seemed to me I have gone faster on Farmer Motham's horse.'

'I am sure not. Mr Motham's horse was more carthorse than racehorse. Anyway, you should thank His Lordship for such a wonderful experience and we will allow the new passengers to get on,' she spoke quickly, hurriedly seeking to open the door as though in a sudden need to leave.

'Thank you,' Ignatius said with dutiful politeness as a gentleman outside opened the door.

'And Ignatius, after we exit, you will not examine the engine.' Miss Carstens spoke in brisk tones, the mantle of governess slipping seamlessly into place.

'How did you know I wanted to?' Ignatius asked.

'Sixth sense,' Miss Carstens said as she stepped out of the carriage. 'Lord Lansdowne, I thank you also. The excursion has been interesting and educational.'

Dolph nodded. 'A pleasure.'

And that odd moment dissipated like steam from the boiler. She was again a practical governess. He was again a bored member of the ton and this apparatus more circus toy than any mechanical marvel.

He was both thankful and regretful.

Chapter Four

Of course, Mrs Harrington and her daughter greeted them as though they had forged a raging river, fought a dozen lions or escaped a burning building.

'That was so exciting,' Miss Harrington said. 'Indeed, I almost fainted merely watching you.'

'I am glad you did not,' Ignatius said with obvious relief. 'That would have made you even more of a ninnyhammer than I took you for.'

Miss Harrington glared at her brother, who seemed happily oblivious to her irritation. Had he and Madeleine been like this, Dolph wondered? Ignatius and his sister bickered but their genuine caring was apparent. It seemed unlikely that Madeleine would unbend sufficiently for such squabbles. Perhaps the years apart were too great or their personalities too different.

And Barnaby? He remembered boyhood scrapes, squabbles, games and laughter. Then everything changed, one action spurring on the others. Barnaby broke his arm. Dolph went to school. Everything changed. And Barnaby was lost behind a wall of perfection.

Dolph sighed. He wished now that they had been as honest in life as in death.

With a flicker of irritation, he pushed the memories away. The apparatus behind them clanked and hissed, readying for its next circuit. A queue had formed. Ignatius was jumping on one foot and announcing to no one in particular that it was a momentous event and well worth the shilling. His joy was so open, so spontaneous and without pretence.

Dolph realized that, for the first time in for ever, he'd felt something like joy on Trevithick's engine. The experience stood out like a candle in what had been a dark night. It was not just the ride but the shared experience with Miss Carstens, as though momentarily lightening that familiar dull, flat feeling.

Now, as he manoeuvred the party through the small crowd, he was aware again of this typical flatness. The penalty for feeling joy was its antithesis, he thought, as he welcomed the dull flatness again. Better the familiar than the alternative.

He glanced towards Miss Carstens. She was walking on his left with Iggy while the Harringtons walked a little in front. Her lips were curved into a happy, spontaneous smile.

'Gracious, do I have a smudge on my nose?' she asked.

'Pardon?'

'You were looking at me rather quizzically so I feared I had a smudge.'

'No, I suppose I was wondering what you were thinking.'

'I was wondering whether this marvel will eventually replace the horse and carriage. It seems impossible, given that it runs on tracks and it would be a lot of work to build tracks all across the country. But then roads and wheels and carriages likely seemed impossible when first developed.'

'So has it inspired you to invent something?'

She shook her head, laughing. 'Likely it will have inspired Iggy so I better keep an eye on the chicken coop. My aim is to perhaps teach an individual who might create such a thing.'

'You plan to continue to work as a governess? You couldn't join Miss Harrington for any part of her come-out?'

'Mrs Harrington would like me to do so but I would prefer to teach. And you? Are you still balancing vehicles on wheels?'

'No,' he said, too sharply for good manners. 'Unfortunately, that resulted in an accident which dissuaded me from future attempts.'

'So what do you dream of?' she asked in that direct way of hers, fixing him with her clear gaze.

'I—' He should say some platitude. Good lord, he knew enough. Yet it seemed oddly wrong, and disrespectful to the moment. Like swearing in a church.

A life without the constraints of society, without the dullness, the emptiness, the ritualized routines, the lack of purpose...

'I am not certain if I do,' he said.

She frowned, her expression disapproving. 'But you should. You must.'

'Why?' he asked.

'Because I suppose everyone needs to have hope and to have purpose.' Their gazes met.

'Good heavens, Miss Carstens, what a dreadfully old-fashioned notion,' he quipped.

They walked through the narrow entrance between the fencing. Martin pulled forward the carriage and, dismounting, swung open the door. They ascended. Ignatius pushed himself into a corner, pressing his nose to the window as though hopeful to see a final glimpse, despite the tall fencing.

The carriage moved forward. Mrs Harrington and her daughter both expressed their delight in the excursion, but both displayed a certain restlessness.

Mrs Harrington shifted as though discomforted, learning forward and then back, clasping and re-clasping her gloved palms, her expression one of earnest intensity.

'Lord Lansdowne,' she said at last. 'I do not wish to be forward but your kindness has led me to hope...'

'That we can go again tomorrow?' Ignatius asked, twisting from the window.

'What? No, of course not,' his mother snapped. 'It has led us to hope that perhaps we can count on your kinship to help us with my dear Lucy's debut.'

'Ah, yes,' he said.

He glanced towards Miss Carsten's averted profile. 'As I recall when I first discussed the prospect with Miss Carstens, she worried that I would not be sufficiently blunt.'

He felt her stiffen, turning quickly towards him, her brows contracted. 'No, it is not that—'

'Therefore, I must reassure her. Miss Harrington, may I enquire whether you are merely ornamental or do you possess intellect as well?'

'Um,' Miss Harrington said, flushing prettily, 'I can paint, a little, and play the piano.'

He sighed dramatically. 'I thought as much but do not worry. The ton has little interest in a woman's intelligence and you are pretty enough. Is that sufficiently blunt, Miss Carstens?'

'Blunt and rude,' Miss Carstens retorted. 'I thought that good manners were revered in high society.'

'Oh, they are. I merely sought to prove that I can rise above the limitations of my birth.'

'So you will introduce us?' Mrs Harrington asked, reminding him of Ignatius with her perseverance on the issue deemed paramount.

'My introduction may not be of greatest use. However, I will inveigle my sister to do so.'

'Truly? We would be most grateful and would greatly enjoy making her acquaintance.' Mrs Harrington reached forward so dramatically that he feared she'd slide from her seat and onto the carriage floor, should they encounter a rut in the road.

'Her company is not that enjoyable. However, I have one condition.'

'Please, name it,' Mrs Harrington begged.

He leaned back against the cushions, pressing his fingers together and inhaling, purposely drawing out the moment.

'I find society dreadfully dull and, peculiarly, Miss Carstens appears to lessen the dullness to a limited extent. Moreover, while currently a governess, it would seem that she might aspire to more, given her father's profession and her own education. Therefore, I suggest that she join us on appropriate social activities.'

Chapter Five

For a split second, it seemed to Abby that everything and everyone paused. Even the horses' hooves slowed as if suspended.

Abby gaped. She felt her jaw drop. Lucy's favourite novels used this phrase and she'd not thought it anatomically possible. But now she felt it, a wide-eyed, breathless, facial slackening. 'But...but I am not really very social.' Her voice was unusually high even to her own ears.

'Fiddlesticks,' Mrs Harrington said in her strident tones, clapping her gloved hands together. 'An inspired and lovely idea! Miss Carstens is quite superior, as you surmised. Her father was a clergyman from Scotland. Her mother grew up in my own village and was my very good friend until she passed. She told me that she had relatives in France. Unfortunately, they lost their heads and really everything else. Although the heads were the worst of it. However, dear Abigail can speak French quite well. She was also very well educated by Miss Brownlee.'

'But I don't want to attend social events,' Abby repeated more forcefully, pushing out the words with physical effort. 'I would be...be quite like a fish out of water. Besides, I have no funds and it will be hard enough to alter Lucy's clothes with sufficient time.'

Lord Lansdowne waved a dismissive hand. 'If I am to involve myself in this debut, I will, naturally, pay.'

'And, Abby, it would be so wonderful to have you there. Indeed, it is everything we dreamed about when little.' Lucy reached across the carriage, squeezing Abby's hand tightly.

Abby returned the squeeze although cognizant that this had been Lucy's fantasy and not her own. Her recollection was more of enduring social rigmarole until her mother's death when she had embraced new-found freedom.

However, no one else appeared to have any reservations. Lucy looked enraptured while Lord Lansdowne and Mrs Harrington were discussing dressmakers.

'Madame Aimee is quite excellent. I will forward your name. She will make dresses for you all,' Lord Lansdowne said.

Mrs Harrington gave another clap. 'My lord, I have heard that Madame Aimee is quite the *modiste de jour.* Indeed, you are so kind. Your mother always said that you were!'

He shrugged, and Abby caught sight of that crooked, slightly rakish smile which both attracted plus irritated. 'Pray do not spread such a rumour. My motives are entirely selfish. It will amuse me. And irk my sister.'

Abby straightened, trying to regain some element of control. 'Lord Lansdowne, let me assure you that securing a position as governess or schoolmistress is quite the height of my current aspirations. Moreover, I am certain that your sister would be sufficiently irked if required to sponsor Miss Harrington. Including me is an unnecessary annoyance and expense. I am not even a relative. It would be far better if I remained home. With Ignatius.'

'I do not need anyone at home with me,' Iggy announced, without turning his head from the window.

'He will be quite fine,' Mrs Harrington said. 'Mrs Fred will look after him.'

'Don't need that either,' Iggy muttered, fogging the window with his breath and then drawing shapes or diagrams.

'Please, Abby, it would be so lovely to have your company. I would be so relieved. I am quite shy,' Lucy explained, addressing this last comment towards His Lordship.

'And I will not be particularly helpful. Social chit-chat has always been challenging.'

'Enough,' Mrs Harrington said, quite stridently. 'Lord Lansdowne is offering an opportunity. Wasn't Miss Brownlee always suggesting that one seize opportunity? Carpe diem or something like that.'

'She was also a strong advocate for free choice,' Abby remarked tersely.

'Well, maybe you'll run into that Wilberforce fellow you like so much.'

'I am not certain if he frequents debutantes' balls.'

'Please,' Lucy said.

'I—' Abby glared at Lord Lansdowne, who stretched out his long legs, smiling complacently.

'I am certain you would not want to disappoint Miss Harrington,' he said.

To say his sister was not best pleased was an understatement.

Madeleine's facial expressions seldom suggested contentment but now her frown and pursed lips suggested an even stronger emotion.

'I do not see why you would want to involve yourselves in the lives of nobodies from Harrogate!'

'Would nobodies from elsewhere be preferable?' he asked, seating himself on her satin settee within her gilded salon. It felt too low, making his knees angle awkwardly. 'I am certain I could find some.'

'Must you mock everything? You have become insufferable since Mother's demise. It was bad enough that Mother had such foolish charitable notions but now you follow suit. And why? Merely to drive me to distraction?'

He pretended to consider the matter. 'Of course, that is an added benefit. However, I believe my primary motivation is to ensure that I do not too closely resemble our dear papa. Or maybe it is possible that I am developing a sense of familial duty. Wasn't it only yesterday that you suggested I take a greater interest in my niece and nefarious nephew?'

'Jason is not nefarious. Merely young. Besides, you should want to do so, given that he is your heir and your current lifestyle is hardly suggestive of longevity.'

'Good lord, do not send to be measured by the undertakers quite yet. And which of my pursuits, pray tell, might cause me to shed my mortal coil on such an expedited schedule?'

'You have participated in two horse races since you inherited the title. Plus you drink like a fish every night.'

'But there are nights when I only drink like a small fish, a minnow perhaps.'

His sister made an irritated tsk, raising her eyes to the ceiling.

'I suppose I should be thankful that you drink at

White's, as is proper. Jason shows less sense. He gambles at quite dreadful places,' Madeleine said, snapping her lips together.

'Lud, are there rules about everything? Even where one may lose one's fortune?'

'Jason will not lose his fortune,' she said in the tone of voice one uses to reassure oneself as opposed to convince the listener. 'However, he is young, not yet twenty. He needs male guidance and, given Lord Stanhope's demise, I suppose you'll have to do.'

'You flatter me. That is a heady role. Will I need to reform myself, marry or something equally tedious?' Dolph teased.

Madeleine turned to him with a narrowing of her eyes as she tapped her fingers more quickly on the arm of her chair.

'Marriage might be good for you, although you've indicated that you'd rather be burned at the stake or something equally dramatic. Wasn't Mother forever suggesting suitable young ladies?'

'Mealy-mouthed debutantes.'

'Well, you can hardly marry one of your operatic courtesans or somebody already married,' she retorted tartly.

He sighed. 'But respectable ladies are so dreadfully dull.'

'Respectable ladies are suitable for your station. And, if you do intend to take such a dramatic step, you must forgo the mantle of rake and act like a gentleman of the first water. We must ensure that your duchess is a lady of lineage, good countenance and deportment.'

'Good Heavens, such a marriage sounds a dreadfully dull enterprise. Indeed, even finding such a paragon sounds tedious.' He feigned a yawn. 'I will content myself with young Jason as heir. Indeed, I will even show an avuncular interest in your offspring.'

'That would be appreciated. I know we are not close, given the ten years between us, but we are both somewhat lacking in relatives.'

'I will be a model uncle and attend Susan's come-out and inspire Jason with my wisdom.'

'Thank you. I am hopeful Susan might make a match with Mr Trollope. They know each other well.'

'A dull way to start a marriage.'

'And you will abandon this nonsense with these Herringbones?'

'Indeed no. If I am to take this avuncular interest, I will need some entertainment.'

Besides, if he abandoned the project now, Miss Carstens would likely say *I told you so.* Generally speaking, he cared little for another person's opinion but it seemed surprisingly important that he should not disappoint her.

Or perhaps there was something appealing in continuing his mother's good work, as though it might make him feel closer to her and ensure he differed from his father.

'And are they entertaining? The Harringtons?' Madeleine asked with obvious suspicion.

'Not exactly.'

'More to the point, is either girl likely to be named an incomparable?'

'Heavens no, Miss Harrington is pretty enough, but insipid. And Miss Carstens is no beauty at all.' He smiled, even as he said the words. It was true. Although there was something arresting about her. It was the intelligence, the eager interest and lack of pretence.

'Then why are you smiling?'

'Natural amiability?'

Madeleine let her hands drop to her lap with a slight thwack, her expression even more suspicious. 'You've taken a fancy to her.'

'What? Miss Harrington? Good lord, I couldn't stay awake long enough.'

'No, the governess. Miss Carton. You cannot be introducing her into society if you intend to bed her. We can't have a scandal. I have my Susan to consider—'

'Miss Carstens? Of course not. Miss Carstens is

not that sort of female at all. Far from it. And your Susan might actually learn something from her.'

His sister said nothing for several seconds, which was quite worse than when she was loquacious. 'You speak with unusual vehemence,' she said at last. 'I have seldom heard you compliment a female with such fervour.'

'Well, you and I are hardly confidants. Besides, the ladies I could discuss with my sister are determinedly dull and those who are not, I cannot discuss.'

'And this Carstairs female? She is not dull?'

He remembered Miss Carstens wrestling with the dog, her fascination with invention and her sharp, acerbic tongue.

'I have not been bored in her presence, but rest assured she is not of the operatic variety, so you need have no worry for Susan's morals.'

Chapter Six

'An evening in London! Our first event of the Season!' Lucy said in tones breathy with excitement, hardly able to stay still despite Madame Aimee squatting at her feet and painstakingly pinning her hem.

'Indeed,' Mrs Harrington agreed from her seat by the small fire within her bedchamber. 'Seeing the locomotive was exciting but we did not meet a lot of people. And the noise and excitement made conversing difficult. Although I did see Lady Abreu.'

'Was that the lady carrying that fierce little dog?' Lucy asked.

'Little dogs are often much fiercer than big dogs,' Mrs Harrington said. 'Although upon reflection, I believe Lady Abreu was wearing a fox stole. Its eyes looked decidedly glassy.'

'Ugh, that is even scarier.' Lucy wrinkled her nose. 'Thankfully, it is unlikely she will come to a debutante's ball. Abby, I am so happy you will be there. It will be just like when we all had tea parties.'

'I could put a spider in someone's teacup to make you feel completely at home.'

Lucy giggled. 'Remember how Annabelle squealed! Although I know you did that just so you could be sent home.'

'True enough, I became better behaved as I got older and when my mother got sicker. I didn't want to disappoint.'

'She was proud when you and Miss Brownlee helped the villagers.'

'Yes,' Abby agreed. Although she was glad that her mother had thought they merely delivered ox-tail soup, and not babies. She doubted Mother would have viewed the latter as a suitable thing for her twelve-year-old daughter to do.

She glanced at Mrs Harrington and Lucy. Her mother and Mrs Harrington had been good friends and Mrs Harrington had done everything possible to help both during her mother's illness and beyond.

Nor had life with Mr Harrington been easy. He was deaf and had gout, and both afflictions had severely limited his good nature. Even as a small child, Abby remembered tiptoeing so as not to disturb his rest.

But they'd opened their home to her after her father's death, even before the tutor had so precipitously quit, allowing her to repay their kindness in some measure as governess.

Yes, they deserved good fortune.

Moreover, despite her initial reservations, Lord Lansdowne had stuck to his word. Bonnets, fans, shawls, shoes and all manner of other finery had been trundled inside over the last few days. New gowns were being made for both Lucy and her mother, and the promised introduction to Lady Stanhope arranged for this very night.

Abby had rather hoped she might stay home with Iggy but this was not a popular suggestion. Of course, Lucy and Mrs Harrington were motivated by kindness. But what of Lord Lansdowne? Why had he wanted to involve her? He scarcely seemed the altruistic type. Was she there merely as entertainment, like a court jester, an antidote to his own boredom?

'Turn a little, mademoiselle,' Madame Aimee said to Lucy from her position on the floor, her voice made guttural by the pins clenched between her teeth. 'And do not fidget! My ladies do not fidget.'

'Sorry, Madame,' Lucy said in contrite tones.

Despite her diminutive stature, Madame Aimee was formidable.

'I think you will do well enough,' Madame Aimee announced, replacing the pins within her pincushion and standing, her knees creaking with the movement.

'It is beautiful,' Lucy said with obvious sincerity, giving a twirl. 'And I am glad that I do not have to wear white. I know that debutantes usually do and it is suitable for mourning but I get so pale when I am nervous that I always look like a ghost.'

Madame Aimee made a muttered tsk. 'My ladies do not resemble ghosts, *non!*'

'Indeed, I am too excited to feel very ghostly. Abby, I do wish you would have accepted Lord Lansdowne's offer of a new gown.'

'There is no reason for Lord Lansdowne to pay for my gown,' Abby retorted. 'The new lace will quite revitalize this one.'

'You couldn't just accept good fortune. Like Cinderella?'

Abby chortled. 'Lud, do not cast Lord Lansdowne in the role of fairy godmother. He would abhor it.'

Or perhaps it would amuse him? She could imagine that glint of humour and a slight, sardonic twist of well-sculpted lips. His jawbone, chiselled cheeks and firm mouth all spoke of an intelligent strength.

She did not like strength without intellect. Such people tended to be bullies, unable to restrain base impulses.

'At least choose my pink gown. That grey makes you look positively fustian,' Lucy said, quite making Abby jump.

'I am too old for pink.'

'You are only eighteen months older than me. You always make yourself sound ancient,' Lucy complained.

'It would not suit her,' Madame Aimee announced in tones which would permit no contradiction. 'Pink, maybe, but not *that* pink.'

'But I love that pink dress,' Mrs Harrington said.

'Indeed, it is vibrant, *madame*. However, the grey is a better choice. It suits your eyes, Miss Carstens. The cloth has undertones of purple. We could improve that hair. A few curls, *peut-être*? You have too much chin, nose and cheekbone.'

'All of which are quite serviceable,' Abby remarked.

'But your hair could be improved,' Mrs Harrington said.

'I've always had it this way. It is easy to manage and sensible.'

'Which matters not one wit at a ball,' Lucy said.

'It is not a ball. Merely a gathering so that you can meet Lady Stanhope and her daughter.'

'We,' Lucy emphasized. 'So that *we* can meet them and it is vital that we look our best. I refuse to have you looking sensible.'

Abby shrugged. 'Very well, but only a few curls at the front. The rest can go into a net. I do not want it dangling down my neck and getting in my way.'

'Getting in your way? You will not be baking a cake,' Lucy muttered.

Madame Aimee took a brush from the nightstand, uncoiling Abby's thick hair while Lucy looked on as though expecting a transformation of biblical proportions.

'It is quite thick, *oui*? The colour is a pleasant chestnut. It has natural waves when not dragged back into that dreadful bun.'

'It is a wild mop when not in a bun.'

'I think, *mademoiselle*, your aim has been to disguise your good looks.'

'Miss Carstens believes that the world cannot see a pretty woman as intelligent,' Mrs Harrington said.

'It can't,' Abby said. 'They are mutually exclusive. The former is lauded while the latter despised.'

Mrs Harrington had pulled out a piece of needlework which appeared to have no discernible pattern. She stared at it as though hoping it might provide its own inspiration, before casting it aside.

'I liked Miss Brownlee a lot,' she said. 'However, I am not certain she was correct in that surmise.'

Madame Aimee ran her hands over Abby's hair, eyes squinting and head cocked at a critical angle. 'Perhaps, *mademoiselle*, it is up to you to demonstrate that a beautiful woman can also be quite brilliant, *oui*?'

The seamstress picked up her scissors, brandishing them with singular determination.

'Indeed,' Mrs Harrington agreed. 'I am certain a few curls would be the very thing. I see absolutely no reason why you might not meet your Prince Charming this very night.'

'Only that I am not looking for him,' Abby said. 'That is the problem with fairy tales—they always put females in ludicrous high turrets and expect rescue. I aim to have my own ladder'

The night had an auspicious start.

As promised, Lord Lansdowne sent a carriage. This was opulent with high-stepping matching greys and ducal crest. The cushions were of a soft crushed velvet and, unlike the Harringtons' elderly vehicle, the interior had not even a hint of mustiness.

Abby's gaze flickered towards Lucy and Mrs Harrington. Their excitement was tangible. Indeed, it seemed as though they held their breath for the entire ride, perhaps fearing any exhalation might disperse the magic.

'I am quite certain that this is a different coach than the one used to transport us to Torrington Square,' Lucy said, in low tones as though fearing to be overheard.

'The fact that it is upholstered in a different colour is suggestive of this,' Abby agreed.

'Can you imagine the wealth one must have to possess two coaches?'

The carriage moved sedately through the narrow streets which characterized their neighourhood and into an area with wider streets, trees and large houses, their facades dimly lit by flickering gas lamps.

As they neared their destination, the street became more congested. Peering out curiously, they noted other carriages, uniformed footmen and sleek horses.

They stopped. Abby was aware of an expectant hush as the hooves and wheels stilled. The groom opened the door. A cool breeze whistled in. Glancing out, Abby noted the house's gracious dimensions, the wide staircase and uniformed servants.

Indeed, Abby felt a slight wobble in her stomach, somewhat like Mrs Fred's blancmange. The black lacquered door, complete with brass door knocker, reminded her of Ashleigh Hall.

'Why are you looking so worried?' Mrs Harrington asked in one of her loud whispers as they walked up the wide staircase towards the black lacquered door with a lion's head door knocker. 'And sighing like Mrs Elder when she thought the hymn selection too lively. Please try to enjoy yourself.'

'I will,' Abby promised.

After all, she had no wish to lessen either Mrs Harrington's or Lucy's enjoyment. And this was in no way like Ashleigh Hall. The last time she had been to Ashleigh Hall was after her father's accident.

The Ashleighs had been kind enough, offering vague support before removing to London.

The door swung open. Two liveried footmen stepped forward to take the ladies' wraps and, after dispensing with these vestments, they stepped into the entrance hall. Everything seemed larger than typical. The hall alone was mammoth, twice the size of the entire house on Wimpole Street. A massive chandelier hung low and large portraits of dour relatives flanked the wall leading to the second storey.

They followed the butler to the top of this staircase and he pushed open another door.

'Mrs Harrington, Miss Harrington and Miss Carstens,' he announced.

They walked into a chamber which, while smaller than the outer hall, was still of impressive proportions. The high ceiling was painted with a seascape of Neptune, brandishing his trident, and rising from the waves.

The air felt chill, the fire flickering in the grate having little impact. Two women sat, one on either side of the hearth. The elder was thin and appeared to be tall with dark hair now woven with strands of grey.

The younger resembled the elder but whereas Lady Stanhope's height and aquiline features made her formidable, her daughter appeared merely awkward, as though her nose had grown too much, leaving her other features in a race to catch up.

Lady Stanhope acknowledged their presence with a slight tilt of her head, her gaze sweeping critically across their faces. 'Welcome, Mrs Harrington and Miss Harrington. My brother says you are related to our mother.'

'Indeed, on my father's side,' Mrs Harrington said. Lucy sat beside her on a small couch, sitting close as though unwilling to take too much space.

'We do thank you for your generosity. I am so glad to meet you,' Lucy said, glancing at both mother and daughter.

Lady Stanhope gave a slight shrug. 'Your manners seem pretty enough. Although you are better looking than Lord Lansdowne's description had led me to suppose.'

Her gaze turned to Abby, who had found a seat somewhat separate from the group, behind the couch.

'You must be the governess,' she said.

'Miss Carstens is a family friend really,' Mrs Harrington said. 'I knew her mother when we were children and her father was a parson. He died and she came up with us to London. Indeed, she has been a great comfort and help.'

Lady Stanhope nodded acknowledgement of this

statement, before continuing her scrutiny. 'Your hair could be improved. The fringe is well, but a few ringlets would be advised.'

'I don't like ringlets. They tickle my neck.'

'Good lord, girl. It does not matter what you like.'

'Given that it is my hair, I rather thought it did.'

'I hope you are not pert.'

'Heavens, no,' Mrs Harrington hurriedly intervened. 'Indeed, she is not. She occasionally has a…a…whimsical sense of humour but is kind and eminently practical. Everyone said so in the village. Indeed, she was like a ministering angel, if angels came supplied with chicken soup.'

'Well, despite these rural accolades, I worry that you don't fully appreciate your good fortune and may spoil your chances with an ill-conceived remark. Humour is not generally encouraged in the young.'

'I will endeavour to maintain a serious disposition,' Abby said.

'But smile. No need to look melancholy. You have much to learn if you hope to make an advantageous match.'

'Oh, I don't.'

'Pardon?'

'Intend to make a match, advantageous or otherwise.'

To say that Lady Stanhope looked shocked might

be an understatement. Her mouth opened and then closed—much like a freshly caught trout, Abby thought, before she could stop whatever imp had entered her brain.

Mrs Harrington, uncomfortable with silence, burst in with a volley of speech. 'Do not mind her. She is eccentric. Intelligent. I always think intelligent people are odd. A good friend of ours, Miss Brownlee, was very intelligent but odd. And she is related to French aristocrats. I mean Miss Carstens is, not Miss Brownlee, except they lost their heads. I don't mean that they acted foolishly but that they lost their heads in a more literal sense. Anyhow, what I meant to say, is that Miss Carstens has occasional whims to which we pay no heed.'

Following this speech, Mrs Harrington thankfully ran out of air and was forced to lapse into silence.

'Does your mother always talk so much?' Lady Stanhope addressed this comment to Lucy.

'No, my lady.'

'Good, I would suggest a rest for her vocal cords. Follow me. We will step into the ballroom. We have a dance floor set up with an orchestra and a few guests. Not many, just those who would be suitable. I believe the gentlemen will meet us there. It is an opportunity for you to practise your steps and your manners before presentation at court or more lavish events.'

* * *

As Dolph finished his cognac and stepped out of the study and towards his sister's ballroom, he was aware of an unusual anticipation. This was, he acknowledged, out of character. Since his brother's death, he could not remember anticipation or an emotion even close to anticipation. Indeed, his every activity had felt touched by the grimness of obligation or a frenetic energy as though by drinking, galloping or gambling, he might find an illusion of peace.

It was even odder that he should feel anything akin to anticipation for a debutante's ball. Dancing with his niece and a gaggle of girls was scarcely an alluring prospect. And while Dolph did not precisely dislike his sister, she was quite ten years his senior and her company provided limited entertainment and considerable aggravation. As for his niece, he bore her no ill will. She appeared to have a pleasant disposition but she was still too young to be interesting.

Therefore, any sensible man would bolt into a carriage and hide in White's or some such establishment. Instead, Dolph stepped into the floral air of his sister's ballroom with something closer to curiosity than dread.

The ballroom, like the rest of the house, was steeped in history. The Stanhopes could trace their lineage to William the Conqueror or some such notable and had tapestries and portraits to prove such pedigree.

His father's family had a similar ancestry but a lot less money, leading to his parents' unhappy match, secured as a way to save the Lansdowne fortunes. Encouraged by their father, his sister had married the now deceased Lord Stanhope with the aim to wipe away the distaste of her mother's plebeian ancestry.

This had worked well for Madeleine, who now, with lineage, money, style and a crafty intelligence, ruled London society, making or breaking reputations.

The decor of the ballroom spoke to her good taste. It was not overly extravagant but more moderate, as was suitable for an event aimed at young ladies taking their first foray into society. A large fire burned in the hearth, chandeliers and several lamps provided a flickering golden glow, while chairs were grouped along the walls to provide seating for mamas or unfortunate wallflowers.

A pastel collection of debutantes swirled and twirled within the centre of the room. The air would warm later but currently felt cool. It was a huge space, rife with drafts, and heated only by the massive fireplace.

In addition to the pastel melange within the chamber's centre, he noted clusters of debutantes chatting over lemonade proffered by nervous gentlemen.

Meanwhile, their mamas kept keen eyes on their charges while sipping lemonade or exchanging gossip. A small orchestra was set up under an oversized palm tree on the left side of the room, and a mix of music, chatter, the swishing of gowns and tapping of feet filled the air.

'Lord Lansdowne! How delightful!' Mrs Harrington bustled towards him, her kindly round face red with excitement. She was followed by her daughter and Miss Carstens.

He made his bow to the three ladies. Miss Harrington looked less bland than he had anticipated, but it was Miss Carstens who caught his attention.

She looked different. Indeed, it was hard to reconcile this woman with the sparkling blue eyes, flushed countenance, low neckline and full bosom with the somewhat prim female from earlier encounters.

He frowned.

Her dress was too tight. And low.

His frown deepened.

'Your Lordship,' Mrs Harrington said in her loud, voluble tones, apparently oblivious to his ill temper. 'This is truly the most wonderful event. Indeed, I do not know how we can thank you, or your dear sister. Although might I suggest that we sit for a moment? I daresay Madame Aimee is correct that these shoes are a fashionable delight, but I do have a slight tendency to bunions and they are just a little aggravated, don't you know?'

'Of course,' Dolph said, leading the company towards the perimeter so that they could sit in straight-backed chairs.

'Perhaps you also have bunions?' Miss Carstens murmured to Dolph in low tones with a wry, mischievous smile, again speaking to the humour under her sensible facade.

'Pardon?'

'You are frowning at me quite ferociously. Bunions can have a bad effect on one's disposition.'

'I do not— Did Madame Aimee make your gown as I instructed?' he asked as he took Mrs Harrington's arm to get her settled in the chair.

'No, it used to be Lucy's,' Miss Carstens said, also sitting.

'I told Madame Aimee to make you a new gown.'

'There was limited time and this is quite adequate.'

For some reason her nonchalance irritated him even more. Didn't she know that she was in that odd, tenuous middle ground of the unmarried, impecunious female likely to appeal only to impoverished widowers with too many children?

The thought of her bright spirit sentenced to such a life bothered him.

The fact that it bothered him, bothered him.

'I was quite clear with my instruction. It is out of fashion. Besides it is revealing,' he said irritably.

'Except I hope to attend very few social events so a new fancy dress seemed somewhat of a waste. And it is not half as low as the young lady's over there, in the pink.' Miss Carstens angled her head towards the lady in question.

It was Miss Plymouth. She was decidedly flat chested. Miss Carstens was not, a fact made all too obvious by the gown. Indeed, he found his gaze too frequently drawn to the pale creaminess of her skin, her cleavage, an enticing furrow disappearing into the new lace, and the shadow of her breasts visible under the fabric.

'That is besides the point,' he said abruptly. 'Miss Plymouth has a dowry which will likely hasten a marriage proposal. You are not so fortunate.'

'Except I really do not want to get married.'

'So you have said. Repeatedly. But you cannot *want* to be a governess. Surely you would wish to have your own household?'

She shrugged, an insouciant movement. 'I would prefer to be a woman of independent means but, if that is not possible, I am quite suited to the role of governess.'

'Are you?' He thought of the dull, grey creatures in his sister's home. 'It seems you might prove somewhat outspoken.'

She laughed, and again he was struck by her genuine humour. Other women practised their every word or gesture so that every event felt like a stage play, every gesture nuanced. 'Apparently you have overcome your predilection for flummery,' she said.

'Touché.'

Abby watched the expressions flicker across His Lordship's face. He unsettled her. In her experience, most people said things that sounded deep and were, in fact, piffle. Whereas Lord Lansdowne said something trite but with hidden depth.

Or maybe not. Maybe the hidden depth was but a product of her imagination. Perhaps she was as bad as Lucy and saw that dark lock of hair and chiselled jaw, immediately casting him as a melancholy hero with deep, angst-filled thoughts.

Lord Ashleigh's son spent more time considering the height of his collar than anything of deeper merit and, in all likelihood, Lord Lansdowne perused similar topics.

It was her own thoughts which gave him depth, not his own.

But that was the problem. He confused her. She found the clarity of her thoughts impacted and her thinking circuitous.

He even looked different. Men fell into categories. Labourers, farmers, small landowners and high-flyers with elaborate neckties, impossible collars and bright waistcoats.

Lord Lansdowne fit none of these categories. He did not have the knickerbockers and expansive waistcoat of the well-heeled landowner. Yet, his dark hair and clothes differed starkly from th of the other gentlemen. Indeed, they appeared but brightly costumed actors, canaries beside the hawk.

'Miss Carstens,' he said, smiling with that quick, disconcertingly mercurial change of expression. 'We cannot have you sitting. And looking so serious. Allow me the pleasure?'

He stood, offering his hand.

'To dance?' she asked startled.

'It is not that unusual to dance at a dance,' he said, gentle mockery lacing the words.

'I am not really a dancer. I never practised. It did not seem productive.'

'And every activity in which you engage must be productive?'

'Yes,' she said, with some asperity. 'Most people do not have leisure for frivolity and idleness.'

'Gracious, that sounds rather grim. And *circumspectly* sensible.'

She found herself both wanting to grin back while still feeling oddly uncertain and wrong-footed.

'I don't know if *circumspectly* is a word. Besides,

one need not be idle to experience many pleasures,' she retorted.

Again his lips twisted with sly humour. 'So what *pleasures* you, Miss Carstens?' He lingered over the words, dragging out the syllables.

Her cheeks became heated, in a way which was unusual to her. She had always floundered socially but in general she cared little for her floundering. She had never before encountered this odd wobbly feeling within her stomach, the warmth in her face or this slight breathlessness.

'I… I enjoy many things…but I am not certain if I enjoy your teasing tone,' she said.

'You don't? Then that settles the issue. I am failing to entertain with my conversation, so we absolutely must dance.'

'I—'

'You cannot refuse me this pleasure. Besides, you might enjoy it. It is always pleasant to introduce a pleasurable experience to someone, don't you think?'

'I suppose. Iggy did enjoy studying the night sky,' she said, which for some reason made His Lordship laugh so loudly that several people glanced their way.

'See, you are a natural. The first rule is always to entertain your partner.'

'And the second?'

'Never display a serious countenance. Rather, you

must appear as though I have said something witty,' he said as they stepped towards the floor.

'Even when you have not?'

'Especially then.'

'How tiresome for you,' she said.

'Why so?'

'Well, it must make you feel as though you're not a real person, but just a lord and you must never know if people are communicating or merely flattering.'

Again, she hit close to the truth and her words had a refreshing quality that robbed them of insult.

'That is true. I had not considered it previously. You have a way of doing that.'

'What?'

'Putting thoughts I never knew I had into words,' he said. Few people saw him as a person. Women never did. His father had seen him as the black sheep and his mother as solace for a broken heart, his brother's shadowy replacement.

And his brother… How had his brother seen him? Barnaby had hidden under so many layers, he couldn't even see himself.

'Now you're too serious,' Abby said as they stepped forward into the first steps. 'Aren't you supposed to look as though I've also said something remarkably entertaining? 'Or does it not work both ways?'

'It does. Indeed, appearing amused when one is,

in fact, dreadfully bored, is a vital skill for any gentleman. Once I had to pretend a fascination with earwax.'

'A lady wanted to discuss her earwax?'

'No, the wax belonged to her spaniel.' He raised his arm and she stepped under it.

'Basil does not suffer from earwax, but I could discuss boils,' she said.

'Boils? Basil suffers from boils?' he asked, so startled he almost mis-stepped.

'No, one of my father's parishioners. My mother used to help and then, when she became ill, Miss Brownlee and I would. I learned about boils and carbuncles.'

'Carbuncles? They sound like a scary cousin to a barnacle. You have my condolences.'

'I didn't mind,' she said. 'Truthfully, I might have more interest in boils than bonnets, although the latter are the more suitable topic. Mrs Harrington suggests that I talk about the weather or fashion, you see.'

He remembered Mrs Harrington's bonnet. 'I am uncertain Mrs Harrington could be considered a fashion expert.'

She laughed, a spontaneous gurgle, as they came together and apart. He caught a whiff of lemon. She smelled of summer sunshine, so different from the perfumed scents of other women. In fact, *she* was different.

He had grown up fearing difference and found her very eccentricity appealing, fascinating...interesting...

'I am afraid that I must concentrate on the next steps so cannot talk. However, I will ensure I keep smiling so that everyone considers you witty,' she said.

'That is appreciated. And silence is infinitely preferable to earwax.'

Truthfully, she was not a bad dancer. She had natural rhythm and he even found the slight, infinitesimal movement of her lips, as though counting the steps, appealing. The fact that she had a comfort with quiet was also unusual. Most people filled every second with conversation.

The dance came to an end and he felt a reluctance to leave the floor, although to stay would cause comment. Miss Carstens, however, had no such hesitation. Indeed, she strode away in her eagerness.

He smiled at her transparency, her lack of guile, so different than the swirling pastel melange of dancers. He should remonstrate, he supposed. Bolting off the dance floor would hardly endear her to polite society. But then he rather liked the fact that she was different from the dancers in their pastel gowns.

'They really are so much alike,' he said, almost surprising himself that he had spoken out loud.

She looked towards them also. 'Society has made them so. We live in boxes. We can be wives, spinsters, mothers, governesses.'

He thought of his brother and even his own days at school when he was *too small, too smart, too odd*. 'I wonder why we value conformity so much?'

'The world is run by wealthy gentlemen. Change threatens your power.'

His? *His?* He thought of his brother dying in his arms and that feeling of helplessness. And of his brother, hiding his truth, unacceptable to society's mores.

'Lud, I think you must have me mistaken for the King or Prime Minister,' he quipped. 'My power is quite limited.'

'You can't vote? You don't have a seat in the House of Lords?' she asked, turning and fixing him with her rather piercing stare.

'Not one that I occupy frequently,' he said.

'And that is just it,' she said, her thick, straight, dark brows snapping together. 'That is what is frustrating about people like you and Lord Ashleigh. You have the tools of power but you make no use of them. Instead, you drink and hunt and racehorses.'

'Given that we are barely acquainted, you make rather a lot of assumptions about my character and activities,' he said. 'And who is this Lord Ashleigh who is condemned to be like me?'

'Local landlord from my father's parish. They neglect their tenants but love hunting.' Her lips pressed together in a firm line.

'Well, that rules me out. I definitely don't hunt. Dreadfully early start.'

'Do you speak in the House of Lords?'

'Gracious, no. I consider it my civic duty not to speak. Too many do already.'

'But there are important things to speak about. Do you know Wilberforce? Are you active against slavery?'

'I am aware that parliament passed the Slave Trade Act last year,' he said.

He wasn't quite certain how he knew this. It was one of those random pieces of information he had acquired while doing other things, he supposed.

Her eyebrows rose slightly, as though surprised, which he found somewhat satisfying.

'However,' she said, 'that act is insufficient. It attempts to outlaw the trade but not slavery itself. I surmise that Britain's parliament has too many vested economic interests for it to, in fact, abolish slavery.'

She paused as though she anticipated an answer or further discussion.

'I must confess, my knowledge of the act is limited to its name,' he said.

'But you can find out more. You can advocate. There are so many things you could advocate for— like educating the poor.'

She spoke with intensity that bordered on the passionate. Her cheeks had flushed and there was a force about her that drew him to her, as though everything within her orbit was brighter or had more meaning.

And yet, conversely, he felt oddly vulnerable. 'Gracious,' he said. 'That sounds dreadfully arduous. And don't the poor have enough trials?'

She looked at him with her intent, direct gaze. 'You're doing it again. You use your wit to prevent serious discourse.'

'The ton does not encourage real discourse.'

His father had not encouraged real discourse, he realized. Agreement, deflection, avoidance was always the safest policy. Sometimes, it seemed he could still feel the bite of the strap against his palm.

'That does not mean you have to follow their dictates. Discussion and debate is how we learn. But you don't converse. You spend more time coming up with your own witticism than listening.'

'You care so much,' he said, again cognizant of his own confusion. 'And you want others to care.'

'And that is wrong?'

'No, just unusual. And,' he added more firmly as though finally reaching solid ground, 'unfashionable.'

She gave a wry smile. 'I have never been accused of fashion. It would have me mince around, warble songs and be witless.'

'Not witless, perhaps more moderate.'

'Moderation would be easier if others were not so apathetic. We live in a world where people hide their real selves under smiles and jokes, Hessian boots, tall collars and fancy cravats.'

She spoke the words with no more emphasis or volume than those preceding and yet Dolph felt them more.

What had been merely conversation became something more. They slammed into him, reverberating through him. They drowned out the other sounds, the orchestra, the laughter, the chatter.

He felt his breath catch. Something tightened within his chest. He heard his whistle of exhalation but was unable to inhale as though all energy and air had been drained from him.

The words were eerily identical. He could still hear them. They still rang in his ears, taking on an almost physical entity. His two worlds collided. The scenes merged into one, the battle and the ballroom. In that moment, his sister's elegant draperies, tapestries and candelabras dissipated into mud, blood, sweat and decay. He felt the weight of his brother's head against his chest and heard the death rattle in his breath.

At least I no longer have to pretend. To hide. Behind smiles and jokes. Looking right but feeling wrong.

'Lord Lansdowne, are you well? You've gone quite pale?'

Miss Carsten's words seemed remote, as though spoken from some great distance, far removed from the ballroom. They echoed in his mind, a blur of sounds, no longer sensible. Usually, he pushed the memories away, stuffing them down, drowning them. It was only in the earlymorning hours that he would lie alone with that single question circling and bouncing in his mind.

Why didn't you tell me? Why didn't you tell me?

And then, inexorably, that question would be followed by that other unanswerable question: what would he have done or said? Would he have loved and accepted his brother as he was?

Or not?

The dancers merged into a swirling, colourful distortion. The orchestra was muffled, as though each instrument was wrapped in cloth.

'Your words reminded me of someone for whom I cared a great deal. He felt he had to conceal a part of himself that was important and I wish he had not.'

'I am sorry,' she said.

'No need to apologize. If you will excuse me, I will get a little air,' he said, pushing the words out from between his stiff lips.

'You look unwell. I will come with you,' Miss Carstens said.

'No need.'

He stood and, with the quick bow necessitated by politeness, exited the ballroom into the welcome coolness of the corridor.

Chapter Seven

Abby hurried out of the ballroom, but found the hallway empty, save for the two footmen at the top of the wide staircase, their expressions mask-like. There were several closed doors but no way of knowing where Lord Lansdowne had gone.

She stood, glancing between the staircase and shut doors, uncertain within the unfamiliar house.

'Good evening, Miss Carstens.'

The voice was cool. Abby jerked about. Lady Stanhope glided towards her. Didn't the woman have feet?

'May I help you?' she asked.

'Yes, I was looking for Lord Lansdowne,' Abby said. 'I believe my words may have upset him. He looked ill and then left quickly. I wanted to ensure he was not unwell.'

'I am certain he is fine, Miss Carstens.'

'He did not look fine,' she said, unduly irritated by this woman's apparent indifference.

'Gentlemen occasionally feel *unwell*.' Lady Stanhope gave a knowing smile, emphasizing that last word.

Abby shook her head. 'If you are suggesting that he has imbibed too much, I am certain that was not so. In fact, we were having a very coherent conversation about the abolition of the slave trade. He was making perfect sense and I could not smell alcohol on his breath.'

Lady Stanhope's haughty, austere expression became more severe. Her eyebrows contracted sharply and there was a slight flaring about her nostrils. 'Miss Carstens, it is totally and completely unacceptable for a young lady to speak of such things. To have any inkling of such things.'

'Which alcohol or slavery?'

'Good heavens, both. Have you no etiquette?'

'Regardless of my social ability, if Lord Lansdowne is ill, he should receive aid.'

'If he is ill, he will go home. Benton will look after him. Meanwhile, it appears you are overwrought and unused to socializing. I will arrange for your coach to be brought around and summon your companions.'

Lady Stanhope nodded to the footmen, who, apparently needing no further instruction, turned and disappeared into the inner depths of the house.

'This way, Miss Carstens,' Lady Stanhope said, walking down the stairs.

Abby followed. There was nothing else to do. She could scarcely stand at the top of the stairs and refuse like a child having a temper tantrum.

She stepped down. Portraits of unhappy Stanhope ancestors lined the wall, their stern gazes seeming to follow her as she moved towards the black-and-white tiling of the hall.

'You must be careful, Miss Carstens. You seem under the misapprehension that you have the knowledge necessary to survive in this world. You do not. Likely you know mathematics or Greek, but they are useless in this milieu. I will leave you here. I am certain your companions will be here momentarily.'

With these words, Lady Stanhope departed, her tall figure again seeming to glide away. Abby was left alone under the watchful gaze of both the dead ancestors and the footman.

She stared after Her Ladyship's retreating form. Sometime in the middle of the night she would think of a wonderful retort.

Right now her mind was blank as a slate board.

Moreover, Her Ladyship was entirely wrong. Abby was under no misapprehension that she could, in any way, cope with London society. She had been unable to cope with little girls' tea parties; therefore the ton was definitely out of her realm of ability.

Except there was a difference.

This time she'd wanted to—if only for the Harringtons.

Or because some odd, perverse, unacknowledged part of her had enjoyed talking to Lord Lansdowne.

But she did not belong and neither trimming her hair nor adding lace to a secondhand gown would help. She was aware of a familiar discomfort, that feeling of not belonging, of difference, of being at odds with her environment.

It had not bothered her before, or only a little during her mother's lifetime. There is a vulnerability which comes with caring and not wanting to disappoint. And there had been a freedom after her mother's death when she no longer had to live up to expectations beyond her ability.

But she felt it now. The feeling of not belonging slid over her, coldly familiar like a wet, ill-fitting coat.

'Are you feeling better now, Abby, dear?' Mrs Harrington asked kindly from her seat opposite as they travelled home.

'Yes,' Abby said, conscious of heavy guilt.

'Were you ill? What was the matter?' Lucy asked.

Abby groaned. 'I just— I should not have come.'

'Nonsense,' Mrs Harrington said firmly. 'You

danced with Lord Lansdowne and I thought you looked quite lovely.'

'Except I may not have "sounded" quite lovely to Lady Stanhope.'

'You had words with her? Lady Stanhope?' Lucy spoke in such stricken tones that Abby was certain she could not have been more shocked if she had confessed to murder.

But then Lucy had been dreaming of weddings and dresses and carriages for as long as they had known each other.

'I didn't mean to and then...' Abby pressed her lips together, remembering the sharp exchange. The thought that her words might have impacted Lucy's happiness made her stomach tighten and her head thump.

'Did you argue? Or say something inappropriate? What if she doesn't like us?'

'She will like you,' Abby said. 'She cannot help but like you.'

'I hope so. She is very powerful, you know, and can either make or break a debutante's debut. We have to make a good impression or she might not sponsor me.'

The words hung within the coach's lamplit interior, their presence almost physical.

'I'm sorry,' Abby said, conscious again of the woeful inadequacy of her words. 'I am sure she wouldn't hold my words against you.'

'I love you like a daughter but there are times when your sharp tongue will get you in trouble,' Mrs Harrington said, which was as close to a reprimand as Abby had ever heard from that kind-hearted individual.

'I know and I am sorry,' Abby repeated.

They continued forward in an uncomfortable silence. Abby looked at Lucy. Her face was pale in the lamplight with dark circles under her eyes. Despite this, she looked beautiful. She belonged in this carriage, nestled on the crushed velvet cushioning in a fashionable gown.

The carriage moved from the side streets and into the narrow roads close to their small rental. As they got closer, the street lamps became sparse and they passed fewer carriages.

Finally, they stopped. The coachman swung open the door and cool, damp air whistled in. Abby shivered, pulling her cloak more closely about her.

'Get some rest,' Mrs Harrington said, in a kinder tone. 'Likely, it will all seem better in the morning.'

Abby nodded dubiously. In her experience the cold light of day had never been particularly comforting.

Dolph retired to the study. He poured himself a cognac. His hand shook. Droplets of amber liquid fell onto the polished tabletop. He dabbed at them ineffectively, before tossing the cognac down in a fiery gulp.

When Barnaby had first joined the regiment, he hadn't understood why. He'd catalogued it under a foolish excess of patriotism. He'd thought it irrational, reckless even. He supposed he still did.

Was following a forbidden love into battle brave, foolish, tragic or a mush of all three?

And how did Barnaby or Miss Carstens or anyone else think that he could, in any way, impact this huge monolith that was society? He poured a second cognac.

The memories pressed against him: mud, the stench of faecal matter, urine, decay, death. It had all felt so hopeless. Indeed, from the moment he'd found Barnaby, injured within the mass of other casualties, he'd felt an absence of hope which he'd never regained.

The knock was peremptory and the door swung open before he'd had a moment to respond. His sister stood, darkly silhouetted against the lamplight from the corridor.

'Are you mad?' she asked, her tone too strident for his head.

'I don't believe so,' Dolph said, wincing as he stretched out his legs towards the small hearth. 'I find myself to be quite coherent and not foaming at the mouth or any other behaviour suggestive of madness.'

'You are sitting in the dark and likely drinking yourself silly in my dead husband's study. You should go home to Benton.'

'He'd tut and tsk with disappointment. Anyhow, shouldn't you be entertaining your guests?'

'They've gone home. A relatively early night. They are just out of the schoolroom, which is why I wanted to talk to you,' she said, lighting the lamp and sitting opposite. 'These Harringtons are worse than anticipated. They have no social graces. Society will make mincemeat of them.'

'Really?' He yawned. 'I did not think them colourful enough to invoke such ire.'

'The daughter is too quiet. The mother is too loud. The governess is rude and odd.'

'Oddity definitely the worst sin of all.' He eyed the bottle and wondered if he had sufficient energy to rise and refill the snifter. Was the required effort sufficient for the reward of more expeditious oblivion?

'As the daughter of a clergyman, I expected basic manners. But she was discussing most unsavoury topics.'

'She is progressive in her views, I find.'

'Progressive? I found her overly blunt in our conversation and she even mentioned—' Madeleine's voice dropped as though sharing a shocking confidence '—alcohol.'

'Never!' he said with pretended shock.

Oblivion was definitely worthwhile. He stood up poured another snifter.

'Do try and be serious,' she said. 'Set this Carstens female up as your mistress if you are infatuated, but do not induce me to sponsor such hangers-on.'

'Good heavens, even at my most rakish, I would draw the line at besmirching the reputation of an innocent. Moreover, I am not infatuated with Miss Carstens. I mean, she is sensible and intelligent and witty, well read and not without pluck and quite comely in that gown but not the sort one would be infatuated with.'

Madeleine appeared about to make a comment but suppressed this, pursing her lips. 'Miss Carstens is not the primary problem. None of them are ready for the Season. And, for this reason, I cannot sponsor Miss Harrington's debut.'

'You sound determined. This decision would have nothing to do with the fact Mr Trollope fancies her and you hope that he will make an offer—'

'That is an exaggeration. Besides, Mr Trollope is not the only suitable gentleman for Susan. She will have numerous offers. However, being associated with individuals having neither title, wealth nor social graces will not help her. And I do not wish nobodies from some benighted northern town to limit her chances. Truthfully, it would be kinder to abandon this project altogether.'

'Damnable nuisance.'

Madeleine leaned forward, an expression of genuine curiosity flickering across her face. 'Why?'

'Miss Carstens rather foretold this eventuality and I did not wish her to be right.'

Madeleine was silent for an unusual length of time while scrutinizing his expression. 'Back to Miss Carstens again. Now, I am beginning to worry,' she said at last.

'Why?'

'Because I cannot remember you ever concerning yourself with any lady's good opinion.'

'Not concerned. Just don't want to prove her right. Know she will be confoundingly irritating.'

'Well, they are not ready. Miss Harrington is pleasant enough. If her mother hired someone to prepare her properly, she could debut next year. As I recall, Mother arranged for Great-Aunt Edith to do so prior to my come-out.'

'Don't even remember a great-aunt Edith. Is she still alive?'

'I believe so.' Madeleine paused, smoothing her skirt with her long, elegant fingers. 'Did you talk to Jason?'

'Yes, had a man to man. Suggested that he might

want to limit his gambling and avoid insalubrious establishments. Will keep an eye on him.'

Madeleine rose. 'I will order your carriage. You can drink in your own home. Or go to bed.' She rang the bell before turning around to him.

'Thank you for talking to Jason,' she said.

Dolph sat staring into the low flames of the hearth within his own study. He felt no more at ease here than at his sister's home.

Worse...now he had his sister's words circling his brain, clashing and spinning with all the other thoughts and worries which kept him up at night.

Madeleine was right, he supposed. Lucinda Harrington, while pretty enough, had spent the evening looking like a frightened rabbit. Her dancing had been awkward and her conversation limited. She curtseyed without grace and in a haphazard manner with no real understanding of etiquette.

He supposed he'd have to tell them next day. And live up to Miss Carstens's worst expectations. That bothered him, he realized. More than was sensible.

He also knew they'd likely have to pack up and return to Harrogate. This also bothered him. He had rather enjoyed conversing with Miss Carstens. There was something about her that he would miss. She was intelligent and compassionate. She did not smile without reason but when she did, her expression transformed in a manner which made his breath catch. And while her mouth was firm, the corners twisted up just slightly, as though she were privy to some inward fancy. And they were well shaped.

Good grief. He stood abruptly, about to reach for another cognac. He paused; perhaps the fact that he was waxing poetic about Miss Carstens's lips was a sign he had imbibed sufficiently for the night.

The door opened and Benton entered, clearing his throat as was typical to announce his presence.

'Why are you hovering? Didn't I tell you to go to bed,' Dolph grumbled.

'Yes, my lord. Indeed, my lord, but I thought you might require my assistance.'

'I can undress myself. Likely you merely wish to supervise to ensure I do not wrinkle my neckties.'

'It is a matter of some concern, my lord.'

'You're still hovering.'

'Yes, my lord. Actually, I wanted to tell you that a Mr Smythe is here,' Benton said.

'A visitor? At this hour? Smythe?' The name was familiar but his thoughts were moving slowly, likely mired in cognac.

'He is very determined to see you,' Benton said, pursing his lips as though even the words were distasteful. 'An insalubrious gentleman—'

'I am not an un-salty whatever!' A somewhat

rough-looking gentleman appeared within the door frame with almost theatrical timing.

'I told you to wait,' Benson said, thunder in his tone.

'And I told you as 'ow I was 'ere to do this gent a favour,' the speaker said with some impatience, apparently inured to the thunder.

'It is fine.' Dolph quickly intervened. 'I now recognize you. Mr Smythe is in my employ.'

Benton wrinkled his nose disdainfully but made no comment.

'And I believe I may need my carriage brought around,' Dolph added.

'Might I suggest that a good night's sleep might serve you better, my lord,' Benton said.

'Absolutely. However, it appears that I may have to postpone the possibility of slumber.'

Benton left, a tutting sound audible under his breath.

The door closed. Smythe was dressed in an older style, choosing knee britches which looked to have seen better days.

Dolph took a seat at his desk, waving his hand towards the second chair, but Smythe chose to stand, shifting his weight uneasily.

'You have information?' Dolph asked.

'Well, yes, you said as 'ow if I ever saw Jason losing and drinking and getting taken by someone wot counts cards that I should come for you, so I did.'

'Indeed, your memory of our conversation is impeccable,' Dolph said, reaching into his desk drawer and handing over several coins.

Mr Smythe studied them. He was a short individual with vast quantities of facial hair as though to make up for his balding head. He frowned, his bushy eyebrows forming a solid line. His scepticism was such that Dolph half expected that he would bite the coins like a pirate. He did not do so, merely pocketing the coins with a cheerful jingle.

'Thanking you kindly, I'll be off then,' he said.

'May I offer you a ride? I imagine we are going to the same establishment.'

'Lor no. Don't want to be seen with the likes of you. More than my job's worth.' And with these words, Smythe turned, exiting the study hurriedly as though fearful that he might be manhandled into the proffered ride.

Moments later, Dolph also stepped into the hall. Benton waited, holding his great cloak. 'The carriage has been ordered, my lord,' he said in a doom-and-gloom tone, as though this news were quite dire.

'Thank you.' Dolph allowed Benton to help him into the cloak, stepping to the door as the carriage wheels rattled outside.

'May I enquire where you might be going, Your Lordship?' Benton asked.

'It appears I am going to a gambling hell with the interesting nomenclature of the Coffee Cauldron,' Dolph said.

Chapter Eight

The Coffee Cauldron was not a prepossessing establishment. Its sign hung from a post, clanging in the wind and impossible to read. Dolph walked towards its entrance and stepped inside.

The interior was quite different than it was during his earlier visit. At that time, it had been quiet, occupied only by several old men supping coffee. Now, every table was occupied. Smoke hung swirling in visible tendrils that twisted up into the dark rafters of the low ceiling. A fire crackled but was drawing improperly, making the air thick, laced with food, beer and sweat.

Dolph was also cognizant that he was being observed although the punters hid this well under blank expressions, their curiosity noticeable only as chatter became muted and tankards remained unsupped.

He nodded, smiling affably while handing a guinea to the man behind the bar.

'I would like entrance to the downstairs game.'

He kept his voice quiet but authoritative as though entering a grimy gambling hell was part of his everyday routine.

The man peered at him, one eye covered with a film as though injured or infected. He shook his head. Dolph reached for a second coin. For a moment there was hesitation before the man reached out, his fingers folding tightly around the silver.

'This way,' he said.

The stairs were narrow, twisting and dimly lit. The lantern hung at the head of the stairs, casting eerie, elongated shadows. Upstairs had been noisy with talk, but the cellar felt different. Sounds were muted, the air cold and stale, its chill broken only by a small, lacklustre fire at the far end of the room. The occupants at the round tables did not demonstrate an opulent cheer but rather a fixed concentration as they huddled nervously around tightly packed tables.

Dolph strolled into the room, his gaze flickering across each table.

'Greetings, all,' he said affably. 'Sorry to interrupt. Just looking for my nephew, don't you know. My sister is so worried about him. Well, you know how it is.'

He saw Jason quick enough. He gave himself away in his quick stiffening and apprehensive stare. The lad was younger than the other players with his collar so high it seemed like to impede his movement.

His hair was cut short as was the fashion and he had long, but still somewhat patchy, sideburns.

'Dolph,' he said, his tone both slurred and lugubrious as his jaw slackened.

'Indeed, in the flesh.'

'We're in the middle of a game, you can get in on the next hand,' the man opposite said. He wore a flamboyant waistcoat of red silk with several gravy stains. There was a bristling bravado about him.

'I am afraid there won't be a next hand,' Dolph said pleasantly.

'Must stay. My luck will turn—' Jason said, the words running together.

'Doubtless but not here.'

'Happy to visit you tomorrow.' Jason gave a dismissive wave.

'I am sure but I must insist that you see me now instead.'

'You're embarrassing me,' Jason said, muttering as though this would disguise his words. His cheeks had flushed with wine and anger.

'You are being fleeced by a secondrate card sharp in the Coffee Cauldron, a third-rate gambling hell. Not certain it is within my power to embarrass you further,' Dolph said.

This comment caught the attention of the man opposite with the red waistcoat and a wig that had, in some bygone era, been white. He stood, the movement sudden. 'What? You're impugning my honour. Who do you think you are?'

'Lord Lansdowne, Duke of Elmsend.'

The man's hands curled into fists. 'I will have satisfaction!'

'Duels are for honourable fools and you are neither,' Dolph said dismissively. 'Leave here.'

'What? And if I don't?' He stepped forward.

'I'll ask you to roll up your left sleeve and show the ace hidden within the cuff.'

This caught the attention of the other players. One man rose, so tall and lanky that he had to stoop to ensure he did not hit the low beams. Another swore while a third lunged forward with such aggression that the first man stepped back, edging into the corner.

'Right, well, best we leave,' Dolph said to Jason.

The boy flushed and stood, stumbling drunkenly across the floor and then up the narrow stairway. From behind they heard shouts, the crash of tables and crockery. There was a thud and the sound of fist meeting nose.

'Seems to be a bit of a dust-up downstairs,' Dolph said, tossing another coin at the server and then stepping out of the establishment and into the cool, maritime and somewhat noxious air of the Thames.

Martin opened the door of the carriage.

Jason got in, his complexion pale within the lamp-light.

Dolph sat opposite, making himself comfortable and eyeing his young nephew. 'Do try not to cast up your accounts. This is a new carriage.'

'How did you know I was there?'

'I had made arrangements to ensure that I would be notified if you failed to live up to our agreement.'

'You didn't trust me?'

'It appears you are not to be trusted.'

'Didn't want you to come.' Jason glowered and Dolph was reminded of a sulky child.

'Didn't particularly want to come. I was well on the way to a pleasant state of inebriation,' Dolph said, fondly remembering his cognac. 'But family obliga-tions, you know. How much would you have lost?'

The boy said nothing, slumping further so that his face was almost obscured by the ludicrous collar.

Dolph remained quiet, merely fixing him with his piercing gaze until an answer was forthcoming.

'One thousand pounds,' Jason said.

'You are not mature enough to play for more than conkers if you cannot spot a cheat.'

'Don't see how you can lecture me,' he muttered. 'Seems you're always in your cups or good as.'

'Difference is, I spot a cheat.' Dolph leaned back as the carriage lurched over the uneven roads. He had not yet closed the carriage curtain and through the window he could discern ramshackle buildings, dimly lit by sparse street lamps which provided small puddles of insufficient light. Poorly clothed children huddled around small fire pits, and beggars held out cupped hands while women in ragged, low-cut dresses lingered on street corners.

He looked away.

'Are you going to tell my mother?' his nephew asked.

'At some point, although she seems to have little influence on you.'

'I'll do better.'

'Hmm…so you said.'

They travelled for some distance in silence, which was not uncomfortable as the boy seemed to have slipped into a drunken doze. In repose he looked so very young.

They stopped in front of Lady Stanhope's house. Jason jerked awake, peering around blearily. 'You coming in?' he asked his uncle.

'Not at present.' Dolph had had enough of Madeleine for the moment. Moreover, the boy looked too nauseous to be of much use.

He watched as Martin helped him out. Jason walked towards the house, lurching unsteadily. The boy had been spoiled. His father had died early and Madeleine had left him in the care of indulgent servants and governesses.

Dolph leaned back again. The carriage moved forward again. He hoped Benton had not stayed up all night.

Outside, the eastern sky was stained with pink and ribbons of light were visible on the horizon. With the advent of dawn, the city would come to life. Barrow boys would push their wares, cart horses would lumber with deliveries and milkmen would put milk on steps as newsboys set up their stands.

Dawn had always seemed a hopeful time. He remembered getting up early with Barnaby and riding their stocky ponies or, bored and unable sleep, they would talk and play and wait for the rest of the world to wake.

It was the promise of a new day, he supposed. Hope had felt absent from his life but, in these last few days, he had felt it growing, unfurling. As he gazed at the dawn sky with its ribbons of light, an idea struck him.

The carriage stopped. He got out.

'Martin,' he said. 'Refresh the horses and be back in an hour.'

'Back, my lord? You're going out, my lord?' his groom said with understandable confusion. Dolph seldom ventured out during the day and never during morning hours.

'It appears I must visit number thirty-one Wimpole Street,' he said.

* * *

Abby slept little. Her thoughts circled. Why? Why had Lord Lansdowne turned so white? Who had he been thinking about? Why had she been so worried about a grown man? Why had she been so impulsive and spoken so freely?

And to Lady Stanhope, of all people?

Why?

She was forever telling Iggy to be less impulsive and consider the consequences of his words and actions, and yet she had been unable to hold her tongue to this woman who held her friend's future within her palm.

And why had Lord Lansdowne even wanted her to come? Was Lucy's future to be sacrifice to her own ineptitude and a man's bored desire to watch her stumble through social missteps, saying things that debutantes should not say.

Or was it planned? Had he guessed that she would be a social disgrace and provide him with an excuse to abandon the project?

Her mind baulked—would he be so devious. So unkind?

And then her mind careened to those moments on the dance floor. She'd felt oddly comfortable, in step, as if moving together in a way which almost seemed instinctual so that she had felt her usual awkwardness slide from her.

And this made her remember the tea parties of her childhood, where everyone had the same script and she'd felt a discomfort within her own skin.

Of course, this raised that old, familiar, niggling guilt. She'd loved her mother and missed her mother but there'd also been a relief.

She supposed that had been her mother's tragedy. She had married a man in a most conventional occupation, out of the need to conform. Except, despite or because of his position, her father did not conform. Mother had attempted to make him the type of vicar she thought the parishioners deserved and Abby had briefly tried.

It hadn't worked and she'd given up, letting him be himself: an academic, an orator, a gambler and a risk-taker.

To thine own self be true.

Miss Brownlee loved Shakespeare or literature of any sort. During mother's illness and after her death, they'd worked together to provide some basic education to the village children within the church basement. They'd delivered soups and bandaged wounds and Abby had continued that work, even after Miss Brownlee's death.

Abby had liked that life. She missed it. There was a simplicity in the provision of physical care. If an individual was bleeding, one bandaged the wound. If there was hunger, soup and bread helped.

She got up, unable to bear her circling thoughts. She peered into the darkness. Already the birds sang in their predawn chorus. Was their song, she wondered, the definition of hope? The ability to sing within the blackness of night, sure in the belief of dawn and a new day.

Indeed, even by the time she'd pulled on her dress and splashed water on her face, she could see the shadowy outline of the hedges and the shimmer of damp cobbles in dawn's grey light.

She walked down the corridor, her feet soft pads within the morning quiet. She'd find Mrs Fred. She would help. She would know what to say. Already Abby could detect the comforting smell of bacon and, as she entered the kitchen, she heard its sizzle, the crackling fire and bubbling kettle.

'You're up early,' Mrs Fred said, poking a fork at the rashers so that they spat and hissed.

'I should never have gone. I made such a fool of myself. And we had to leave early,' Abby said, throwing herself in a nearby chair, much as she had done as a child.

'Rome wasn't built in a day,' Mrs Fred said, which, while comforting, did not seem entirely pertinent.

'I just hope Lady Stanhope will still sponsor Lucy. I mean, she can't blame Lucy for my ill manners.'

'That is a worrisome question on an empty stomach. And I cannot be guessing the ways of one like

Lady Stanhope but you can't be pondering on what other people think. You never have. Best not to start now.'

'I don't care for me but for Lucy.'

'Well, if she has any sense, Lady Stanhope will see the beauty in you both. Now you be going upstairs. I'll bring breakfast to the morning room. You'd best be making up a fire. We don't want you freezing to death. And take up your tea—there's a love. A cup of tea will work wonders.'

Abby carried the tray and sat in the still empty breakfast room. She held the cup tightly, thankful for its warmth. No chamber within the tiny rented house was uplifting but this was the worst. It faced the back alley so she could not see the street. The dull grey light of morning flickered through the panes onto the beige walls with their semicircles of rising damp.

Mrs Harrington had put her last sou into renting this apartment. And Lucy knew her dream. She had no doubts. She was not like Abby, dreaming of women's independence and choice and a host of other things which seemed impossible. She wanted only a husband and family and Abby might well have jeopardized that dream.

Abby sipped her tea with that feeling of both exhaustion and restlessness. Indeed, she was so deep in thought that she was quite unaware of time's passing so the sharp rap startled her. She spilled her tea. With a mutter of irritation, she put down the cup, dabbing at her gown, while looking around nervously as though expecting some explanation from the blank walls.

She hoped it was not Mrs Pollock about her roses. Or Lady Stanhope to heap further condemnation. Although she would be unlikely to be up this early. Or bothering to make a house call in this area of town.

However, Abby reminded herself, she was not of the personality to hide from callers with inventive fears. With an inhalation, she put aside the cold tea, straightened and walked briskly towards the door.

'Good morning, Miss Carstens,' Lord Lansdowne said.

'I… I…' The air left her body in a winded gasp.

Again Abby was struck by his size, the breadth of his shoulders and an odd, peculiar fluttering squeeze in her stomach.

'You'd best come in,' she managed, still clutching the doorknob and gaping, she feared, like a fresh-caught flounder. 'Mrs Harrington will be down soon.'

She turned, leading the way into the parlour although, in truth, she was tempted to slam the door and run back into the dim confines of the breakfast room—except that would be childish and lacking control.

'The hound is secured upstairs?' He angled his head to the ceiling, where a loud barking could now be heard.

'Mrs Fred likely confined him to quarters. She made bacon, you see. You could have some, if you like,' she said, then pressed her hands together, hoping to stop further foolish rambling.

'Thank you. I have eaten,' he said.

'Of course.' Indeed, he did not seem the type to nibble on stray bacon rashers. 'I am certain Mrs Harrington will be down presently. I, um, hope you are feeling better.'

'I am. I came early because I wanted to talk to you.'

She sat down rather heavily. 'With me?'

'I wished to apologize to you for leaving so abruptly last night. I am sorry if I caused you concern.'

'I feared you were ill. I am glad you are better.'

'Yes.' He paused. 'Also, my sister spoke to me last night.'

Bother. She shifted uncomfortably. 'I was outspoken. I will apologize.'

'She was a little shocked,' he said, with that twist of his lips which she always found appealing, as though he was not without humour.

'And doubtless she does not wish me to participate in any future events, which I do not mind. Not at all.'

'There is another problem. She is unwilling to sponsor Lucy.'

'But…' Abby swallowed, aware of a sad sinking feeling. She had tried never to let people down or promise that which she could not deliver. 'I should not have come. Truly, Lady Stanhope must not judge Lucy. It is not fair. Lucy is nothing like me.'

He shook his head. 'It is not because you were outspoken. That is why I came so early. I wanted to talk to you. I didn't want you to blame yourself.'

'Oh,' she said, swallowing, confused but also touched by his consideration. 'Then what is it?'

'She says they are not ready. Lucy is just not prepared. She can't dance very well and is lacking in social etiquette.'

Abby stared. She felt a moment of disbelief oddly mixed with inevitability.

'But they counted on this. Mrs Harrington… Is there no way Lady Stanhope would reconsider?'

'To what end? The fact is—she might be right,' he said.

Abby pressed her hands together. 'But Lady Stanhope would likely have paid little heed to Lucy if it had not been for me. There must be another option.'

'I have an idea.'

'What?' Abby asked.

'You all come to Lansdowne House.'

'Your estate?'

'Yes. It is a short journey. It will not invite scandal as Mrs Harrington will be there. It would not even seem unusual given that they are relatives.'

'But why?' she asked.

'It will give Lucy time. There are ladies who specialise in preparing young women for their debut. Apparently, my great aunt Edith is such an individual. Granted she may be somewhat ancient. But she likely knows someone.'

'And she would work with Lucy?

'Yes. Or someone like her.'

'But why? Why would you do that? Why go to so much trouble for people you don't know?'

Miss Carstens looked at him with that sharp, intent gaze which made him oddly tongue-tied and unable to give his usual glib answers.

'I don't want you to say I told you so,' he said, with a lame attempt at humour.

'Another Banbury tale?'

'Not entirely,' he said. 'I think you would relish it and would be extremely annoying.'

He paused, aware that she was still studying him, her gaze astute.

'And?' she said.

'And I also wish to remove my nephew, Jason, from London.'

'Lady Stanhope's son?'

'And my heir.'

'Why?'

'He is drinking and gambling. I think the country will be good for him.'

She nodded. 'Or he will be most dreadfully bored. Regardless, that need not involve us.'

He paced, standing by the chill hearth and drumming his fingers against the mantelpiece. 'I think you might also be good for him.'

'Me? Me personally?'

'Yes.'

'Because of Ignatius? I am certain your nephew would not want a governess. Good lord, he would run a mile,' she said, sensibly enough. 'Besides, I tried to curtail my father's interest in horses and horse racing with limited success.'

'The vicar?' he asked with some surprise.

'The reluctant vicar, yes. Likely, he could have been a happy thespian, but my grandfather didn't want his second son in the theatre. So Father contented himself with performing once a week. He gave excellent sermons, relieving his boredom with gambling and riding horses too fast.'

She glanced down at these last words, pressing her hands together. It seemed as though she winced at the pain while also picking at an open wound. He wished he could hold her hands, to feel them in his own, to still their movement.

'I'm sorry,' he said.

She shrugged, an insouciant motion. 'I think when people lack choice or control over their lives they self-destruct.'

It was true, he thought.

'Barnaby, my brother.'

'Was that who you were thinking about last night?'

'Yes. He believed there were many things wrong in our society and he felt trapped by its rules and judgement. He wanted to make it better.'

She glanced at him. He felt exposed, raw, vulnerable like she could see through him. 'You loved him a lot.'

'Yes,' he said.

It was a given, a fact, a truth, and yet it also felt oddly good to say it out loud, to state the truth with such stark simplicity. Somehow that simple acknowledgement made the misunderstandings and hurt become less important and more like unimportant noise.

Trivial.

The tight knot of pain in his chest eased, just a little. He looked at her, this calm, straightforward woman with rich chestnut hair, firm features and cornflower blue eyes. No, not cornflower blue. They were a deeper hue, a grey blue. And her skin, while pale, had a luminosity to it so that he wished he could touch her cheek. And her lips looked soft, their fullness contrasting with the primness of her other features.

Odd to feel this connection, this compassion from someone he hardly knew.

A parson's daughter from a far-flung northern town could know nothing of his brother's situation. The thought of a man loving a man would shock and confound her. Yet conversely there was something about her...the hint of a suggestion that she might see beyond the box which was their current society.

'I would like you to come to Lansdowne, not just for Jason,' he said. 'Over the last few weeks, I have been able to think about the future, visualize a future. Maybe it was experiencing the locomotive or even planning for Miss Harrington's debut, but the future seems more possible and less like a dark pit. It seems to me that if I am to be a half-decent uncle or landlord, I need to see a future.'

She remained silent, as though processing the words, discerning the meaning beneath them. He liked that she did not need to fill every moment and was prepared to sit with the steady tick of the clock. The ton feared silence, filling every lull as one might plug a dam.

'You see I have to go back,' he continued. 'To

Lansdowne. I haven't been back since my mother's funeral. Barnaby died some years ago. Then my father. I was starting to think about the estate and my duties to it. Then Mother died. I haven't been back.'

'I'm sorry.' She stood, walking to him.

'Yes, I was rather careless with my relatives.'

'Don't,' she said. 'Don't hide.' They stood in front of the hearth. She was considerably shorter than him. Her eyes held a kindness, an intelligence and an understanding.

He smiled. 'You wish to break a habit of a lifetime? That's what we do.'

'The upper classes are emotionally constipated. That doesn't mean it's a good thing,' she said in those firm, blunt tones which broke the tension but were oddly comforting.

He laughed. 'Have you always been so outspoken?'

'Yes, at least, since my mother died. So why now? Why do you want to go back to Lansdowne now?' she asked with that typical persistence.

'I have to. For my brother.' He felt the words come out with difficulty, jerky and uneven.

There was an angular beauty to his features, also marked with a stark pain. She reached to touch his cheek, the movement involuntary. Her fingertips grazed against his skin, sensing both its warmth and the slight roughness of his unshaven cheek.

'I'm sorry.' She dropped her hand.

'Don't be.' He spoke so softly that she wondered if she'd dreamed the words.

He took her hand within his own. She could feel the strength and warmth of his palm and just the slightest roughness on his fingertips.

They stood close. She could hear his breath and smell the tangy scent of tobacco. She could see the single dimple, the strength of his jaw line and his lips, firm but with that slight self-deprecating twist.

They were cocooned within the early-morning stillness.

'You have a quality, Miss Carstens, that…' He paused as though trying to find the words. 'That makes me want to hope again.'

His tone was one of wonder, as if describing alchemy.

She lifted her eyes and met his gaze. His eyes were a dark flinty grey with flecks of green. His expression was not that of his usual sardonic humour. Instead, there was a heat, an intensity, a vulnerability. It seemed enthralling and absorbing so that he could not look away. Instead, he felt her body sway, just a little closer.

He lifted his other hand, running his thumb along her jawline. Her heart quickened. She heard its hurried beat, a fast shushing against her ears. She felt his touch. It scorched her skin, as if all sensation started in that spot, growing and winding through her.

He moved forward. She heard the rustle of fabric. She touched the strong line of his jaw and felt the roughness of stubble against her fingertips again. She swallowed. Heard her own light gasp, and her lips parted.

A clock chimed, and she pulled away.

He dropped his hand, and she heard the soft thwack of his palm against his leg. She stepped away.

'I apologize, Miss Carstens,' he said.

'Yes. Well…um…no matter.' Her voice sounded hoarse, breathless, even to her own ears.

She knew a need to escape his company and the strange, foreign feelings he evoked.

Her limbs and brain lacked their usual control so that it took an almost conscious effort to walk back to her seat and remain still, straight backed as she clutched her hands together as if, without restraint, they would reach for him.

'I will speak to the Harringtons later. You will convince them to come if they are reluctant. Even if it means missing a part of the Season?'

'I—' She found herself unusually bereft of words. The thought of staying in the same house as him made her feel…odd. The word was pitifully inadequate.

The thought of packing up and returning to Harrogate made her feel empty and bleak. Those words were also pitifully inadequate.

Besides, it was a good idea. It would help Lucy. Moreover, there was no need for them to even see each other. His house was doubtless vast. He might well stay in London. She would teach Iggy. She would spend time with this great-aunt and Lucy and Mrs Harrington.

'Yes,' she said. 'I'm sure they will be pleased to come. '

He nodded, walking towards the door.

'Dolph— I… I mean, Lord Lansdowne. If they ask why, tell them that Lady Stanhope thought my manners should be improved. It is true enough. I don't want Lucy to lose her confidence.'

He nodded, bowed, then walked away. The door closed behind him with a muted sneck. His footsteps retreated into quick clicks against the hardwood as he walked through the hall.

Basil barked. The sound was laughably prosaic. The front door opened. And closed.

She inhaled. It felt as though she had forgotten to breathe. Her exhalations were uneven.

Slowly, as though needing to consciously orchestrate the movement of her limbs, Abby rose. She went to the hearth. She gripped the mantel. The wood felt solid, pressing into her palms. She liked its hardness. It seemed to connect her to the earth, to what was real.

One was changed by experience, Miss Brownlee had said.

She felt changed.

And yet, nothing had happened. There had been no experience. A gentleman had touched her chin… held her hand. And she had touched his jaw. Twice.

It was no earth-shattering event.

How many hands had she held while teaching in the village or ladling soup? How many ankles had she bandaged?

Yet this felt more. Different. Viscount Ashleigh had tried to hold her hand once. She remembered the damp, distasteful moisture of his palm.

But today…but today felt different, was different. As though something fundamental had shifted.

With an almost violent movement, she swung from the mantel. She needed to get away. To forget today. It had meant nothing. It was nothing.

Good lord, there was nothing to forget.

Nor was she the type of female to get her head turned by a handsome man. She did not believe in fairy tales. She did not believe that women should sit passive and wait for rescue. Her aspirations had never involved a man, be he honourable or dishonourable. Her dreams were not of love, marriage but of autonomy.

A peculiar thump sounded from upstairs. There was a scrabble of paws and a crash.

With a muted groan that was half relief, Abby turned towards the door. She'd best earn her keep and prevent the destruction of the small rental by her charge.

Chapter Nine

Thankfully, the journey was much shorter than that their travels from England's north. Moreover, Lord Lansdowne had kindly provided his vehicle and it was considerably more luxurious than the Harringtons' rather ancient contraption.

However, that did not mean that it was pleasant.

In a moment of maternal weakness, Mrs Harrington had promised Iggy that he and Basil could travel with them, rather than coming in the second carriage with Mr and Mrs Fred.

Naturally, Iggy was bored and therefore peppered them with questions and further ideas for inventions. These became more far-fetched as the day dragged and his tedium grew.

Meanwhile, Basil insisted on standing on their laps to peer out of the windows, his sharp claws painful on their legs, while his feather duster of a tail wafted in their nostrils. This activity was interspersed with retching sounds, necessitating all too frequent pauses.

Iggy also felt sick, bored and otherwise indisposed, nor was he of a stoic disposition. Therefore, the trip was not quiet and involved much stopping and starting.

Lord Lansdowne was not travelling with them. He had gone ahead with Jason and Benton, in an attempt both to prepare the house and keep Jason away from further gambling hells.

Abby found his absence both a relief and yet not so. It seemed that he possessed her thoughts so that she could think of little else. When she closed her eyes, she saw his face or remembered things he'd said. At times she reached far-fetched interpretations or could see nuanced meaning. Then, moments later, such conclusions seemed the height of foolishness.

She felt giddy and, simultaneously, her stomach would drop, leaden with apprehension. She both hoped for his quick return to London and that he would remain at Lansdowne.

It irritated her that a man she hardly knew should so occupy her thoughts. It irked that her own self-control appeared limited and her ability to manage her own thoughts undone. Even the calming repetition of Latin declensions in no way soothed her mind nor banished the memory of his fingers on her skin, the intensity of his gaze and the angular strength of his jawline.

By late afternoon, the sun had slipped behind the hills and the countryside was obscured, the fields becoming a vast darkness dotted with pinpricks of light from homes and barns.

Eventually these flickering lights multiplied and it seemed as though they were going through a more populated area, a village perhaps. Through the window, she could see buildings, their shapes outlined under weak puddles of light. The wheels of the carriage rattled as if travelling over cobblestones until they swung sharply to the left.

In contrast this road was rutted and the carriage lurched uncomfortably over uneven ground. The springs creaked. Branches scraped as they struck and scratched the exterior and Abby could discern no lights breaking the gloom, save those from their own carriage.

'Gracious,' Mrs Harrington said, speaking in a low voice as Iggy had fallen to sleep. 'It does not seem well maintained. I hope we do not get stuck or lose a wheel or some such.'

This slow, uncomfortable progress continued until, at last, they passed through two huge gate-posts which opened into a courtyard.

Abby pressed her face against the cool pane. A large courtyard was visible in the light of numerous torches lit about its perimeter. A massive stone structure hunkered at one end, its entrance guarded by stone lions.

'Thank goodness,' Mrs Harrington said as the carriage stopped. 'I am that stiff. I tell you a body is not meant for inactivity.'

Iggy was roused with difficulty while Basil bounced and barked in a mad cacophony of euphoria. Abby quickly grabbed his rope. She had no wish to chase a lively dog or Iggy in his attempts to catch the dog.

At close quarters, the house proved neither ugly nor beautiful. Rather it had presence. She could feel it in the proportion of a single turret, the intricate masonry about the doorway and the wide arch of the porte cochère.

'Looks like it could be haunted,' Iggy announced with a yawn, taking Basil's rope from her as they descended from the carriage.

She had to agree that there was a certain desolation. Moss grew over the flagstones and steps, several of which were cracked and uneven. One of the windows was broken and tufts of grass grew at the base of the walls while ivy covered a portion of the turret.

'Welcome. I hope your ride was comfortable.'

Abby startled. Her breath caught in a husky gasp. Lord Lansdowne stood in the doorway at the top of his stairs. His elevation and the light from inside made him appear taller and more imposing.

Abby's mouth felt oddly dry and her tongue awkward, as though unable to properly form her words.

He stepped down, and that single lock of hair fell into his eyes.

'I am glad you are here,' he said.

'I am glad—' she started, her voice oddly squeaky.

Mrs Harrington hurried forward. 'Lord Lansdowne, thank you so much for this invitation and personal greeting. Indeed, it is so kind of you. Our ride was very comfortable.'

'I am pleased to hear it,' Lord Lansdowne said. 'This is Benton. We are a little short-staffed but he is hiring all manner of people and will ensure your visit is comfortable.'

A tall elderly man appeared in the doorway. 'You are most welcome.' He spoke in rather formal tones. His jaw, Abby thought, looked a little swollen.

It was good to notice such details, she decided. Much better than to focus on the wobbly feeling in her stomach, the dryness in her mouth or that peculiar breathlessness, despite the fact she had not exerted herself in any way.

They walked into the hall, which, like the courtyard, was a mix of beauty and decay. Iron chandeliers hung from a domed ceiling. The candlelight flickered, creating odd, mobile shadows adding an eeriness to the space. A fire roared within a massive stone hearth, taller than a man, and yet despite this, the air was cold. Thick columns, wide as an oak's trunk, supported the roof and the walls were interrupted only by heavy tapestries and suits of armour.

'Can I try—' Ignatius started.

'No,' Abby said.

'How did you even know what I was going to say?'

'You were going to ask if you could try on the armour.'

'How did you know?' Ignatius asked, his tone disgruntled.

'Might I suggest that you and your canine companion go to the kitchen, Master Ignatius?' Benton asked, allowing his formal expression to soften. 'Cook will likely have some food which might tempt you both.'

'Basil doesn't take much tempting. He'll eat anything,' Ignatius said.

'Indeed,' Lord Lansdowne agreed. 'As I recall, he has a particular fondness for roses.'

'He didn't eat the roses. He just liked digging them up,' Ignatius explained, while he and Basil followed a footman down a long corridor towards, she presumed, the kitchen.

Abby heard Iggy's retreating chatter and the clatter of claws with a certain relief. Regardless of the other stressors involved in their stay, it was good to know that Basil was out of London and away from the temptation of Mrs Pollock's roses.

As they stepped further into the hall, Abby became increasingly aware that it felt less like an abode and more like a stone castle from a bygone era. Their footsteps echoed, rebounding from the walls and making the space seem the more cavernous, and she was conscious of a chill draft.

Abby pulled her cloak more closely about her person.

'This is the medieval part,' Lord Lansdowne said. 'Quite frigid, particularly in winter. It dates from the 1300s. Fortunately, other parts are more habitable.'

They clambered up the stone staircase that followed the curved contour of the wall. Of course, it had no banister and Abby found herself instinctively clinging close to the stonework, brushing against the faded tapestries, doubtless shifting the dust of the ages.

She had thought she loved history, but her experience had been with dusty texts or neat exhibits. There was a rawness here, something uncivilized which seemed bigger and more overwhelming than the present.

It also made her all the more aware of his ancestry and lineage. Lord Lansdowne had relatives that had likely arrived with the Normans. They had built this medieval monster. They were rooted in history and steeped in pageantry. As she glanced at the tapestries and armoured knights, she also gained a sense of what it must be like to be part of such a family with an obligation not to the future but to the past.

Several corridors led away from the top of the landing into what appeared to be a newer construction. As they reached the top, a footman approached, passing a message to His Lordship. Dolph nodded and Abby thought his expression appeared briefly anxious.

'I hope you will excuse me. I must attend to another matter. However, I know that Benton will make you comfortable. We had thought that, given the late hour, you would prefer a small repast in your chambers. I will see you in the morning.' He made his bow, walking briskly down the stairs.

Abby found herself watching as he strode away. Oddly, she felt both bereft and relieved. She had been waiting the entire journey to see him but now his absence felt like a reprieve. At the same time, she knew that, layered under the relief, there was disappointment.

And maybe worry...?

Not that Dolph would welcome or needed her concern.

At the end of the passage, a kindly individual met them, introduced as Mrs Lamprey. She was of short stature with bright eyes half-hidden within the pouches of her plump cheeks.

'She will show you to your bedchambers so that you can freshen up,' Benton explained. 'And I will, as mentioned, arrange for a light repast.'

He turned. As he did so, his cheek caught the light and Abby felt quite certain that his jaw was not only swollen but inflamed. She would investigate tomorrow. Her mother had made a poultice and she'd used the recipe herself in her father's parish. While not a miracle cure, it had helped.

'This way,' Mrs Lamprey said, leading them further along the corridor. 'We have your chambers close together. Ah, here we are, Mrs Harrington and Miss Harrington.'

Mrs Lamprey stopped, opening up two doors and escorting both ladies inside.

'Why, this is quite lovely!' Mrs Harrington exclaimed from inside the room. 'It was all feeling a little medieval earlier but this delightful.'

'Thank you,' Mrs Lamprey said. 'Miss Carstens, we thought you might be comfortable opposite. Also, Lord Lansdowne suggested that it would be helpful to have support with Master Ignatius, so I asked my niece in for tomorrow, thinking as how you might all be tired.'

'How kind,' Mrs Harrington said, stepping back

into the corridor. 'Lord Lansdowne thinks of everything. Such a kind man!'

'And your niece, is she experienced? Iggy can be rather a handful,' Abby asked.

'Eldest of eight. Six of them boys.'

'And we cannot be relying on you to look after him all the time. Not when His Lordship has arranged for one of his relatives to come in and provide you with an improvement in your manner. Your mother was all things delightful, as are you, of course, but there are moments when an individual might find you the merest bit abrasive.'

'I will naturally listen to His Lordship's aunt or whatever,' Abby said, turning and following Mrs Lamprey into her bedchamber with an exhalation of relief.

'Now, I can send up one of the maids to help you get ready,' Mrs Lamprey said. 'I know your staff isn't here yet.'

Abby chuckled. Their 'staff' consisted of only Mr and Mrs Fred.

'I am fine. Thank you,' she said.

'Right. I will send the tray up and you can explore the house in the morning. Best ring for a maid to guide you down to breakfast. It can be a bit of a labyrinth.'

Mrs Lamprey left and Abby sat down on the comfortable bed, the baleen springs creaking. Refreshment, warmth, rest and solitude would surely provide some relief to her confused, chaotic thoughts.

Labyrinth proved an apt description. The house was as massively convoluted in the morning light as it had seemed the night previous with a vast collection of corridors sprouting from its medieval core like the limbs of a mythical monster.

Abby was up before either Mrs Harrington or Lucy and followed the maid towards the scent of bacon and coffee, which wafted pleasantly through the hallways. The breakfast room was a bright, pleasant apartment within the newer part of the building. A fire crackled pleasantly within the hearth. The weather had also improved and beams of morning sunlight flickered across the floor, through somewhat grimy windowpanes.

The chamber was unoccupied except for the footman and she felt a telltale flicker of disappointment, as though she was constantly looking for Lord Randolph only to feel a confused muddle of disappointed relief.

'I hope Master Ignatius was not too much trouble last night,' she said to the footman, now recognizing him from the night before.

'No, Miss.'

'Is he up yet? He tends to get into trouble when left to his own devices.'

'Indeed,' the footman said. 'So Mr Benton advised. I took the liberty of suggesting that he take the dog for a walk and Mrs Lamprey's niece will be accompanying them.'

'Thank you. Perhaps if they both get sufficient exercise, it will improve their behaviour.'

'Yes, Miss. Cook fed them breakfast and sent them off with a morning snack. She is a great believer in fresh air, exercise and food for growing boys.'

'Right, well, thank you again,' Abby said although she was also cognizant that she now had time on her hands. She had never feared time before. Indeed, Miss Brownlee had always assigned numerous readings and, even after her death, she'd had endless chores about the village and church.

Time, she supposed, had first become uncomfortable after her father's death. Strange how something, once treasured, could become unwelcome. Then, of course, she'd taken over Iggy's education and really that was such a full-time occupation she'd had little time to dwell.

But now she felt a discomfort. She felt unsettled and while the house spiked her curiosity, she did not want to explore it and risk running into Lord Lansdowne. Although, conversely, she found herself wondering where he was and when she might next meet him.

The lack of logic in her reasoning was unfamiliar.

It appeared that emotion was overwhelming cognition. Such confused uncertainty was foreign.

There was, however, Benton's tooth. She remembered this satisfaction. Given his swollen jaw last night and discoloured skin, she felt quite certain that he had a toothache and should, out of human decency, provide care.

'I must see Benton,' she announced with sudden enthusiasm. 'After breakfast.'

'Of course, I will inform Mr Benton that you wish to see him, Miss,' the footman said.

'And what is your name, by the way.'

'Giles, Miss.'

'Thank you, Giles.'

Abby was helping herself to breakfast when a second individual entered the room. This person was young, with a pale face, blond hair and clothes that seemed too fashionable for country living.

'You must be Jason,' she said.

'Yes,' the young gentleman said monosyllabically. He added for the sake of manners, 'Miss Carstens, I presume. Pleased to meet you.'

'Giles, do get Lord Stanhope coffee,' she said, kindly keeping her voice soft.

Jason grabbed at the proffered cup, much as a drowning man might cling to a life raft.

He stood at the sideboard, as though needing its support, and took several sips before garnering sufficient strength to venture the few feet to the dining table. Upon making this landmark, he slumped into the seat with a muttered groan.

'Perhaps get more coffee and dry toast,' Abby said to Giles.

Abby looked at Jason with sympathy. He seemed younger than she had anticipated and his clothes, with their high collars and intricate neckties, quite overwhelmed so that he was more clothes than person. This again served to emphasize the gangly slimness of a boy who had not yet filled out into a man.

'Giles will be back with the toast shortly. Dry toast will prove helpful,' she said. 'A cold bath can help to lessen the effect of too much alcohol. I also can make you a beverage with several herbs which are likely within the kitchen garden.'

He stared at her groggily as he went to a chair, lowering himself into it, the movements suggestive that the room was still spinning. 'Are you even supposed to know about such things?'

'Likely not, but I have a bad habit of talking before properly limiting my knowledge to that which others expect. My father used to gamble rather a lot and drink on occasion.'

'Heavens, and Dolph thinks he will be able to make you proper?'

'I might be a lost cause, although I will try for my friend's sake.'

'Right. Good to meet you. Hope I wasn't rude. Did not expect someone up so early,' he explained, rubbing his temples as though that might serve to clarify his thoughts.

'I quite understand. I was myself rather rude recently and regretted it. However, that does rather lead to the question as to why you are up so early. It appears that you might be more comfortable if horizonal.'

'Uncle Dolph! Told Benton, who told Giles, to get me up with the rooster. Thinks country hours will do me good.' Jason spoke with some disgust.

'You disagree?'

He shrugged. 'Can't see it will make much difference. Did you try it with your father?'

'My mother did. She tried everything. And, no, it didn't work.'

'And where is Uncle Dolph? Perhaps he should follow his own advice.'

'There is some wisdom in your words. There could be benefit in modelling appropriate behaviour,' Abby agreed.

'Indeed,' Jason said approvingly. 'Maybe he should try country hours though glad he is not. He can be very grumpy in the morning.'

'A family failing, perhaps?'

Before they could continue this conversation, Benton entered. He bowed, his forehead wrinkled in concern. 'You wished to see me, Miss? I hope everything is satisfactory. I know His Lordship wanted you all to feel as comfortable as possible.'

'Indeed, you have all worked so hard. It is only that I noticed last night that you had a toothache. I wanted to ask after it.'

'How— It's much improved, Miss,' Benton said, quickly hiding any expression of surprise.

'Your jaw is swollen, as I surmised last night. Indeed, in morning light I can see that it's quite inflamed and must be painful,' Abby said with blunt sympathy.

'Er…just a little, Miss.'

'Well, I've finished here, so I'll make you a poultice.' Abby stood abruptly. 'I am certain Lord Stanhope would appreciate some quiet. Which way to the kitchen?'

'The kitchen, my lady?'

'Yes, we must go there and also to the kitchen garden so that I can get the correct ingredients. I can also make something for your head, Lord Stanhope. It used to help my father considerably.'

'Generally speaking, guests and family do not go downstairs, Miss. I could send the cook up to you if you require something,' Benton said.

'No, it would be much too complicated to explain,' she said, walking briskly to the door.

'It is most unusual, Miss,' Benton said, his face set in a lugubrious expression.

'Indeed, but I have yet to believe that unusual is necessarily bad,' Abby said.

The kitchen, like everything else at Lansdowne, was immense—double the size of that in the rectory. It had a red flagstone floor, a ceiling studded with heavy, dark beams and a grey stone hearth taking up a good half of the far wall. Again it had that feeling of antiquity; it was in the smoky discolouration of the plaster between beams, the roasting spit, large enough for whole pigs, the hearth with small alcoves where one might sit.

Still, it smelled like a kitchen right enough. Moreover, it had an energy absent from the rest of the house and felt less like a mausoleum and more like a home. The air was moist and warm, scented with a mix of onions, bacon and yeast.

'Miss, were you needing something?' Mrs Lamprey hurried forward, rubbing floury palms across the starched white cloth of her apron, her face flushed.

'Mrs Lamprey, I thought you were the housekeeper?'

'No, Miss, I was just helping out. Mr Benton is being quite wonderful and hiring staff but we don't quite have a full complement yet. We hope to have a housekeeper soon. It has all been rather sudden. Lord Lansdowne has been away for a while but we are glad he is back.'

'You must have your hands full and I don't want to bother you. I'm looking for chamomile and some other herbs.'

'I'm sure I could make anything you would like, Miss.'

'I'm making a poultice for Mr Benton's tooth. While at my father's parish, I helped with some minor medical needs.'

'Mr Benton has been suffering,' Mrs Lamprey said, nodding her head to affirm this premise. 'It started a few days ago. As soon as he got down here. You think you can help?'

'I will do my best. Might you have a large pot?'

'Yes, Miss.'

'Good. If you could boil the water, I'll go outside and pick the herbs. Better yet, get a second pot and we will brew up a beverage for Lord Stanhope to help with his head.'

'We only have the one scullery maid, Elsie. She is out at present but once she returns, I am sure she could pick the plants, Miss,' Mrs Lamprey suggested.

'Gracious, no. She might not know a dandelion from a parsnip and I need the right things if the poultice is to work. Benton should have gone to the tooth extractor.'

'He would not. You know, gentlemen are not as tough as they would have us believe.'

The cook flushed slightly and Abby wondered if she might have feelings for Lord Lansdowne's valet.

'Have you known Mr Benton long?'

'Oh, yes, he came here twenty years back, but for the last four he has been in London with His Lordship. Until the last few days.'

They did say that absence could make the heart grow fonder.

'Point me in the direction of the kitchen garden and we'll get started,' Abby said.

Mrs Lamprey led her through the scullery and into the overgrown garden, looking about it with a sad shake of her head. 'I am afraid we had to let it go rather. Our staff was limited.'

'Quite understandable and I am used to finding the ingredients in all types of settings. So do not worry.'

Once outside, Abby inhaled, glad of the country freshness. The garden was overgrown. Weeds seemed omnipresent, sprouting between paving, suffocating plants and winding tenaciously up disused garden frames. Still, it was good to get away from London. While the air was not exactly fresh, it had a country scent of earth, animals and vegetation.

Indeed, even an overgrown garden is infinitely pleasanter than a city street.

Lord Lansdowne had not enjoyed his morning ride. His head hurt. He had been up late. Thus far, the country had served only to bore Jason, fuelling his drinking. Last night Dolph had been summoned by the innkeeper to escort Jason home.

This summons had meant that he'd left the Harrington party soon after their arrival, which bothered him to a peculiar degree.

The estate was in much poorer condition than he had realized and it was all too evident that it had been mismanaged. Cottages were empty, or poorly maintained, fields bare and animals malnourished and tenants poor.

When had the neglect started? It seemed unlikely that it could have become so derelict since his mother's death. How had he not noticed it during her funeral? But then he had stayed only one night and drunk sufficiently to keep everything blurry.

As Dolph strode into the deserted hall, his irritation grew. He frowned, tapping his hand impatiently against his breeches.

'Benton?' he shouted irritably.

There was no answer. The place remained eerily silent. He went into the morning room. Jason was up, holding a cup rather tightly between his fingers and peering blearily above its rim.

'Must you bellow at such an ungodly hour?' he muttered.

'It might not seem quite so ungodly if you did not drink so much.'

'Pot…kettle…' Jason muttered.

Just then, from the depths of the servants' quarters, Dolph heard laughter. 'What's that?' he asked.

'Laughter, I supposed. Unheard of in this family,' Jason said.

Turning from his nephew, Dolph went into the hall, pushing through the baize door. He heard chatter and another chortle of laughter that sounded suspiciously like Miss Carstens.

For some reason, this made his mouth dry, hastening his pace down the remaining steps.

At its base, he froze, surveying the scene before him.

Benton sat on a high stool in the centre of the kitchen. A towel was draped around his neck and shoulders. Meanwhile, Mrs Lamprey and Miss Carstens appeared to be applying greenish slime to the man's chin. Lucy Harrington was also present, while the other servants hovered close as though expecting a miracle of biblical proportions.

'Good morning,' he said, his tone quiet but with an edge.

The servants instantly dispersed with a rustle of bobbing curtsies and shuffling feet. Miss Harrington hurried upstairs, flushing and begging him to excuse her and adding something about breakfast.

Abby, however, showed no such anxiety, looking up and saying in her firm tones, 'Mr Benton was suffering from a toothache but I have made a poultice which should help.'

'So I see. If you are finished, may I escort you upstairs?'

Miss Carstens nodded but paused, addressing the cook. 'Do make certain that Mr Benton keeps this on for at least ten minutes and let me know when Lord Stanhope's beverage is ready.'

'Yes, Miss.'

'Beverage?' Dolph questioned as they started up the stairs.

'Yes, Jason has been imbibing too much but I have an excellent remedy. You might benefit as well,' Abby said. 'You are looking a little indisposed.'

'I am fine,' Dolph said, pausing on the stair landing. 'Miss Carstens, if you will grant me a moment in my study?'

'Naturally, my lord.'

They went past the knights with their shining, sightless visors, down a smaller passage and into the study.

Of course, his London study suited better. It had fewer memories.

In fact, this study remained disturbingly unchanged since his childhood when his father had been its absolute sovereign. The same leather-bound books filled the shelves, the same desk and leather furniture. It even smelled the same, the air infused with leather and smoke.

More than anywhere his feeling of displacement was centred in this room. He glanced at his father's portrait over the mantel. In many ways, he still seemed alive within these walls.

Not that his father had spent a lot of time at Lansdowne. In early childhood, Dolph had few memories of him. Mother had frequented the nursery on occasion but his father had been in London. To Dolph, he had been but one of many blurry adults for whom he was occasionally paraded.

It was later, in the years after the nursery and before adolescence, that his memories turned from abstract, hazy images to memories so harsh, stark and jagged that he felt himself flinch from them.

'How was it? Coming back here?' Abby's voice startled him, as though the past had muffled the present.

He jerked around, glancing about the room, peopled with ghosts. 'Fine,' he said. 'Right as rain.'

'Indeed,' she said, looking at him with eyes

slightly narrowed. 'I usually find that the use of clichés correlates to obfuscation.'

'Pardon?'

'My father had a habit of horse racing, gambling and other risk-taking pursuits but would always tell my mother that his day was "as dull as ditchwater", "dry as dust" and "nothing to write home about".'

He shrugged. 'Yes, well, I suppose this place brings back memories.'

He looked to the hearth, now unlit and neatly laid. The wooden struts of his contraption had made a splintering crack as his father had broken it apart. He'd thrown the pieces into the fire like so much kindling. Dolph remembered the heat of the flames, the way they'd snaked hungrily along the boards and twisted through the wooden wheels.

Dolph looked up at the portrait. His father's unsmiling features stared down at him, his expression judgemental. When had his father's features first sharpened into focus? When had he first realized that he was the 'other' son?

'I think it was when I took apart the clock,' he said.

'You took the clock apart? You sound as curious as Ignatius,' Abby said.

'Too much like him. Father feared that I might take after my grandfather.'

'And that was bad?'

'Yes.'

'Why? I mean your grandfather was brilliant and wealthy. He is greatly respected in Harrogate.'

'Indeed, Grandfather had neither status, fashion or social graces. Even his education was limited. Yet, through his brilliant mind and business acumen, he made so much money that he could buy his daughter access into one of Britain's best families. Of course, the families made the arrangement. My father had little choice. He had little in common with my mother and hated being indebted to one he saw as his inferior.'

'Sad for your mother.'

'Yes,' he said. 'Marriage seems a sad affair.'

Her children were her compensation, although that had also brought her pain. After Madeleine and Barnaby there had been two more boys who had died in infancy before his own birth.

And then she'd lost Barnaby also.

'What was he like? Your grandfather?'

Dolph turned away from the mantel. Abby stood quite close. Her expression was one of interest, not a superficial interest but one of genuine curiosity.

'You know, I think you would have liked him. He smelled of tobacco and wood. He had a huge itchy beard, like Father Christmas. He liked questions as much as my father hated them. He died when I was quite young.'

They stood so close that he could see the three freckles on her nose and hear the intake of her breath and see the chestnut glint in her hair, caught in a beam of sunlight.

'Yes, I broke several edicts. I reminded him of my grandfather. I failed to protect my brother and I had a crazy idea for a contraption that the village boys could use to bring grain to the mill. I thought it would save money and horses.'

'We...are...not...involved...in trade,' his father had said, his words pushed out between clenched teeth as he struck Dolph's hand with every word.

Reflexively, Dolph rubbed his palm.

'He whipped you,' Abby said softly, a statement more than a question.

'Just a switch.'

'I am so sorry.'

She stepped forward, taking his hand between her own. The gesture surprised him and yet he did not want to pull his hand away. There was a sense of comfort. She ran her fingers across the palm as though to feel for bygone welts. Her touch was gentle and yet there was an intensity which seemed to penetrate his being, through skin and bone and tissue.

'Is that when they sent you to school?'

'Yes... Eton,' he said jerkily.

He still remembered the sting of the switch and his mother's cries from outside the study door. 'Stop your weeping and wailing, woman,' his father had shouted. 'You've mollycoddled him long enough. We'll send him to Eton and make a man of him.'

Dolph pushed the thoughts away. He never allowed himself to dwell on the maudlin.

'Anyhow, enough reminiscing. I am sorry to bother you with my sorry tales.'

'But we need to feel the sad in order to feel the joy. We weep tears both of sadness and joy.'

'My father did not believe in tears. He would—' Dolph paused. It had been so long ago he had forgotten.

'What?'

'He would strap me longer if I cried.'

He felt her wince, her fingers clasping his hand more warmly. Her touch drew her to him and yet he felt a vulnerability, a need to bolt as an unbroken horse might.

He disengaged her hands, moving from the hearth. She also stepped back quickly, her movement jerky, as she rubbed her hands against the cloth of her dress as though awkward or discomforted.

'Right, well,' he said. 'I did not ask you here to discuss my childhood. I wanted to talk to you on more serious matters. I think we are both agreed that we wish for Miss Harrington to have a successful come-out.'

She nodded.

'Therefore, we must ensure that Miss Harrington's manners are acceptable to my sister and society. And I cannot think that it is customary for a young lady to discuss libation or lather servants with slime, for that matter. Therefore, we should eschew such activities in her presence.'

He could feel himself plucking at long words and formality, using them like a shield as though they would distance him from both this woman and, more importantly, the vagaries of his own emotions.

'When you say "we," I presume you mean "me." Moreover, Miss Harrington was not there when I spoke about alcohol and the slime was not "slime" but a poultice. I would also suggest Miss Harrington's challenge will be saying two words in front of your sister, as opposed to discussing libation.'

She spoke tartly and he felt a relief as though he had been drawn too close to hot flame and had escaped.

'As her friend and governess, it is important that you model appropriate behaviour, which doesn't include kitchens or slime.'

'A poultice. My mother made them all the time for the villagers, so I see no reason for raised eyebrows. Mr Benton had a toothache and is fearful of having his tooth extracted.'

'Fearful!' Dolph couldn't imagine Benton as fearful. 'Did the man give you his life history?'

'Mrs Lamprey confided in me. I think she likes Mr Benton. By the way, is he a valet or butler?'

'Both, at present. You think she likes him?' Dolph looked at her blankly. He could not imagine Benton as being the recipient of romantic feelings.

'She appeared quite flushed.'

'She was in a hot kitchen,' he said.

'Anyway, the most important thing is Mr Benton's health. I will continue with the poultice and, of course, encourage him to have his tooth extracted.'

How had Miss Carstens managed to know the intricate matters within his household while he had not recognized that his estate manager, Trask or Trent, was an incompetent if not a criminal?

Again, he had that confused feeling of wrongfootedness and an irritation which he knew to be out of proportion to the situation.

'I am merely saying that if this is going to work, both you and Miss Harrington must learn some manners,' he said.

'And I am merely saying that providing care for one's staff is hardly scandalous.'

'Except your particular way of doing so is unusual.'

'And society hates difference,' she said more softly.

The tone, the words, the tiny smile, touched with sadness, made the ground unfirm again.

He glanced up at the portrait. 'Indeed. And Miss Harrington cannot risk it during her debut.'

Miss Carstens also glanced up. 'Just because one is very passionate in one's beliefs does not necessarily mean one is right.'

'No, but it does much to convince the rest of the world that one is.'

Abby startled at Jason's abrupt knock and Dolph swung around as he entered.

'Lord Stanhope, did Mrs Green bring you something to drink?' she asked, speaking quickly with the unfamiliar need to fill the silence.

'Yes, vile stuff.' Jason slumped into a nearby chair, shoving his feet towards the unlit fire.

'It will help your head.'

'Hope so,' Jason muttered.

'And don't tell me off for mentioning Jason's bad head. Miss Harrington is not here,' Abby said to Dolph.

Jason gave a chortle of laughter. 'She has you there, Uncle.'

'I take it you two have met? Miss Carstens is a friend of the Harringtons and currently acts as the governess to their son,' Dolph said.

'Poor fellow. I remember giving my tutors a dreadful time.'

'I find that believable,' she said tartly. 'I encourage Iggy to go outside. We do letters in the morning and then collect leaves or do experiments in the afternoon.'

'That does seem jollier than the schoolroom,' Jason conceded.

'Entirely so. I base my philosophy on Aristotle. He taught his students how learning is all about perceiving this reality and then interpreting it through thorough logical inquiry.'

Jason gave a theatrical groan, rolling his eyes heavenward. 'You lost me at Aristotle.'

'Well, we were going to work on his butter churn this afternoon, if that is of greater interest,' Abby said.

'His butter churn?' Jason raised an eyebrow.

'Or some form of a mixer for cakes or bread. He hasn't quite decided. We hope to find a lake, as it is powered by water.' She turned to Jason. 'Why don't you come?'

'Just the thing for you, Jason,' Dolph said. 'Fresh air will do you good.'

'Why do people always say that? I will likely get cold feet and sneeze,' Jason complained.

'You should come too,' Abby said to Dolph. 'Your nephew might learn from your good example.'

Dolph laughed. 'Touché,' he said.

Jason glanced between them, his expression curious. 'Perhaps this excursion might not be so dull as

I had thought. I mean I am a great fan of Aristotle. Better than remaining indoors. I will change. Don't want to spoil my jacket. New, you know. Weston.'

He left and they were alone. She felt again that tingle of awareness, both of the physical man and of their emotional connection. Strange to feel this odd closeness to an individual so disparate from herself, an individual who also irked her half of the time.

And appealed to her the other half.

She glanced away, taking in the chamber, the books with their embossed titles, the desk and chair so huge it appeared throne-like.

If Lansdowne was haunted then this was its epi-centre. It seemed imbued with sadness.

Abby glanced at Dolph. His expression, perhaps because of his earlier vulnerability, appeared more shuttered.

Before Dolph, England's peerage had been carica-tures to her, personified by the Ashleighs with their house parties and that innate entitled knowledge that such an existence was not luxury but birthright.

When Dolph had first arrived on the doorstep at Wimpole Street, she had seen him like that. Except now that caricature had taken dimension and the person had become more than the flat image.

She still did not know if she actually liked him or not, but he was more than that. He was more than or different from the Ashleighs and their wilful neglect. The thought of his losses and of his father's harshness hurt her. His interest in science and the mechanical intrigued her. His kindness to Miss Harrington, Iggy and Jason appealed to her.

And the physical man, his shoulders, dimple, smile, the dark eyes and wayward lock of hair confused her...unsettled her...appealed to her.

'You should come,' she repeated.

'You don't think going over the ledger to determine how this estate got in such a sorry condition would be a better idea?'

'Yes, that needs to be done,' she agreed, glancing towards the overgrown courtyard, rife with weeds and moss. 'But this is important too.'

'Iggy's contraption will earn vast sums and save the estate?'

'Doubtful,' she said. 'It is more likely to cost vast sums. But you and Jason could spend time together. You've lost a lot. Maybe you can help each other?'

'You have met Jason?'

'I have. I met a boy who has lost a father, an uncle, a grandfather and grandmother. It seems you might have a lot in common.'

By late in the morning, they were all assembled. Given the number in the party, Dolph had ordered the carriage, although Mrs Harrington and Lucy had wisely chosen to remain at home. Dolph had insisted that Basil stay also, which meant that the excursion consisted of Dolph, Abby, Jason and Ignatius.

They stood in an uncomfortable cluster waiting for Martin to bring around the coach. Jason looked bored, already staring sleepily as though regretting his decision and wishful only of a comfortable nap.

Iggy, meanwhile, had brought out the pieces of his churn, a wheel of approximately two feet in height, a trough, a barrel and a structure including a wooden paddle which was meant to rotate inside the churn.

Dolph eyed this array of equipment, his expression demonstrating limited enthusiasm. 'I did not realize your churn was quite so large or involved so many pieces.'

'I hope that there will be sufficient space in the carriage,' Iggy said. 'Perhaps it is as well that Basil is not coming, although he would have loved a swim. Surprisingly he likes swimming, despite nearly drowning when he was little.'

'Perhaps we can put some items on the floor and squish up together,' Abby said, although she was reluctant to squish, remembered the trip to the locomotive and her unusual awareness of this man.

Their gazes briefly met. Abby looked away, momentarily convinced that he had the same thought, as though there were two tracks of interaction, the obvious and something existing only between them.

A foolish notion.

'Iggy, you can squish up with me,' she said briskly.

'But—'

'Without argument,' she said with a look which usually got compliance.

They entered the carriage. Iggy handed the pieces of his apparatus inside and they placed the churn on the floor and other parts on the cushions, like honoured guests.

'Did Martin remember a bucket?' Iggy asked, jumping back out of the carriage with the urgency of this request.

'Yes, Master Ignatius,' the groom called out.

Iggy clambered back into the carriage, sitting beside Abby and opposite Jason as they waited for Dolph, who appeared to be providing lastminute instruction to Martin.

There was a luxury in watching him without observation, Abby thought. He had fluid, easy movements; even his country clothes seemed to emphasize the breadth of his shoulder and length of his leg.

Jason gave a yawn.

'You are not excited by my invention?' Iggy asked in a somewhat accusatory manner.

'No, um, not so much, although given the lack of diversion in the country, I suppose it is better than nothing.'

'Better than nothing? It will be exciting,' Iggy said in an aggrieved manner.

'Our definition of excitement may differ somewhat.'

'What is your definition?'

'Winning money at a card game.'

'That would be exciting,' Iggy admitted. 'We don't have a lot of money. I am hopeful that my inventions will work and make money. I think your grandfather made money.'

'Great-grandfather,' Jason said.

'I have several inventions, although I haven't been able to work on the actual models in London because Miss Carstens was too busy and we weren't close to any ponds. But I worked on the designs.'

'Mother says that invention is for the middle classes. It aims to help business and is below us,' Jason said.

'That sounds quite daft,' Iggy replied without heat but merely making, what he considered, a statement of fact.

Jason gave a half smile. 'I would love to see you tell that to Mother.'

'If she comes to visit, I will do so,' Iggy said. 'Is it more socially proper to win money playing cards than inventing something?'

'Cards, as long as you don't count 'em, I suppose,' Jason said with another yawn.

'I am good at counting.'

'Good gracious,' Abby said, turning hurriedly

from the window. 'Do not get any ideas. Perhaps we should discuss something you enjoy other than gambling, Lord Stanhope? What else do you like?'

'I am not certain if *like* is quite the right word. Generally, don't really like anything. Just seek diversions,' Jason explained.

'That sounds dull. Miss Carstens always says I get in my worst trouble when bored,' Iggy confessed.

'It appears we might have something in common.'

Before this line of conversation could be further explored, Dolph got in. Martin picked up the reins and the carriage moved forward.

As on their trip to Torrington Square, Abby was again struck by the intimacy of a carriage. Thankfully, she was not sitting beside Dolph but that, of course, meant that she sat opposite and if she glanced up, she would look directly into his gaze.

There was something arresting in that gaze.

And if she looked down, she became aware that he sat opposite with only a few inches separating their knees and that his hand rested on his leg. And then she remembered holding his hand. She remembered its size and warmth within her own. She recalled their proximity and how they had been so close that she could smell the outdoorsy scent of him, see the dark smudges under his eyes and hear the whisper of his breath.

She pulled her gaze away, looking at the scenery outside with an unusual intensity as they swung through the gateposts and down the rutted lane.

Again, the neglect was evident. The roadway was uneven, the trees overgrown and, in the gaps between them, Abby could discern several fields badly drained, the fencing collapsed. At the end of the drive, they turned to the left, moving towards what appeared to be a small, woodsy area. On either side, there were fields and a few cottages, although some were deserted.

A flash of colour caught her eye and, leaning forward, she saw several young lads running over the fields beside them. They loped, waving and jumping over the uneven land, with the bobbing, uncoordinated movements of childhood. Gradually, the carriage surpassed them and they dropped from her view as they neared a body of water which, in Abby's mind, appeared more puddle than lake.

They pulled to a stop and Iggy was already sliding off the seat as Martin got down, opening the door for them.

'It is muddy,' he warned but Iggy was out, his feet sinking into the mud.

Abby got out more carefully, followed by Dolph and Jason.

'Glad I wore my second-best boots,' Jason muttered.

While not large, the lake was pretty. A cool wind

whistled across, ruffling the water. Several ducks swam at the far end and weeping willows grew around the muddied bank, their graceful limbs dragging into the water.

'Thought country air was supposed to be fresh,' Jason said.

'It is fresher than London.' Abby said, inhaling the marshy scent of a countryside in early spring.

With a squelch of muddy feet and rustling of foliage, the group of boys burst into the clearing. They stopped short, mouths slightly open, as though in their madcap dash to catch up, they had failed to consider what they might actually do or say if they achieved their objective. They stood like an ill-dressed, somewhat awkward welcoming committee.

'Hello,' Abby said.

'You don't have shoes,' Dolph said. 'Or proper clothes.'

His face looked so stricken that she felt moved to comfort. 'You can order some.'

'I have shoes,' one boy said, obviously taking this as a criticism. 'Only they don't fit. So my brother uses 'em.'

'Do you live in the village?' Dolph asked.

The boy nodded. He had a round, freckled face with fair hair so tufted that it seemed have been stuck at indiscriminate angles on his head.

'What's your name?' Dolph asked.

'Albert. Are you Lord Lansdowne?'

'I am.'

Dolph's gaze caught her own. 'I should not have stayed away so long.'

'You will make things better.'

'I will,' he said.

'What are you doing with that?' Albert asked, nodding towards the waterwheel that Martin still held, somewhat awkwardly, his feet sinking into the mud.

'I am glad you asked because you might be able to help, if you know the lake well,' Abby said.

The boys moved closer. 'We knows the lake,' Albert said.

She nodded. 'I thought you would. You seem knowledgeable. We are doing a scientific experiment. But perhaps we should introduce ourselves. This is Ignatius. I am Miss Carstens. You have met Lord Lansdowne and, this is Lord Stanhope.'

'Hello, Miss,' they said in unison, nodding their heads to emphasize the response.

'This 'ere is Harry and Thomas. So what's this about a science 'speriment?' Albert questioned, obviously wishing to get introductions over and move to more important matters.

'We hope to use water to power a butter churn—'

'Or a mixer,' Iggy interrupted.

'And we require a flat place close to the lake where

we could place the churn.' She nodded towards the barrel-like apparatus that Martin had still held.

'Flat? The rock what we use for fishing is flat,' Albert said.

'Which?' Iggy asked, scrutinizing the bank. 'I see nothing but mud.'

'Over here. Under the willow. Come on.'

The group, now with Ignatius, ran to the left, almost disappearing under the long willow branches. '

'And this is considered school?' Jason asked.

'Indeed, one learns geometry and physics and then applies the theory to a practical application,' Abby retorted. 'Besides, it tires him out.'

'Your approach is interesting. Is it based on Plato or Aristotle,' Dolph asked. 'I mean, Aristotle was his pupil.'

'Miss Brownlee and I used to debate that very issue. It is hard to separate their ideas.'

'Right, well, now it seems like school,' Jason said.

Iggy and the rest of the boys reappeared from under the willow. Mud now seemed to come up to their kneecaps, but all were oblivious to this, their expressions merely demonstrating lively interest.

'Come on, Iggy said. 'We have found a suitable location. Lord Stanhope, can you bring the bucket? Martin, bring the churn.'

'My second-best boots will be ruined,' Jason grumbled but complied, grabbing the bucket.

Dolph took the trough and Abby managed the waterwheel. Burdened with the churn, Martin took up the rear, a rhythmic clanging accompanying his every move.

'This will do,' Iggy announced. 'I'll get the water.'

He hurried to the edge of the bank. Each footstep made a sucking noise as he stepped into mud. The rock jutted out from the mud banks as though nature had intended to provide a place to fish. Marsh grass grew on either side, rustling in the breeze.

Abby had intended to take greater control of the experiment but, with typical impulsivity, Iggy was already squatting, dangling the bucket into the lake while the other boys clustered about him.

Once filled, he placed the bucket on the flat rock, before focusing his attention on the churn and waterwheel. With an expression of intent concentration, he bent over both, carefully fixing the trough so that it was angled above the waterwheel and then connecting the waterwheel to the paddle.

'Lord Lansdowne, if you could come and steady the churn and Miss Carstens, pour the water into the trough so that I can better observe the wheel's motion.'

They each took their role while the village boys stood around, wide-eyed as though expecting mystic magic. The water poured, splashing onto the trough, which then moved the waterwheel. Its rotation, in turn, made the wooden paddle move, clunking against the inner walls of the churn.

'It's working!' Iggy announced, his face flushed with excitement.

He got up, grabbing the bucket again. 'If we get the balance correct it will work. We just need enough force to move the waterwheel but not so much that it floods. I'll just get a second bucket!'

Without waiting, he stood, grabbing the bucket and running to the far end of the rock.

'Be careful!' Dolph shouted.

Of course, Iggy did not pause. That was Iggy's problem. He because so focused, he seemed oblivious to any remonstration.

'Ignatius!' Abby shouted. 'Scientific experiments are done with care. Slow down.'

He looked around. For a moment, he was outlined against the shimmering lake water. Moments later, with his arms flailing like a windmill, he toppled backwards. The bucket flew in a perfect arc back towards the bank. Iggy slithered, teetering backwards.

Abby grabbed her skirts, rushing to the water's edge as he bobbed up, spluttering. Then, likely slipping again, he plunged under the surface.

'I'll get him,' Dolph said, lunging after him. He grabbed Iggy's hand, dragging him upwards, and steadying him as he regained his balance 'Are you all right?'

'Of course,' Iggy said as if insulted by any assertion to the contrary.

'What were you thinking? Come on. Let's get you on dry land.' They waded out.

'It's not deep,' Albert said.

'Even in the centre, it is not deep,' Harry averred.

'But it is muddy,' Thomas said.

'Indeed.' Dolph's tone was dry as he looked down at his muddied boots and sodden britches.

Abby glanced away.

'Martin, get the blanket from the carriage and tell the footman that we'll return home immediately. We will leave this clobber here. You can get it later,' Dolph said.

'Not clobber. My churn,' Iggy said. 'I don't see why you are making such a fuss about it. I am just a little wet.'

'You are soaked to the skin. And could have drowned,' Dolph said.

'In two feet of water?' Iggy expostulated. 'How could I drown in two feet?'

'By hitting your head on the rock,' Dolph said.

'I think it is the responsibility,' Jason said to Iggy as though in confidence. 'He has taken to fussing over me, as well.'

'Likely because neither of you seem to have an

ounce of common sense between you,' Abby said. 'Ignatius, we are getting you dry before you catch a chill. We can collect the churn later.'

This had the desired effect. Both Ignatius and Jason headed towards the carriage. Martin handed Iggy a blanket.

'Let's get that around you. We don't want Lord Lansdowne's carriage to be entirely covered in mud,' Abby said.

'We can bring back the churn, if you're wanting?' the boys suggested.

'That would be kind,' Abby said. 'I think perhaps I should rethink experimental learning, at least when it involves Iggy and mud.'

'I don't know,' Jason said. 'I actually almost enjoyed the experiment.'

Dolph washed and changed, leaving Ignatius to Abby's care. He ate with Lucy, Jason and Mrs Harrington. Jason had changed and, while still grieving his second-best boots, seemed less bored, eating with enthusiasm and conversing with something bordering on animation.

Mrs Harrington was, naturally, as loquacious as ever while Lucy remained quiet. Indeed, Dolph rather wished Mrs Harrington was as quiet as her daughter since she seemed determined to keep up a steady monologue, even as she sipped her soup.

'I truly thank you for such a delightful invitation to your delightful estate,' she said. 'And for your help in preparing Miss Carstens for the Season. I know she will tell you that being a governess is her only option. However, I cannot agree. Indeed, I would not be living up to my obligation as her mother's best friend if I did not encourage her to embrace this opportunity. I was so very close to her dear mother, now sadly deceased.'

After this long statement, Mrs Harrington inhaled and then took several restorative sips of soup.

'I am certain my great-aunt will have many ideas. She plans to arrive shortly. I was thinking that she might also help Miss Harrington, as well,' Dolph said.

'In what way?' Miss Harrington asked a little nervously.

'Practising dance steps and titles and curtsies. You know, that sort of thing,' Dolph said.

Mrs Harrington nodded. 'Indeed, that would be ideal. They have been best friends for ever. Indeed, it might hope my dear Lucy be a little less shy. She never says much.'

'I wonder why,' Dolph said drily.

'Confidentially, we have hopes that Mr Trollope might have an interest,' Mrs Harrington added.

Her words, Dolph thought, would see more confidentiality if she did not speak at such volume.

'Mother!' Miss Harrington said, flushing in some discomfort.

'Well, you are corresponding with him, which is an excellent sign. Now, as far as Abigail is concerned, I have been exploring widowers. I mean, she does have a way with children. I mean, consider Ignatius. He has a dreadful habit of driving his tutors quite distracted and she has a way with him. Therefore, given her financial situation, I think that marrying a widower would be quite her best option. There would be several suitable. Perhaps your aunt might know?'

'Perhaps,' Dolph said, although he suddenly felt irritated.

He had been rather enjoying Mrs Harrington's garrulous chatter but now found it foolish. He wasn't quite certain why, but the emotion was strong and even the excellent repast did not soothe his feelings.

After lunch, Dolph had intended to go through the limited accounting provided by the absent estate manager but found himself restless.

Indeed, he wasn't certain where to start. Moreover, there were even more papers which had been sent up to London.

He glanced out of the window. Tufts of grass pushed through the cracked bricks and cobbles in a way his father would not have allowed. Benton had suggested that the grooms weed. However, every animal on the estate appeared malnourished, so getting feed seemed the priority.

His mother would have been sad with Lansdowne's condition. In many ways, she had cared most. His father had kept it maintained out of pride or duty but his mother would notice things. She would see the child without shoes, the widow struggling to feed her children or a man limping after a fall. Much like Abby, he thought, ministering to Benton and his sore teeth.

He smiled at the memory. He did not think that he would ever get over the sight of the rather proper Benton draped in a towel with green stuff on his cheeks.

His mother had made a few tinctures as he recalled. Indeed, when in residence, his mother had been involved. She had arranged flowers for weddings and funerals, judged jams and pies at the fair and donated books and clothes.

A local horticulturalist had even created a new variety of rose in her honour. As he recalled, the colour was a dark purple but looked closer to black, which, as his mother had said, was quite an admirable colour for a carriage or horse, but less appealing in a rose.

She had laughed when the 'Lady Lansdowne' had failed to place at the fair.

Of course, that was years ago, before Barnaby's death, when she had withdrawn to London as though the big city made his passing more bearable.

Dolph stood, pushing the chair back with uncharacteristic force. He couldn't sit under his father's gaze, in his father's chair and look at a mossy driveway all afternoon. He needed to do something. He needed to escape the ghosts.

He got up, striding into the hall.

'I'm going into the village,' he announced to Benton, who appeared to be hovering again.

'Yes, my lord.'

'What's Jason doing?'

'Lord Stanhope and Master Ignatius are walking around the grounds in search of Burley, a small pony, if you recall. Apparently, Lord Stanhope has a fondness from when he used to visit with his mother.'

'Is Miss Carstens with them?' Dolph asked. 'Jason and Ignatius unsupervised might cause disaster. Particularly if Basil is also part of the excursion.'

'Indeed, Miss Carsten was indisposed but I alerted Martin and sent Giles with them.'

'I hope Miss Carsten was not unwell.' Dolph felt a flicker of unease.

His mother's death had happened so suddenly. His brother had been shot by a French cannon. His father had been old, ill and irascible. His mother had caught a cold.

And died.

'I believe she might be better able to answer than myself,' Benton said.

Dolph turned. Abby was descending the staircase. He had not expected to see her and found himself briefly startled. Her hair appeared damp and was not as tightly restrained as was typical. Instead, it was tied loosely at the nape of her neck while several tendrils had escaped and now framed her face. Her cheeks also appeared somewhat more flushed than usual.

'I hope you are not ill?'

'Not at all,' Abby said. 'I was merely having a bath. Basil escaped while Iggy was washing and jumped into the water with him. Of course, I had to wrestle with him, leaving me quite soaked to the skin so I took a bath.'

'Right,' Dolph said rather abruptly because he was suddenly thinking about her skin, soft, smooth and luminous. The warm bathwater would make her flush—her cheeks, her neck and chest. Her hair might be undone and would drape about her shoulders, half covering her breasts while the soapsuds would cling to her skin.

'...retrieve it.'

'Pardon, I apologize, I was not attending,' he said, foolish like an adolescent schoolboy.

'No matter. I was just saying that I would check

on Iggy and perhaps see if the boys have brought his churn before he dashes off to retrieve it.'

'Of course. Allow me to accompany you,' he said. 'I was going out anyway.'

When she nodded, he felt that conflicting emotion: anticipation and apprehension.

The road through to the village was unchanged, save for additional ruts and puddles. Dolph saw shutters hanging loose and broken fences. Several chickens walked on the road and a cow stood close to the verge, its hip bones protruding.

'You must think I'm like the landlords in your father's parish,' he said, seeing the landscape as it must seem to Abby.

'The Ashleighs? I don't know yet.'

'You don't know? Their estate was worse?' he asked.

'No, better, but the question is will you make things right?'

'I will,' he said.

'Then you are not like the Ashleighs,' she said in her blunt way, as though stating a truth or certainty.

They continued to walk. He glanced at her calm, composed features. There was a steadying, intelligent strength about her and an allure which seemed all the greater because it was obscured, seemingly hidden under the sensible and circumspect.

'I have heard that turnips can help restore a field,' she said.

He laughed, the image a of lithe goddess overshadowed by a root vegetable.

'Turnips amuse you?'

'Only when combined with Aphrodite.'

She frowned. 'I like Greek mythology as much as anyone, but given the current situation, it is best to concentrate on the estate.'

'Indeed,' he agreed. 'As soon as the estate manager returns, I will find out more.'

'What do you know about him?'

'I hired him. Or approved his appointment,' he said.

Truthfully, he'd met Trent once, in London, following his mother's death. The previous estate manager had retired and Dolph's man of business had found Trent. Dolph scarcely remembered the appointment. He had a blurred recollection of a slim, middle-aged gentleman, well dressed but with sufficient blandness to fit in to almost any environment.

'I found that after Father's death, there were big holes in my memory. I would do things, you know, normal things like arranging flowers or packing, and yet I couldn't properly remember. I felt frozen.'

'Numb,' Dolph said. 'That's how I felt. How I have been feeling. Particularly after Mother's death—it was so unexpected.'

Like death had neglected to issue an appropriate warning.

'Sometimes I felt like I was someone else,' she said. 'Or had two selves, a before and an after.

'I remembered making arrangements, going through the process, talking to the vicar. But I felt like an actor. No more real than a London stage play. '

'Ignatius helped me.'

He laughed. 'Just when a conversation is getting serious you do have a way of adding levity. What did Ignatius do exactly?'

'Gave me purpose. Maybe the estate could do that for you?'

So what would you suggest?'

'Me.'

'Yes, you said you were always telling the Ashleighs how to make things better. What you would say to me, as a landlord?

She looked at him, full lips slightly pursed, brows raised in question, as though trying to determine if he was serious in his request.

'My guess is that Mr Trent is embezzling funds or managing the estate extremely poorly. This means that there is no investment being made in seed or materials. Therefore, you need to look through the finances. As you noted, the animals are malnourished so food is a priority. The boys also looked quite thin, so I would question whether some of the tenants are also struggling to feed their families. Doubtless someone in the village will know who is in need. Does the estate have its own livestock?'

'I don't know,' he admitted.

'Get dairy cows and chickens. Then you can ensure that the village children always have sufficient milk and eggs. Make certain that seeds are purchased for the upcoming season. Also there are several fields which appear to be lying fallow but, as mentioned, they might well support turnips.'

Her words sparked his own ideas and he felt a surprising rush of excitement. 'I will close the London house for now. The servants can come down here. I have already ordered boots and shoes. They can bring some down and also provide additional support. Of course, they are not used to the country but could help to hand out food or repair fences.'

'While I am here, I am happy to help.'

'Mrs Harrington will not want you to miss any instruction from my great-aunt.'

'She is coming?'

'Yes, I got a letter. Apparently she is alive and eager to help. She stays with relatives, rotating through the year, and is quite happy to add me to the list.'

'You realize that you may become a permanent part of the rotation.'

'It is entirely possible.' He smiled.

He looked around, towards the small church at the crest of the hill, the fields and cottages.

'I am going to make this better. After Barnaby died we all stayed in London. My father was ill. My mother was heartbroken. Thank you for your ideas.'

'I always have ideas,' she said.

He smiled and felt a pulse of something pushing away the ennui and the numbness.

He felt hope.

Abby watched his face. He seemed different from the world-weary aristocrat in London. He seemed less remote, less likely to hide behind the brittle joke or glib words. They walked with surprising compatibility, up the slight incline towards the church.

'St David's on the Lake,' he said.

It was a simple structure, with a single spire, nestled under a large tree. Its branches were still bare but touched with green and the inherent promise of new growth. A graveyard was visible to the left, a patchwork of moss-covered graves. The church itself had a somewhat dilapidated appearance. Slates had fallen from the roof and the northern walls shone green with moss but it was not dissimilar to her father's church and brought with it comfort.

'Are your parents buried there?' she asked as they approached the structure.

He shook his head. 'No, in the mausoleum on the estate. But their names and Barnaby's are engraved on the family pew.'

The side door opened and the vicar came out. She watched him approach, the familiar black cassock flapping in the wind.

'Greetings, Lord Lansdowne, I had heard you were here.' His voice had the slight huskiness of the elderly.

The dark cloth rustled with his movement and, as he approached, she saw that he had a stooped figure as though old and shrunken with the years.

'Mr Walther, let me introduce Miss Abigail Carstens. Her father was a vicar.'

'A great pleasure to meet you, my dear,' he said, something in his tone making the platitude seem genuine. His face was like a net of wrinkles fanning out from blue eyes, still bright despite his years.

'You as well,' she said.

'Now, Lord Lansdowne, I take it this is not a social call. How can I help you?'

Dolph smiled. 'You never did mince words.'

'At my age, I find it best not to waste time,' he said.

'Do you know what is happening here? Why is the village so derelict?'

'You are also direct. More direct than I recall.'

'I have learned the skill from an expert,' Dolph said, glancing at Abby.

'Poor harvests, weather, competition from other estates, mismanagement by Mr Trent,' the vicar said succinctly. 'I did write to you.'

'I— My man of business must have thought it a personal letter. Apologies—I have got behind in my correspondence,' Dolph said.

Abby noted his discomfort. He shifted uneasily but what struck her more was that he had allowed it to show, instead of hiding it under humour.

'Lord Lansdowne has many plans for the estate now,' she said, almost as though wanting to defend him.

'Indeed, I am glad to hear it.'

'I will also help financially to set the tenants back on their feet. Do you know if there are any tenants really struggling'

'Mrs Kent. You might recall her—she manages the flowers and really everything else. She will have a list in her mind. But I'd say the Tatlocks are my primary concern. The father died of pneumonia, leaving Mrs Tatlock and her three children, Albert, Eloise and—' He paused, shaking his head. 'I cannot recall the little girl's name. What is my memory coming to?'

Abby remembered the bright boy with the freckles. 'We met an Albert this morning. He had sandy hair, a little messy, and freckles.'

'Sounds like one and the same.'

Dolph nodded. 'He was with two other boys. I am getting them shoes and clothes.'

'That would be Harry and Thomas. Where you see one, you will see the others,' Mr Walther said with fondness.

'Do they have sufficient food?' Abby asked.

'Mrs Kent and I do our best to make sure their bellies are not too hungry and their pride is not too hurt.'

'I can help. I mean while I'm here. I used to help in my father's parish,' Abby said.

'I am certain that would be appreciated though you'll have to mind how you go.'

'I will ensure that Mrs Kent feels that she is doing me a great favour.'

'That's the idea.' The vicar smiled, his blue eyes almost disappearing within the pouches of his wrinkled cheeks.

'Is there a school?'

The vicar shook his head. 'Not for a few years now.'

Dolph glanced at her, a smile flitting across his face. 'I will make that a priority, I promise.'

'You are keen on education, Miss?' the vicar asked.

'Yes, it provides opportunity. A poor boy with education might access the halls of power,' she said.

'You have progressive ideas?'

'I believe that there will always be inequity but that education is likely the best, the only way, to help lessen it.'

'My tutor used to say things like that,' Dolph said, surprising himself.

'I recall Mr Jennings,' the vicar said. 'Your father fired him, I recall.'

'Yes, after I'd made my creation—you know, the wood on two cart wheels.'

'I recall your brother had an accident with it.'

'Yes,' Dolph said.

'And you never saw him again?' Abby asked.

Dolph laughed. 'Oh, no, nothing so dramatic. He gained employment at a boys' school. I met him for a drink when I went to Cambridge.'

'Oh, that is a relief.'

Except oddly it wasn't. 'We had nothing to discuss. I think the stodginess of the porridge served at his school was the highlight of the conversation.'

'That must have been hard.'

It was, although he did not know why. Mr Jennings had been hale and hearty. Robust even. Why did it seem sadder than if he had been some frail poet, starving as he clung to his ideals?

The vicar brought him back to the present. 'So,

Your Lordship, will you be staying here for a while then?'

'Long enough to make certain things have improved.'

'I am glad,' Mr Walther said. 'If I might add, my lord, that you do belong here, you know.'

Dolph stiffened. 'I am aware of my title and responsibilities.'

For a moment, the vicar said nothing, pressing his gnarled fingers together and studying Dolph's face as though his expression might provide a clue or information.

'Do you mind if I speak freely, my lord?'

'You have seemed able to do so thus far,' Dolph said.

'I can let you talk,' Abby said, feeling perhaps her presence was intrusive.

'Good heavens, we have already established that I need to pull up my socks as landlord. I don't think I have any other dark secrets.'

'Loss and grief do odd things to a body,' the vicar said.

'Also not a revelation. Nor will I use it anymore as an excuse. I am the landlord and I will ensure that the tenants are not hungry or barefoot or uneducated.'

'Indeed, but I was not referring to your grief, although I believe it to be very real. I saw your parents bury three children.'

'My brothers.'

'When you were born, you were a such a small, tiny mite of a thing. Would never believe that to look at you know.'

'An infant's size does tend to change in thirty years.'

'They didn't expect you'd survive. I remember I was called in right quick for the baptism,' he said.

'I do like to surpass expectations.'

'It made them frightened to love you properly, I think. Or take their eyes off Barnaby. At least during those early years.'

'Is that why Mother did not visit frequently and Father stayed away?'

'A part of the reason, I would guess. Strange how fear can make you love one son all the more and yet the anticipation of an infant's death can prevent one from properly loving that child. That is why I wanted to say. You do belong.'

'Thank you,' Dolph said.

Chapter Ten

The next few days were oddly pleasant. Mrs Kent had provided a list individuals that were lacking in basic needs. The staff from London arrived with provisions. Martin located animal feed and had bought, pigs, cows and several hens. The latter purchase was not entirely successful as the hens refused to lay and Mrs Fred felt that Martin had been bamboozled.

To be fair, Martin had grown up in London and was likely not fully proficient in hens or their laying habits.

Meanwhile Abby, Lucy, Mrs Fred and Mrs Kent organized a method for distributing these goods and Dolph kept himself busy making arrangements for his aged relatives travel, organizing work parties and going through the ledger. He found that the financial information was scant but sufficient to prove that the estate had been poorly managed, even if there was insufficient evidence for criminal changes.

Therefore, the moment Trent returned, Dolph had asked that he be brought immediately to the study.

'Mr Trent, my lord,' Benton intoned from the study door.

One could always tell Benton's opinion of a visitor by the tone of his voice. It would appear that Mr Trent had not impressed him.

'Thank you,' Dolph said pleasantly. 'Do come in.'

Mr Trent entered. He still appeared somewhat bland. His face was pale, except for his nose, which was red and laced with a pattern of tiny veins. His eyes were a very light blue but also bloodshot, and his hands looked white and doughy as though unused to physical labour.

He crossed the floor, seating himself in the chair opposite. His clothes, while of decent quality, were dirty and Dolph could detect the smell of whiskey, mixed with sweat.

'I will have to release you from my employ, Mr Trent,' Dolph said without preamble.

The man started, either not anticipating these words, or at least not stated so bluntly. His mouth opened slightly and he licked his lips as if they were suddenly dry.

'I—we have had a run of bad luck, my lord. Poor weather, poor harvest, sickness among the animals. Indeed, I have done my utmost,' he said

'No doubt,' Dolph said. 'However, your utmost appears to have involved rather a lot of alcohol.'

'I have a few drinks while getting supplies for the tenants, seeds and the like. I mean, that is the way of the world. Likely got them a better price, you know, by being sociable,' he said, adding to these words by tapping his nose with his forefinger.

'I look forward to seeing the seeds. However, I doubt you got a better price by purchasing drink for the farmer. It is more likely you got a worse price because your faculties were impaired.'

'My faculties? My faculties are not impaired.'

'I am glad of that. However, I intend to be more involved in the estate now, so your services are not required.'

'Involved, Your Lordship? I am not wanting to be rude but I question how much you would be knowing about running an estate.'

'Likely not as much as I should. However, I know sufficient not to drink the profits and that the seed you brought is less than needed and of poor quality.'

Trent stood, now embracing moral outrage. 'Your Lordship, I have never been so insulted. If you are accusing me of a crime, do so now so that I can answer the charge within a court of law.'

'That seems unnecessarily melodramatic. I had decided not to involve the law. However, if you insist, I suppose I could pursue a legal route.'

Mr Trent gaped, looking somewhat like a fish out of water, gulping in an attempt to breathe.

'I mean, I quite understand that, being a man of honour, you feel the need to answer in a court of law. I have taken a cursory look through these.' Dolph tapped the ledger with a forefinger. 'However, I am certain that my man of business will be able to make a more complete accounting and that the results should be sufficient to support a case against you, if you would like.'

Mr Trent closed his mouth, pursing his lips. 'Your Lordship has obviously made up your mind. I will not stay where I am unwelcome and where my abilities are so unappreciated.'

'Indeed, so shall we agree that you are dismissed without reference? And if you could remove yourself from the manager's cottage by tomorrow that would be most welcome.'

'I certainly will not remain anywhere I am not wanted.'

'Good to hear.' Dolph rang the bell. 'Benton will see you out.'

Mr Trent left. Dolph heard his voice complaining to Benton as they crossed the hall.

He got up. Truthfully, the interview with Trent had left him restless. How could he have even hired the man? Or had he not cared?

It was a pleasant day for early spring. He walked

up towards the small knoll which overlooked the estate. He'd gone there often with Barnaby as a child. They'd climb the huge oak tree at its summit. He remembered once trying to make a swing by tying the hemp rope about the bough. Then, clinging like a monkey, he had swung on it, until the branch had snapped, spilling him onto the ground.

He hadn't been hurt. As he recalled, he and Barnaby had found it hugely funny, giggling so much that they could not stop.

His life had been divided into chapters, or maybe all lives were. There had been the chapter of his childhood, which had ended with Barnaby's broken arm.

Then the summons from his father after Barnaby joined up to follow his friend Stanley. That summons, he supposed, had marked the end of his youth, of being the carefree second son.

He remembered going into the study and seeing his father sitting behind the desk. The furniture had seemed larger. Or perhaps his father had seemed smaller. Dolph had seldom been invited into the study. It had been the place for lectures and punishment.

'Your brother has chosen to join the army. I have arranged for you to join his regiment. Talk some sense into him,' his father had said, his words crisp, sharp and with little preliminary greeting.

'Why? I mean why did he do that?' Dolph had asked.

'Do they teach you to ask questions in the military?'

'No, but—'

'Then don't.' His father had ground out the words, hunching his shoulders. 'Just bring him back,' he'd said.

Afternoon sunlight flickered through the high clouds. Dolph strode up towards the oak tree, enjoying the fresh air and the familiarity of the path. From this distance the fields, lake and pastureland looked much as they had in his youth. The disrepair, obvious up close, was less visible.

At its summit, he paused, inhaling as he gazed at the house with its medieval turret and mismatched add-ons. From there he could see the lake and, further on, the village with its church, store and graveyard.

A movement caught his attention. A woman strode purposefully along the pathway at the base of the knoll. Abby, of course. Even before he could properly discern her features, he recognized her movement, her long strides and the no-nonsense swing of her shoulders.

Perhaps she was taking a well-deserved respite or searching for herbs with which to create a poultice for the vicar or Benton. Truthfully, Benton seemed much improved, although he hadn't yet had his tooth removed.

Dolph smiled. A flare-up could well lead to additional treatment and he might again see Benton with his jowls covered in slime.

Dolph's lips twitched.

He wondered how the romance was going. He must ask Abby if there was any further development in that department. That was the thing about women like Abby or his mother. They cared. They noted details. They saw a downcast expression or wishful glance. They brought heart. Dolph could reinvest in the estate. He could mend fences and buy boots, but could he ever hope to bring that?

As though cognizant of observation, Abby glanced up and waved, walking towards him. Her hair had loosened from her bun, giving her a tousled appearance. Her cheeks were flushed with exercise.

'Truthfully, I didn't know whether to come up or not,' she said as soon as they were close enough to talk. 'It is so uncomfortable when one sees someone but is not close enough to be heard. I realized that you likely came up here for solitude but it seemed rude to just carry on.'

She sat on the ground, a sudden, rather ungraceful movement, seemingly careless of grass stains.

He sat also. 'I am glad you came. Indeed, I wanted

to thank you again for your hard work and mention that I dismissed Trent.'

'That's good,' she said. 'We will do much better without him.'

He liked the way she slipped in the pronoun *we*.

'Mrs Kent is quite remarkable. She seems to know everything about everybody. She is very organized. And Jason has been quite wonderful with Ignatius.'

'Somehow they both make each other more mature,' Dolph said. 'I am not certain how that works.'

'Yes, Iggy is forever quoting Jason.'

'I mentioned Great-Aunt Edith will arrive tomorrow?'

She nodded. 'I can't say I am looking forward to the event. I mean I am certain that she is delightful but I rather fear that I will no longer be doing important work but will be practising my curtsey.'

They were silent for a moment. He leaned back. The trunk felt firm against his spine.

'I forgot how much I loved this place.'

'It is beautiful.'

'You know after Mother died, I tried to pretend Lansdowne didn't exist. I shouldn't have. I should have come earlier.'

'After Father died and before the Harringtons moved to London, I'd avoid going to church even though the new vicar was nice enough and I loved the parishioners. I think we all do the best we can, you know, to cope and to survive.'

'Thanks.' He looked towards the lake as it glistened under the pewter sky. 'Barnaby and I used to fish. We'd sit for hours, threading worms onto hooks, and he'd tell me all the things he'd do when he was landlord.'

'He'd had a long time to think about it,' she said gently.

Dolph nodded. The estate looked like a patchwork in different shades of green.

She leaned into him. She smelled of springtime promise. 'What was he like? Barnaby.'

'I don't know.'

'What do you mean?'

'He worked so hard to be exactly as he was supposed to be. The perfect heir.'

Dolph had envied him. Barnaby was head boy and cricket captain. He was tall with the facility to say the right things, wear the right clothes, intelligent and articulate but not too intelligent or articulate. In contrast, Dolph had been slow to grow and had then shot up like a gangling, scrawny weed, all legs and arms.

'He even looked like my father. He fit in,' Dolph said, although he was aware of the irony within those words.

'And you went with him? Into battle?'

'Yes. You know, he didn't have to go to war. He followed…a friend. My father never forgave him for dying.'

'Or you for living?' she said softly.

He hadn't been alone with Abby for several days. Iggy and the needs of the estate had superseded these moments but he was struck by the ease of their conversation.

It felt right to lean into her and feel the comfort of her presence.

'I was with him on the battlefield. When he died… It was the first real talk we'd had in years. I wish we'd had it sooner. It made me realize how much I didn't know or understand.' He spoke disjointedly, pain threading through the words.

'You knew you loved him and he knew that too.' She took his hand. Again, he was jolted by her touch even as he was comforted by it.

'Yes.' There was the wonderful simplicity of that statement. 'I loved him.'

'My father used to say that humans make things complicated. We tie ourselves in knots. He loved that verse in Corinthians. You know, "Though I speak with the tongues of men and of angels, and have not charity, I am become *as* sounding brass, or a tinkling cymbal." It was his favourite part of the Bible. One of the few parts, he said he never doubted.'

'Your father was an unusual minister.'

'Yes, but that is true. That is the only part I never question or doubt, and my father wasn't the minister my mother wanted him to be. Or likely even the minister the Church of England wanted, but he was loved.'

Dolph stared at the estate spread out before him, fields, trees, hedges and roads crisscrossing like an intricate design.

'Perhaps unusual isn't always a disadvantage,' she said softly. 'You don't have to be landlord in the same way as your father or even your brother.'

'I suppose not.'

And in that moment, he felt something shift or realign, and the feelings and thoughts for which he'd had no words now found expression.

'My father got me assigned to Barnaby's regiment to keep him safe. I rather failed that assignment.' He gave a mirthless laugh.

Abby leaned forward, her expression one of intent concentration, her blue eyes shimmering in sympathy.

'It was an impossible task. It wasn't fair to ask you.'

'A last-ditch effort,' Dolph said. 'He tried to stop Barnaby from going but Barnaby was determined. He had…a friend, Lord Stanley. His family was angry with him. They disowned him because…'

He left his sentence unfinished.

'They loved each other,' she said, simply and shockingly.

'Yes.' He closed his eyes. 'How do you know such things?'

She shrugged. 'I studied the Greeks. Education opens one's mind.'

'Barnaby didn't regret anything. He said to me that death was better than pretending. He didn't want to pretend anymore. He'd been pretending for ever.'

Dolph turned so that he was facing her. He inhaled. He felt her hand in his own. 'I've never told anybody that.'

'I'm glad you told me.'

'I felt I failed him. I wish he had trusted me more. Perhaps he would have told me and then he wouldn't have felt so desperate.'

She reached for his other hand too, her grip tight and warm. 'He told you when he needed you most. He trusted you and you were there for him. Society failed him but not you.'

'But would I have understood? Would I have accepted or would I have judged?'

'I don't know. But we know that you loved him. You were there.

'"Every man is a creature of the age in which he lives, and few are able to raise themselves above the ideas of the time,"' Dolph said softly.

'Voltaire.'

'You studied him?'

'A little,' she said.

'You are...' He couldn't find the words.

She laughed, letting go of his hands and lightening the mood. 'A bluestocking?'

'A fascinating woman.'

A strand of hair had loosened from her typical bun. He reached forward, gently brushing it behind her ear. He heard her sharp exhalation at his touch, the tiny gasp audible. There was something about her, that lack of pretence, her blunt honesty, her humour, the deep blue of her eyes, the sensual fullness of her lips at odds with her otherwise prim appearance. He again felt that allure, that desire no less because she trying to hide or down play her beauty.

He ran his fingers along the soft line of her chin.

Her lips parted. They were pink, moist, perfectly shaped. Her gaze met his, blue orbs framed with long lashes.

He wanted this woman.

The knowledge blasted through him. Perhaps he'd known it on some level from the first moment but now it was explicit, intense, deep and primal.

He leaned into her, cupping her chin, so close his lips were almost touching her own. 'I think I've wanted to kiss you since you and Basil ran into me on the front steps.'

'You have?' Her forehead puckered in concentration as though solving a complex algebraic equation, then she smiled. The mesmeric change in her expression was heart-stopping and appealing. 'I think I have too,' she said.

Her blunt, unusual honesty fuelled his desire more than the blandishment of others.

She bit her lip. 'I mean it is hard for me to know because I have never been kissed. However, I have been thinking about it. With you.'

He was so close that he could see the three tiny freckles on her nose, smell the fresh scent of her hair and feel the loose strands tickle his cheeks. His lips touched hers, gently. Then his kiss deepened, his tongue teasing. He felt her startle and that tiny gasp. Her fingers rose, instinctively gripping his shoulders, and, more wonderfully, her mouth opened under his own as her body arched sinuously into him.

Thought and reason ceased, swamped in a wild, driving, growing need. Nothing mattered, nothing existed, save for the touch of her lips, that instinctive sway of her body and the eager press of her fingers on his shoulders, winding into his hair.

He pulled her closer. His hands spanned her back. His fingers slid up her spine. He touched the soft skin at the nape of her neck and the silky strands of hair, not captured in the bun.

He felt...alive.

For the first time in for ever, he felt totally, completely alive and not a half shell of a man broken by memories.

His fingers moved, exploring her curves. He heard her soft, muted groan. That moan, her eager unschooled fingers tracing his shoulders and the needy arch of her body increased his desire.

Restraint slipped. Coherent thought scattered. Desire invaded, driving and propelling. His blood roared. Dolph wanted this woman. He wanted to peel away the layers of reserve, to pull her hair free from the tight bun so that it fell cascading down her back. He wanted to kiss the creamy, soft skin of her throat, to remove the practical, plain grey dress, to overwhelm sense with passion, memory with experience, to feel her…to hold her…

He wanted her naked. He wanted her naked and beneath him.…

Her hand moved to his shoulders, slipping inside the jacket, tentative exploratory fingers pressing through his shirt. His heart thudded. He felt an urgency, reminiscent of adolescence. They moved together with primal instinct. She arched against him, pressing herself closer with an impatient, inexperienced eagerness.

Inexperienced…

She was an innocent. He could not…would not… let lust swamp reason. He could not allow this vortex of emotion to take control.

He pulled away, shifting back. It took a physical effort which felt huge, as though fighting against every desire and instinct. He sat, breathless against the tree trunk. His heart thundered against his ears, his body shaken.

'I didn't want you to stop,' she said, breathless, her voice husky with passion and surprise.

'I know. I did not want to stop,' Dolph said. 'I am drawn to you in so many ways.'

And then the past, present and future made sudden sense, fitting together like the parts of puzzle.

It felt like a click in his brain, like a bolt unlocking, an answer, a pathway.

'Marry me,' Dolph said.

'Huh?' Abby felt winded, bereft of language.

Momentarily, she couldn't react, like his words were solitary units of sound and could not be strung together to make sense.

'We should marry,' he repeated, his voice stronger.

'Because…we…kissed?' she asked, the words disjointed.

'Yes, but more than that.'

'What? I— You are not being sensible.'

She stood. Her movement was abrupt and yet she was also aware of the action of each limb and muscle as if needing to make a concerted, coordinated effort. Her body shook, vibrating with sensations and needs, making it foreign to her. Her emotions were equally chaotic, a confused mush of anger, vulnerability, desire…

Her world had been rendered unrecognizable. She couldn't make sense of her own feelings—never mind this sudden, crazy, overwhelming proposal. She had only just discovered this foreign part of herself and now he was talking of marriage. Marriage?

It made her head spin. Like the time she'd drunk too much elderberry wine thinking it was juice. The feeling was dreamlike, euphoric, elating but foreign.

'We can't,' she said, grasping on to this statement as a single immutable fact.

'Why?' He stood also. 'Because we did not think of it before? You have another husband hidden in the closet?'

'What? No.' She paced across the grass. 'No—no, of course not. But the idea is not sensible. I do not want to be a wife. I did not dream of being a wife.'

'And dreams can't change?'

'No, I mean, I don't think so. I am not social. I am a governess. We are too different. Our worlds are too different.'

'You are only recently a governess and fit in this world better than I.' He gestured towards the village and lake.

She shook her head. 'I am adequate with children, nothing more. I am no duchess. I don't want to be a duchess.'

'I didn't want to be a duke.'

She shook her head. 'This conversation is not sensible. Maybe you feel that you are honour bound to offer because we kissed. Gentlemen are foolish about honour. But you aren't. No one saw us. And pray do not insult my intellect and say that after one kiss you have fallen madly in love with me.'

'Perhaps not "in love". Not in a romantic fairy-tale way. But I feel as though I have been sleeping and I am awake. It is more than desire. I am drawn to you. I respect your intellect to a degree I find unexpected. I like you. I desire you. I feel—' he paused as though trying to sift through his feelings to find the right word '—whole. And better.'

She shook her head. 'I feel as though I was awake and am dreaming. Another person cannot make you whole. My parents learned that. And I cannot be your conscience. I don't want to be anyone's conscience. Not even Iggy's. I saw my mother do that as well.'

'Maybe I am not explaining it right. But we could help each other and we could help these people. You know that.'

'I know that we were both broken and hurt. And maybe we have helped each other heal but that is not enough. And I am not enough for the role.'

'You care about people. You would have more freedom than as a governess. Or will you let my sister and Mrs Harington marry you off to a widower with a dozen children?'

'No, but—'

You could open a school, work with the tenants. This could work. This could be a workable solution for us both.'

'I—' She was no fool. She knew the drudgery that could befall a governess or schoolmistress.

He stepped forward, taking her hands within his own. She was conscious of his strength but also his vulnerability.

'Think about it,' he said.

The thought of being married to this man…it both excited and scared her. She swallowed, her throat dry.

'I will think about it,' she said.

Abby walked back. Thankfully, Dolph had gone straight to the estate office. Abby considered herself an individual not easily flustered, but the ability to walk calmly with the man who had just proposed marriage after kissing her with such thoroughness was beyond her.

The front hall was a welcome, blissful quiet, the silence broken only by the rhythmic tick of a clock from somewhere within the interior.

She stood quite still, staring at the high ceiling, the painted sky and billowing clouds, as though the chaos of her mind prevented physical movement or perhaps she hoped that a depiction of Greek heaven would bring her calm.

It didn't.

Her thoughts bounced, a million balls loosed within her skull. His words circled, reverberating like an echo in an empty room.

This proposal in no way resembled the pretty speeches that Lucy had imagined or read.

And yet, Abby did not doubt Dolph's intent.

Nor would Abby lie to herself. She was physically attracted to Lord Lansdowne, Duke of Elmsend. She enjoyed his kiss. No, *enjoyed* was a misnomer...an understatement.

She felt altered...made different.

One was changed by experience. She was changed. She was changed by his kiss. This was another before and after in her life.

Abby had never previously considered the physical side of marriage or that, by remaining single, she might miss something integral to the human experience. However, she was too honest to hide from the stark fact that Dolph had awakened a part of herself which would no longer lie passive.

She would have lain with him, there and then, in the open, on the hillside under an oak tree. Indeed, she still would. She could feel it in her body, in the memory of his touch and in an achy neediness.

Previously, Abby had not believed that anything could make her so forget herself, to be so immersed that all else dwarfed in comparison. As a sentient being, this confused and unnerved her.

But did that mean they should marry?

Or did it mean that they shared physical needs similar to most young, healthy creatures? However, strong the physical, it could not or should not overwhelm sense, nor alter the dreams of a lifetime.

Because Abby had never dreamed of marriage as most girls did. Lucy built castles and imagined princes. She would see this as a fairy tale and concoct a romantic story no more real than her beloved novellas. Lucy had always dreamed of handsome men, and wedding bells. She was designing wedding gowns while Abby deciphered Greek.

Abby's dreams had more closely resembled Miss Brownlee's. Miss Brownlee had read books with her feet on an apple barrel and shouted at apple thieves with words she should not know.

She had not dreamed of waiting on a rescue like Cinderella. Miss Brownlee needed no rescue.

Abby wanted to forge her own way, make her own decisions and put her feet on the apple barrel or ride astride.

A duchess could not shout at thieving apple pickers. But then nor could a governess.

Abby groaned. She could not stay here staring

about the hall like a startled rabbit. Besides, Ignatius was still in her charge and usually found trouble when insufficiently occupied. She could hardly expect Jason to always keep him company.

She went up to the nursery but Ignatius was not there. Likely Mrs Fred might know his whereabouts. With this in mind, she went to the housekeeper's apartment, where the Freds were staying, at least until a suitable individual was hired. As always, Mrs Fred had created a pleasant space. A fire crackled in the hearth. Basil lay sprawled on the rug, thumping his tail in greeting while Mrs Fred sat on a comfortable chair, knitting.

'Gracious, is Basil actually tired?' Abby asked, glancing at the exhausted animal. 'He is not jumping around for once.'

'He has had a lot of exercise,' Mrs Fred said, without slowing the fast movement of her hands so that her knitting needles provided a constant rhythmic clicking. 'I am uncertain if the ducks will ever be the same. Did you have a nice walk?'

Abby flopped heavily in the chair, stretching her feet towards the warmth. 'He asked me to marry him. Lord Lansdowne!'

It was a relief to say the words but also odd to hear them. Like she was acting. Saying things aloud sometimes made the information feel more real but not this time. Conversely, once voiced, they felt more surreal.

Besides, such an announcement should not be said within the housekeeper's suite, voiced by a governess wearing grey with a mobile hearthrug flopped upon the floor. Any of Lucy's favourite authors would have staged it better. Lucy would advise a pink gown and elegant surroundings, candles, flowers and crystals transforming the light into rainbows.

Albeit the dust motes were dancing in the single ray of sun peeking through the rather grimy window.

Mrs Fred paused, eying her critically and momentarily slowing the rhythmic movement of her hands. 'Well now, I can't say that I am entirely surprised.'

'You what? Does nothing surprise you? You thought he'd propose?'

'I thought there was a spark.'

'A spark!' Abby almost spat out the word. 'A spark? You thought there was a spark? How did you know there was a spark when I did not?'

Mrs Fred laughed, resuming her knitting so that the click-clicking of the needles merged seamlessly with the crackling fire. 'Perhaps because you are not particularly familiar with sparks. Or you didn't want to see there was a spark. Or you discount yourself as not the sort of individual to experience a spark.'

'Well, I am not. And there is no...no spark. Likely he is shocked by the state of the estate and thinks I could help, which is very practical, dutiful even, but not a spark,' Abby said.

'Yes, dear,' Mrs Fred agreed. She had the annoying habit of being agreeable just when one wanted to argue most.

'Anyway, he drinks too much. He can be irritating and smug. He has this habit of using humour to deflect, which is annoying. Granted, he is intelligent and much more responsible than the Ashleighs. Indeed, I think he will prove a good landlord and I am glad of it. However, none of this would make marriage a reasonable or sensible suggestion.'

'He is certainly occupying your thoughts to a surprising extent given your apparent lack of interest in the gentleman.'

'I just received my first ever proposal. From a duke. It is hardly surprising if it somewhat preoccupies my thoughts,' Abby retorted, getting up and pacing more quickly.

'We could adjourn to the Great Hall. It will give you more room to pace.'

'No, that is not necessary,' Abby retorted, sitting again, keeping both feet flat to the floor with a conscious effort. Her boots were muddy. She'd got her first and likely only proposal in dirty shoes.

But would the proposal feel any more believable if she wore pink, had blond hair and clean slippers?

Yes, it would, she thought, because it would mean

that she was the type to wear pink and have clean slippers, and not the sort to sit with a miscreant dog leaning against her ankles and a ribbon of brown mud about her hem.

'Anyhow, regardless of Lord Lansdowne's motives or…or sparks, I am not the marrying sort of female. All I have ever wanted is independence,' Abby said.

'You'd likely find more freedom as duchess than a governess,' Mrs Fred said prosaically.

Abby shook her head. 'Freedom that is given to you like a gift is not true freedom because it can be taken away equally fast. Every person should have freedom because we are people. It is our right.'

'Sounds like one of those letters you used to write to Mr Wilberforce. And I can't argue with the sentiment but then I don't run the government. I'd say the female of our species cannot be too picky about the type of freedom one acquires.'

Abby stood again. She could not help it. She walked to the small window and back. 'You don't understand. You think you have freedom because Mr Fred will always do whatever you say and will never stop you from doing something. But that isn't true freedom. It is not universal but rather individual to you because you have a nice husband. But we should all enjoy that freedom because we are people. It does not matter whether one is female or male, single, married, rich, poor, old or young. Freedom is a right.'

'Lud, I have missed your diatribes, and I can't say I disagree, but Rome wasn't built in a day.'

'Ugh, what does that even mean? I hate clichés.'

For once, Mrs Fred's unruffled demeanour was not comforting. There was only so much solace one could gain from tea and homilies.

Abby pressed her hands together. 'I've never thought much about marriage. If Mother had lived longer, I would have had to. But when she died, Father let me be me and Miss Brownlee actively encouraged me to follow a different path. Of course, Mrs Harrington has long hoped I might marry. But that is only because it was my mother's wish. I admit I thought she'd be so busy getting Lucy married that my own marital status might seem of less import.'

Abby sighed. Of course, that had been before Lord Lansdowne, his sister and some ancient great-aunt got involved. With them in the mix, her control was slipping, like sand through an hourglass.

'Other than your need for whole societal change, have you any other reservations against the married state?' Mrs Fred enquired, pausing to count her stitches.

Abby turned from the window, wrinkling her nose. 'Just that it seems to involve a lot of dinners, jams and shopping for bonnets. All things I am quite dreadful at.'

'There are some other aspects to marriage,' Mrs Fred said.

'Mrs Fred, do you love Mr Fred?'

'Yes,' Mrs Fred said easily. 'We have become accustomed to each other. Like old slippers.'

'Lord Lansdowne is not the "old slipper" type.'

'Oh, you don't want them as an old slipper at your age. You want some spark.'

'Back to the spark,' Abby grumbled. 'Although I suppose there is a bit. You know, spark, with me and Lord Lansdowne.'

'Tell me something I didn't know,' Mrs Fred said, chuckling.

'But is it enough?' Abby was conscious that her cheeks had flushed and sweat prickled her palms.'

'Maybe not on its own. But then you're forgetting the most important ingredient in a marriage.

'What?'

'Being there. Showing up. I'd say you're good at that.'

'I suppose,' Abby said.

'Ignatius is missing!' The words blasted through the room.

Abby and Mrs Fred jerked around. Jason and Mr Fred stood in the doorway. Mr Fred's face was

flushed, beads of sweat visible. Jason's tie was undone and his hair rumpled.

The knitting fell to the ground. Basil jumped up
with a wild cacophony of barks. Abby stood, her
muscles tensed as though poised to take action.

'What? Did he go to the lake?' she asked, cold
fear clutching at her stomach.

'No,' Mr Fred said quickly. 'Calm yourself. We
checked and left the groom there to keep watch. But
we think he might have gone to London.'

'You what?' Abby's fear morphed into disbelief,
making her almost giggly with incredulity. She sat
heavily of the chair. 'That is ludicrous.'

'Augustus Cornelius Fred, have you been imbibing more than you should? Shame on you. And it is
not yet evening. And Basil, how did you get tangled
in my knitting?'

Abby pulled the bell. 'I'll get Giles to look after
Basil. Then you can explain what this is all about in
a sensible manner.'

Giles came promptly and Basil, his snout still be-
ribboned in pink, was removed. Mr Fred and Jason
sat on the couch, breathing heavily but appearing
calmer.

'Right. From the beginning,' Mrs Fred instructed.
'It sounds as though you two have let your imagi-
nations run wild and we do not want to start an

unnecessary panic. Mrs Harrington already being hysterically inclined.'

Jason began, rubbing the ends of his misused necktie nervously between his fingers. 'As you know, Ignatius and I have been spending time together. I quite like him. We did some fishing. Didn't catch much. Lake not well stocked. Anyhow, two friends of mine came to take me back to London. Planning to go to the Coffee Cauldron. Had mentioned to them I was bored. Nice fellows, Herron and Bellamy. You're not likely to know them, though Uncle might. Anyway, I decided not to go. Said I should stay here. Didn't want to upset Dolph. Sent them away. They were not entirely pleased, having come all this way.'

'Right, I am glad you didn't leave,' Abby said. 'But where does Iggy fit in?'

'We think Ignatius hid in the carriage when they weren't looking and went with them,' Mr Fred finished.

Mrs Fred asked, 'What possible reason would Ignatius have to hide in a carriage and go to London with strangers? No, this is a fairy tale and that you may tie to.'

'It is just that he had been asking a lot about gambling,' Jason explained, the cloth of his necktie making a rough scritch-scratching sound as he rubbed it more vigorously between his nervous fingers.

'He asks questions. He is curious but that doesn't mean he would hide in a carriage with people he doesn't know,' Abby said. 'I think we are being alarmist.'

'They were mighty specific,' Jason said even more unhappily. 'The questions.'

'About what exactly?'

'Counting cards.'

'What?' Granted, Ignatius enjoyed card games and chess but he had never shown any particular interest in the less savoury aspects of the game. 'Why?'

'Said he'd be good at it. That he could keep numbers in his head. I told him it was against the rules. Shouldn't have told him so much. Kept asking questions. So constant that it was just easier to answer, don't you know.'

'Yes, he does that,' Abby said somewhat grimly.

'And I saw him near the carriage,' Mr Fred said. 'I didn't think anything of it at the time. I mean, you know how he likes to investigate things.'

'I do,' Abby said. 'And I still think it is more likely that he is exploring something here as opposed to hightailing it up to London. Has anyone spoken with Mrs Harrington or Miss Harrington? Maybe he is with them.'

'I took the liberty of sending a maid up to enquire. She said that they were both resting but that Ignatius was not there,' Mr Fred said.

'Right.' Abby was conscious of a sinking feeling in her gut. She knew logically it was not sensible to assume that Ignatius had hidden in a carriage to play cards in a London gambling hell. However, far-fetched or not, she could not dismiss it.

'We'd best talk to Lord Lansdowne,' she said.

They rose and went to the Great Hall, where they were met by Dolph, Mrs Harrington, Benton and Lucy, all converging from separate corridors within its centre.

Both Mrs Harrington and Lucy appeared in distress. Lucy's eyes were red rimmed, as was her nose, and she clutched a handkerchief in her hand.

'What is happening?' Dolph asked.

'Ignatius is missing,' Jason announced.

'He what?' Mrs Harrington appeared shocked, which made Abby wonder what had distressed them earlier.

'Jason is being dramatic. But we have no reason to believe any harm has come him,' Abby said.

'The lake,' Mrs Harrington whispered, her face a chalky white, as Abby's had been a few moments earlier.

'No, not that,' Abby said hurriedly, taking her arm. 'They checked it.'

'And we left a groom stationed there to scout around,' Mr Fred said. 'Spoke to the village boys also. They had been fishing and said they had seen neither hide nor hair of him.'

'Well, that is a relief,' Dolph said. 'There are few other natural dangers in this area. We will, of course, put together a search party immediately. However, it is most likely he has wandered off, perhaps lost his bearings. Fortunately, the weather is not cold. We will stay calm and get searchers out there.'

'Thank you,' Abby said with some relief. Mrs Fred was practical but did not have Dolph's resources and the others seemed quite hopeless in a crisis.

'We think he may have gone to London,' Jason said.

'London?' Mrs Harrington said, her tone quavering. 'How?'

'Friends of mine. In a carriage,' Jason said, running his hand through his rumpled hair.

'And you think they would have taken Ignatius?' Mrs Harrington asked.

'Not on purpose, of course. Don't like children, I am certain. But he might have hidden,' Jason explained.

'But why?' Dolph said. 'Abby, you know him well. Do you put any credence to this?'

'I don't know—it is far-fetched, but he does get fixated on ideas and I can't see him wandering around the estate without Basil. It is possible. He has developed an interest in gambling and has been asking all sorts of questions about gambling, counting cards and making money.'

Lucy made an audible gulp and might well have fallen if Benton had not procured a chair and offered a steadying arm.

'It's my fault,' she said. 'All my fault. I got a letter from Lady Stanhope. She was outlining all the things that I should improve before she would sponsor me and how I should make great use of your great-aunt and it all felt overwhelming. I got upset and said I wished we had our own money and didn't have to rely on Lady Stanhope.'

'Did Iggy hear this?' Abby asked.

'Yes.'

'And Iggy decided to find a way to make money,' Abby said, that sinking feeling growing.

'I did see Master Ignatius looking at the carriage,' Benton said.

'As did I,' Mr Fred added.

'I should have been keeping a better eye on him.' Abby flushed, avoiding Dolph's gaze.

'Let us do a thorough sweep of the house and lands. If we don't find him, we can proceed to London.'

'I know it seems unlikely and far-fetched,' Abby said. 'But truly I feel he might be in London. I don't think we should delay.'

Dolph glanced at her and then nodded. 'Very well.

Benton, order the carriage. We must take steps to cover all scenarios. Benton and Mrs Fred will organize a thorough search of the house. Mr Fred and Jason will get every available servant and tenant to search the estate. Miss Carstens, Mrs Harrington and Miss Harrington, wait here at the house. I will go up to London.'

'I will go with you,' Abby said.

'You are not going to London.'

'I must. Ignatius is my responsibility. I cannot stay here. '

'It makes no sense for you to go. The Coffee Cauldron is no place for a lady. '

'And no place for a child.'

'Which is why I will make speed to remove him,' Dolph said.

'But I can help.'

'And I can't allow it. It would be disastrous for your reputation. And quite possibly dangerous.'

'My reputation is less important than Ignatius's well-being,' Abby said, stepping forward so that they stood but a few feet from each other.

'And I am well able to look after his well-being. At least that way I will not be looking after your well-being as well.'

They gazes met. She saw his determination, his unquestioning expectation of obedience, and knew that for a myriad of reasons, this was important.

'I do not need to be looked after but I do need to go. Iggy will react better if he sees someone he knows well. Besides, how would you take care of him after you find him? He can be very stubborn, particularly if he is scared.'

'I'd take him to my sister, I presume.'

'He doesn't like your sister and would run away again.'

'He is a nine-year-old child. I can manage a nine-year-old child,' Dolph said.

'No.' Abby shook her head. 'Iggy is not the typical nine-year-old. He is brilliant but not sensible. He doesn't always manage change well. He will be exhausted, likely overwhelmed and maybe scared. If he is in London, I need to be there. I am going to come, whether it be in Mr Fred's carriage or your own.'

Dolph met her gaze, struck by her stubborn strength of will. He had no doubt that she would do just that. It was a long time since he had been opposed. He did not like the feeling, although he felt a grudging respect.

Anyhow, there was no time to argue. Besides, it would be easier to ensure her safety in his coach than another. Not to mention that the Harringtons' carriage was a lumbering vehicle and slow.

'Fine, I'll take you with me, but we'll have to

travel fast. With few stops. We need to get there before Iggy gets lost in London.'

'Sounds fine to me,' she said.

'You are irritatingly stubborn.'

'Only when I'm right,' she said.

'And have you ever encountered a situation where
you felt you were wrong,' he muttered before turning
to Benton. 'Send a note to my sister. Tell her Miss
Carstens will stay with her tonight. Let her know
that Ignatius might also be there.'

'Very well, sir.'

'And organize a search here. Remember it is still
entirely possible that he is somewhere in the house
or grounds.'

Mrs Harrington stepped forward. Her usually
round, ruddy face was pale and almost gaunt as
though she had gained years and lost pounds within
the last minutes.

'Thank you, Lord Lansdowne, and please bring
him home safely,' she said.

'If he is in London, we will find him,' Dolph said.

Chapter Eleven

The infuriating woman looked irritatingly composed. She was settled against the pink cushions, in a practical, dark cloak and with her countenance quite calm as though it was sensible to be dashing off to the London slums in the late afternoon to chase an errant child who had decided to take up cards. Maybe.

'You do realize that the Coffee Cauldron is in one of London's least salubrious neighbourhoods,' Dolph grumbled.

'I hadn't but all the more reason that we follow Ignatius with all dispatch,' she said.

'Agreed. However, I will lay out a few ground rules. When we get to the Coffee Cauldron, you need to listen to me. Follow my lead. No arguments.'

'Because I am female?'

'Yes,' he said. 'And because you have never set foot in the Cauldron, I presume. Therefore you have no understanding of its layout. You don't know that area of London or even its danger. You're from a country village, likely the greatest threat is an irascible cow.'

'Cows are seldom irascible. Goats are more irascible. And we had brawls in pubs on occasion.'

'The brawls at the Coffee Cauldron would be considerably more serious than whatever occurred in your local tavern. Besides, you are under my protection and I'd rather you not risk life, limb or reputation.'

'And I would prefer the freedom to go about my business as I have always done, as opposed to explaining my every decision' she snapped.

'Well, you can't.'

The words hung in the carriage. He wished he could reel them back.

'If we marry, you mean?' she said.

The words again reverberated around them, almost taking on a physical entity. He both felt a discomfort but also knew a relief that they had been said and were no longer hidden. It would have been worse to travel to London with this huge, unacknowledged thing between them.

'Yes, but even if we don't get married, there is bound to be change. That is life. You moved to London—that brings vulnerability. Whether you acknowledge it or not, there are dangers. We are travelling in a carriage which suggests wealth which also increases risk. As well, you are beautiful—'

'Heavens, you exaggerate.'

He felt a flash of frustration, kindling with something else. 'Abby, you don't see it, do you?'

'What?'

'There is something about you. Maybe it is the very fact that you are so unaware that you are attractive. You represent yourself as some sort of middle-aged spinster but you are not. You are young and beautiful.'

She swallowed, shaking her head slightly. 'Power and autonomy are awarded by age and gender. As a young female, it would seem I would have the least freedom.'

'But is it true freedom if you have to deny a part of yourself?' he asked,

'I...don't know,' she answered, her forehead puckered in concentration. 'It seems that when there are only a few ways of existing in a society, there are bound to be compromises. I suppose this is the one I am willing to make. The only woman I have ever known who was independent was my teacher, Miss Brownlee. I fear that if I am not like her, I might lose the right to make my own decisions.'

They were quiet for a while. He thought of Barnaby. He thought of how he had hated to pretend and how, eventually, he had felt as though he had lost some part of himself in the pretence.

'Abby,' he said. 'It is right that you are here. I have not been entirely successful in keeping my relatives alive and I wanted to keep you safe. However, I think safe also means not having to hide yourself and I do want that.'

She flushed slightly. 'Thank you.' The carriage wheels moved rhythmically. He felt its sway. She looked out into the darkness, running her fingers along the edge of the window frame. 'And thank you for coming so quickly to look for him. I know it seems unlikely, or a long shot, but it just seems like Iggy.'

'I am sorry that my sister wrote to Lucy like that.'

'Likely she meant well. Lucy can get overwhelmed and disheartened.'

'You care a lot for them.'

She nodded. 'They have been very kind. Mrs Harrington stepped in after Mother died. Lucy and I are quite different but that doesn't matter. I suppose we are like siblings and will love each other no matter our differences.'

'Yes,' he said softly. 'I suppose… I suppose nothing can really change that kind of love.'

She looked at him, with that quick direct gaze. 'Nothing can change it. You would have still loved Barnaby. He could have told you about Stanley and you would have still loved him. His choice not to tell you was not about you. It was about him.'

They fell silent again. 'Try to get some rest,' Dolph said. 'It will still be a while.'

She turned to him, tears shimmering. 'I don't think I can. Not when I think that Ignatius might be in danger.'

'He will be fine. We have to believe that. Indeed, he will likely reappear with an idea for a whole new invention. Card shuffling or something.'

She gave a wobbly smile. 'He does have an uncanny ability to land on his feet.'

'He certainly keeps one on one's toes. I might have anticipated a flood or a blown-up chicken coop, but I never thought that Ignatius would decide to gamble,' he said.

She leaned back, letting her eye lids close. He could see the dark smudges of fatigue.

'Use my shoulder as a pillow,' he said.

She smiled and, for a moment, hesitated. Then with a soft sigh she let her head rest against him. Wisps of hair touched his chin.

'We will find him,' he said.

'Thank you. For being here.'

Abby had not expected to sleep but the carriage movement, combined with exhaustion, proved too much. She fell into a sleep filled with convoluted dreams.

When she woke up, she found that she had curled into him, resting her head on his shoulder. For a moment, before the worries about Iggy tumbled back in, it felt nice to wake with her head on his chest and to hear the steady, reassuring beat of his heart and feel his exhalation.

Then she remembered Iggy. She straightened. Her body felt stiff. They must be in the city now. She could feel the bumpiness of the cobbles, the occasional shout from outside and the changing from light to dark as they moved under street lamps.

Pushing aside the window curtain, she peeked out. The houses were tightly packed. People and stray dogs were visible, huddled over fires or sleeping in doorways.

'Don't be looking out. It is not safe,' Dolph said.

She let the curtain fall.

'We are almost there,' he added.

For several more minutes they continued in silence, until they rounded a corner and Abby could feel the carriage slowing.

'Dolph, I need to go in as well. I am not being stubborn but I think it would be best and quickest.'

'Why?'

'I know Iggy. I know the way he thinks. He is likely in his "observing" phase at present. That is the way he does things. He is all about the science, like an experiment.'

'So?'

'Observing can look like hiding. That means that he will not be visible and it will take time to find him. But if he sees me, he would come right away.'

Dolph drummed his fingers against his leg. 'I don't like the idea of you going in there. But I don't like the idea of you staying out here either, even with Martin. And you make sense. The most important thing is to get Iggy out as quickly as possible, if he is there.'

The carriage jerked to a stop. The sudden silence of the hooves and wheels felt eerie. Abby swallowed, rubbing her palms nervously against her gown.

'Put your cloak over your head, stay close to me and don't call too much attention to yourself,' Dolph said as Martin opened the door.

They got out. The air felt cold. It was starting to rain, a spitting type of rain where each droplet was huge.

The building appeared in poor repair. A shutter hung loose. It rattled against the outer wall. There was no moon and not yet the shimmer of dawn. The structures were built so close that their second stories hung over the street, largely obliterating the night sky.

The few street lamps shed weak puddles of light.

A sign hung limply from a post, its lettering obscured by grime. A rat scurried on the pavement, disappearing around the corner. The entrance was lit by a single lamp which provide weak flickering light.

Abby shivered, pulling her cloak more closely about her. She felt both solitary and, conversely that she was watched by a dozen eyes.

They crossed the cobbles. The uneven pavement was wet with large dirty puddles at sporadic intervals. A bird circled overhead, its feathered movement audible. The air felt heavy and damp, each raindrop cold. There was an intermittent drip from the roof or gutter.

Dolph put his hand on the doorknob. The door opened easily with only a tiny creak of unoiled hinges.

They stepped inside.

The door banged shut.

An uneasy, unnatural hush fell over the place, odd for a business of its sort. The narrow entrance widened into a larger taproom. The ceiling was low, criss-crossed with thick, dark beams. Tables and chairs were crammed into odd nooks and crannies. Several were occupied. Men glanced at them with expressionless but slightly malevolent eyes. A large fire burned at one end, but didn't draw properly, so that a thick layer of smoke formed swirling wisps below the beams.

'You taken the wrong turn? We ain't used to toffee-nosed gents and ladies,' a gentleman behind the bar said, winking broadly at his customers.

'I am looking for someone and hoping you might be of assistance,' Dolph said.

'Assistance, is it?' the man said, pulling down on a stained waistcoat which was riding high over his belly. 'Another toff 'ere, gents. We've become right popular.'

'I am looking for three individuals. Two would be fashionable gentleman and the other is a boy.'

'Like I was saying. We gets a lot of gentlemen 'ere. Right popular we are. Mebbe you can narrow that down a bit. Assist with me memory, so to speak.' He gave another broad wink to the punters and smiled. He was missing several teeth and those that remained were stained and uneven. He pushed forward his hand, palm up.

Dolph placed a coin in its centre and the man's fingers curled over it into a fist.

He retracted his arm, pocketing the coin quickly. 'The toffy-nosed fellow is downstairs.'

'And the boy?'

'So, wot does this boy look like?'

'About ten. Very intelligent, with fair hair.'

'Intelligent, eh? Well, we don't 'xactly quiz 'em on

their letters.' He gave a cackle, amused by his own joke. I can't say I've seen a lot of boys in these parts but you are welcome to look.'

He chewed slowly on a piece of chewing tobacco. His jaws made a rhythmic squelchy, liquid sound. Abby moved uneasily between the tables, aware of curious stares from over the tall flagons of ale. As she moved away from the entrance, the air became staler and felt damp, layered with smells gained throughout the centuries.

Goosebumps prickled her skin as though touched by skeletal fingers. The flagstones felt sticky under her boots.

For an awful moment, she could see no sign of Ignatius but then she caught sight of a movement in one of the far corners. He rose as though from a crouching position, appearing very small as he wound between the large tables and chairs.

'Thank goodness,' Abby whispered with an exhalation of relief so huge, her knees shook. She reached for a chair back for support.

'Miss Carstens, you came,' Ignatius said.

'Yes,' Dolph said tersely. 'And now we are leaving.'

For once, Ignatius said nothing, following them, and placing his small hand into hers, an usual gesture.

'You'll be fine,' she said gently.

Dolph opened the exterior door and they stepped from the stuffy air of the Coffee Cauldron and into the stench of the London slums. It was raining heavier. The carriage still stood outside. Martin had suffered no ill effect and the vehicle had a full quotient of wheels and horses.

'Come on,' Dolph said and they scrambled into the coach.

Iggy sat beside her. He smelled of smoke and alcohol. She met Dolph's glance, her relief reflected in his own expression.

Abby shivered. She felt almost shaky as exhaustion and worry caught up with her. 'Ignatius Harrington, don't ever do that again. Whatever were you thinking?'

'I wanted to learn how to gamble,' he said. 'Apparently, it is an excellent way to make money.'

'No! No, it is not. And not for you,' she snapped.

'I am knowledgeable about card games. I have an excellent memory and can hide my emotions. Of course, Lord Stanhope's nephew loses money, but I am a more intelligent and do not drink.'

'You are nine!' Abby said.

'This is true. I find that to be a disadvantage to gambling. And beer tastes bad. Will it taste better when I am bigger?'

Abby again felt that sensation of her jaw dropping as a hundred things flittered through her mind.

'You are not becoming a gambler,' she said firmly, grabbing on to the one fact which was indisputable.

'It appears to take a lot of practice.'

'Practice? Ignatius Winslow Harrington, you are not gambling or practising gambling.'

'Perhaps not. I didn't like it there. It was noisy. There was swearing. The floor was sticky,' he said, his voice trembling on these last words.

'Good, we agree on something,' Dolph said. 'Next we will go to my sister's. I would suggest a bath for you and perhaps some food.'

'I don't like Lady Stanhope.'

'That's fine. You will not need to spend a lot of time with her,' Dolph said.

'She was mean to Lucy. That is why I need money. I heard all about it yesterday. You see, Lucy doesn't know stuff and now Lady Stanhope doesn't want to sponsor her. I mean unless Lucy learns a lot and Lucy is not that smart. So I thought that if I had the money, we wouldn't need to ask her or you. I am the man of the house, you see.'

He addressed this last comment to Dolph.

Dolph leaned forward, keeping his voice gentle. 'Iggy, you are the child of the house. You have grown-ups like your mother and your sister and Miss Carstens who can look after you. And your sister is quite smart enough. Her debut is going to be fine.'

'You think Lady Stanhope will sponsor her.'

'I will do my utmost to convince her.'

'Good.' Iggy yawned. 'I am glad I don't have to gamble.'

'As are we all,' Dolph averred.

Iggy gave a second yawn, his head heavy on Abby's shoulder.

'And, Iggy, don't rush to grow up. You are a child. You have adults to look after you and when you are ready, I will teach you what you need to know,' Dolph said.

'That would be helpful,' he said.

'But you won't do this again, ever.'

'I won't do this again. Ever. It was a little nerve-racking,' Iggy agreed.

'Just a little,' Abby said, catching Dolph's glance

'You're certain we can't go to Lansdowne now. I am missing Basil,' he said.

'No, we have to rest the horses. You will both stay at Lady Stanhope's for now.'

'But I don't like Lady Stanhope,' he repeated.

'So you said. However, we do not like retrieving you from gambling dens,' Dolph said in rather grim tones. 'I think, given the circumstances, you will survive a night with my sister.'

'You come up to London with an unmarried woman to track down a nine-year-old boy and then land them on me. Are you quite sane?' his sister asked, fixing Dolph with a piercing stare from across the rim of her coffee cup.

They had arrived at the London town house close to dawn. Ignatius and Abby had been taken upstairs to rest. The requisite footmen had been dispatched with notes to Lansdowne to reassure the Harringtons.

Madeleine, however, having risen from her bed, seemed unwilling to return and now sat pestering him with questions.

Perhaps he would escape to his London home. Granted it was shut down, without staff or heat, but it seemed better than facing his sister's investigation.

Dolph yawned, stretching his legs. 'Still quite sane, and I will try not to become dispirited by your too regular accusations of drivelling lunacy.'

Madeleine looked at him, her frown deepening. 'Must you always joke? Did you consider what would happen if you had been seen with her? Indeed, you may have been? And what would you do then? Her reputation would be ruined. At best you could buy her off or set her up as your mistress. At worst you would have to marry her.'

'She is a daughter of a clergyman. Even I would draw the line at making her my mistress. Besides, marriage could be a good thing. Miss Carstens has a measure of intelligence and independent thought.'

'A recipe for disaster. You don't want independent

thought in a wife. Doubtless you are merely saying that to irk me and I absolutely refuse to react.'

'Naturally,' he agreed. 'Very restrained.'

'I suppose, on the whole, it was intelligent to come to me. Hopefully, I can save Miss Carstens's reputation, for your sake, if not her own. Running off like that. So ill bred. And impulsive. The lower classes do lack self-control, I always think. And a veritable dowd.'

'One must be fashionable when chasing errant schoolboys?'

'One aims not to chase errant schoolboys. By the way, I have put nanny to work. She is retired but still quite formidable and can prevent the boy from doing anything else foolish until we get rid of them. I'd suggest that they stay here for two days. I will create some story on how she got here. I was going to suggest that we have some people over for dinner tonight, which would send the message that we have nothing to hide. However, last-minute invitations appear so needy. Instead, we will have a more formal family dinner. The Duke of Ayeburn was already attending. You will come also.'

'Of course,' he said.

'She can wear one of Susan's dresses. The duke is Susan's new suitor. Indeed, I have quite gone off Mr Trollope.'

'How unfortunate for Mr Trollope, but wouldn't

Susan's feelings be more pertinent than your own?' Dolph asked.

'You do have foolish notions. The Duke of Aye-burn appears to quite fancy her, which would be an ideal match. You may not have met him. He has a place in Scotland, but one can't hold that against him.'

'Lovely, I will look forward to the introduction.'

Madeleine paused, sipping her coffee and running her finger around the rim of the saucer, and studying its movement with apparent fascination.

'How is Jason, by the by?' She glanced up, vulnerability visible on her strong, somewhat angular face. 'I hope he was not instrumental in introducing the boy to gambling.'

'No, it appears your letter greatly upset Miss Harrington and Ignatius decided to regain their family fortune through gambling. Jason's friends had come down but he chose not to come up with them and, indeed, was very concerned on Ignatius's behalf.'

Madeleine allowed her lips to curve into a brief, fleeting smile. 'That is a relief,' she said. 'And I do thank you for helping him.'

'It was time that I took more of an interest,' Dolph said. 'In general.'

'I tend to agree,' she said. 'How is the estate?'

'Run-down. Impoverished. Ill managed.'

'Father would be disappointed.'

'A familiar feeling for him,' he said. 'But you are right. I have neglected my duties. I have decided to—' He paused. He was not quite certain what to do or how to do it. 'I suppose I have decided to be the type of landlord Barnaby would have been.'

'Barnaby would have done things properly,' Madeleine said. 'The perfect landowner.'

'Indeed,' Dolph agreed. 'Barnaby always tried to be perfect.'

Briefly he remembered those moments, holding his brother. *Death is the easier option. So much less pretence...*

'See you this evening,' she said waving a beringed hand in dismissal.

He nodded. 'Send over a servant to my house. To make the bed and fire.'

He got up and walked across to the door, then with his hand on the knob turned back to her. 'Madeleine, do you ever think that you would have liked more freedom or independence in your life? Or that women, like you, are less autonomous?'

'Good heavens, no. I wield sufficient power here. I make and break reputations.'

'Yes, I suppose,' he said.

Abby woke up with a start. Her head thumped. Her body ached. It felt almost as though she were still moving, the carriage swaying beneath her.

For a confused moment, she could make little sense of the strange bedchamber, as though she had woken in someone else's life. She stared at the blue walls, the ceiling with its puffy clouds and plump cupids. Perhaps she was still dreaming and had imagined this bedchamber while still rattling within the carriage.

As she became more fully awake, events from the day previous rushed into her consciousness. She remembered Iggy's disappearance, the mad dash to the Cauldron, the sights and smells of the London slums and their eventual arrival at Lady Stanhope's home.

Indeed, the arrival was a blur, made all the more surreal by the stark contrast between the slums' grime and the resplendent correctness of the Stanhope establishment. Lady Stanhope had managed to look elegant in a dressing gown at dawn. This had served only to make Abby even more aware that she likely smelled of smoke and sweat, her hair was in disarray and her dress was stained.

And, as a backdrop to it all, was the proposal. Lord Lansdowne's proposal. Of marriage. To her.

A knock startled her, and a maid entered with chocolate and hot water.

'Where is Master Ignatius?' Abby asked, sitting up hurriedly. 'I am his governess. And he can get into mischief if left to his own devices.'

'Yes, Miss, so we heard. Lady Stanhope got

Nanny Owens to take charge. He is in the nursery and Nanny said as how you weren't to worry.'

'Oh.' Abby frowned. 'Thank you, but Ignatius can be a handful.'

'I can help you get dressed if you would like, and you can see him. However, Nanny Owens looked after His Lordship when he was a lad and she can cope with most eventualities. '

'Thank you, I will get dressed.' Abby thrust out her legs into the cool air, looking for her clothes.

'We took your dress for washing, Miss, but brought you up a selection of Lady Susan's dresses. We will select another one for this evening.'

'This evening?'

'Yes, Miss. The family always dresses for dinner and Lady Stanhope said you would be staying.'

'Right. Thank you,' Abby repeated, still feeling dull-witted.

'Did you want me to help you get dressed, Miss?'

'No. No, thank you,' Abby said hastily.

The maid left. Abby exhaled with some relief, thankful to be left alone. Of course, it was logical to remain in London for at least a day but she wished it were otherwise. Or that she were staying elsewhere. Even being alone in the small house on Wimpole Street sounded inviting.

She remembered how Miss Brownlee had described privacy as one of life's luxuries, seldom afforded England's aristocrats.

Going to the closet, she pulled out a simple light blue gown but before she could dress, a second rap at the door sounded and an elderly lady with a stern, somewhat square face entered.

'I am Nanny Owens,' this personage said. 'I will ensure that Master Ignatius is safe and sound until he returns to his mother.'

'Thank you,' Abby said. She should feel reassured. Everything about Nanny Owens's demeanour, her firm, almost masculine jaw and sharp eyes peering from the cushions of her cheeks, spoke of capability.

'Indeed, you just rest yourself, Miss. You are looking a mite peaky.'

'Yes, I will,' Abby said with the irritation one always feels when such comments are made, however kind their intent.

The absence of chores or responsibility, however, was not comforting. Instead, she merely found herself restless. She could, of course, go down and explore the rest of the house but found herself reluctant to interact with Lady Stanhope.

Besides, she needed to think. She could not hide or pretend that Lord Lansdowne had not proposed. And a proposal deserved a response.

Nor could she deny that part of her wanted to say yes. She remembered the eager response of her body to his. And the comfort she'd felt when she'd woken with her head against his shoulder and how he had never hesitated, putting Iggy's safety above all else.

He had shown up, as Mrs Fred would say.

She got up, pacing the room as though her swift, agitated movement could allow her to escape the catapulting motion of her thoughts.

Because another part of her wanted to say no. She could not be the type of wife or duchess that he required. It would be like her parents. Her mother had needed a conventional vicar, the type that didn't drink or gamble and believed the Bible.

Her father had wanted someone with whom he could converse, debate and who might help alleviate his boredom.

She and Dolph would be just such a misfit.

This house, the neat, tidy garden, the ornate ceiling and velvet bed curtains all made this more strikingly obvious.

And these borrowed clothes—she rubbed her fingers across the fabric. She glanced towards the closet. The gowns hung neatly. She stroked the cloth, conscious of the textures, the stiffness of lace, plush softness of velvet and sliding silkiness of satin.

They were gowns for a duchess. They were the gowns for a person who would know where to seat an earl, hire servants and play the pianoforte. They were not for a person who, since her mother's demise, had avoided most social interactions.

They were not for a person happier helping with boils and carbuncles than teacups or who sought to steer one's own ship and not wait like a princess in an ivy-covered tower.

Except, when she closed her eyes, logic dissolved into feeling. She remembered the touch of his lips… the splay of his fingers…the sensations in her body that were part weakness, part need, part excitement…and totally foreign.

Is it true freedom if one must hide or diminish?

Could she go through life as if this part of herself did not exist? This physical need, desire, want was very real. To imagine going through life and never knowing what it would be like to lie with a man… to lie with Dolph—

The knock on her chamber door interrupted these convoluted thoughts. Another maid entered, prim and well dressed, in a grey uniform.

'I am Maria. I am to help you get ready for dinner, Miss,' she said, making a small curtsey.

'So early?' Abby said with limited enthusiasm.

'Yes, Miss. You slept most of the day, Miss. Lady Stanhope said I should curl your hair and that I might have to alter the dress so I thought it best if we get an early start. I recommend this one for dinner, if you like it, Miss?'

Maria pulled out a delicate blue silk creation.

'It is beautiful,' Abby said. 'But isn't it a little fancy?'

The gown was low cut and designed with a high waist and billowing cloth, which seemed quite likely silk.

'Lady Stanhope said as how she thinks you should practise proper evening attire.'

Practise?

'I have been dressing myself since a child. I do not think I require more practice,' Abby said.

'Yes, Miss,' Maria replied.

'Sorry,' Abby said, instantly contrite. 'I appreciate your help. The gown is lovely and so kind of Lady Susan to loan it.'

'Lady Susan has many dresses. She is a little shorter than you but it shouldn't be noticeable for a family dinner.'

'I will keep my feet hidden at all times,' Abby said.

'And both the Duke of Ayeburn and Lord Lansdowne will be coming.'

Abby felt herself stiffen, her stomach tighten. 'Lord Lansdowne?' she said, her voice squeaky to her own ears.

'Yes, I think so. He is Lady Stanhope's brother, you know.'

'I was aware,' Abby said.

* * *

The slippers pinched. Lady Susan must have smaller feet to match her shorter stature. Abby limped towards the salon. Her hair had been curled and tied with ribbons and now clustered in irritating bunches at the side her face. It tickled. She'd tried to dissuade Maria but the girl had looked so worried that Abby feared the maid might be punished. Lady Stanhope seemed the type who would expect her instructions to be followed to the letter.

The house, while nothing compared to the sprawling medieval hallways of Lansdowne, felt even less inviting. The corridor was long and narrow, or perhaps its length was merely magnified by the pain in her toes.

She noted also a lifelessness about it as though it were more museum than home. Even more portraits of dead ancestors were displayed, punctuating the walls at regular intervals. Gold leaf glittered from the ceiling, which was also decorated with clouds, indolent Roman gods and a plethora of cupids.

Indeed, if she allowed fancy to overtake her prosaic good sense, she could feel a certain hostility, as though even the house did not like her and knew that her stockings were ripped under the blue gown.

However, Abby firmly refuted this thought. Houses were not living entities and certainly did not like or dislike their inhabitants or visitors.

A footman opened the door into the salon, which was unchanged since the soirée. Oddly, that night felt both long ago and, conversely, a mere second before. That was the odd thing about time. Momentous events were like chasms, the before and after of life.

Her gaze quickly flickered across the elegant chamber, taking in again the long mirrors, cream couch and marble fireplace. Dolph was not yet there and she felt that instant mix of disappointment and relief and knew that she was both hoping for and dreading his presence.

Lady Stanhope was also absent and only Lady Susan sat on the cream settee, smiling rather nervously. Abby had not paid particular attention to her at the soirée. Indeed, the girl had seemed but a paler version of her mother.

Now, however, they had the opportunity to talk and Abby found her much friendlier than her austere features would suggest. She smiled somewhat shyly and said that she hoped that Abby was enjoying her visit to London and that Mrs Harrington and Miss Harrington were well.

'Indeed, they greatly appreciate your uncle's kind hospitality. How have you been enjoying the Season?' Abby asked.

In her history of enforced social interactions, Abby had found that if she happened on an item of interest, the individual would talk freely. This allowed Abby to listen and nod and she had employed this strategy frequently.

The Season proved to be the right topic to hit upon and Lady Susan did not disappoint. She nodded, clasping her hands together.

'I have enjoyed the Season so very much. I didn't, at first, because Mother was so determined that I should marry Mr Trollope. I like Mr Trolope well enough but he lives quite close to us and I have known him for ever. It is hard to feel romantic about someone you have known for ever. I mean, he once put a frog down the back of my dress. However, I met Lord Ayeburn and I like him very much.' She let her voice trail with these words, leaning forward and clasping her hands more tightly for added emphasis.

'I look forward to meeting him. I understand that he is coming for dinner.'

'Yes, he is very handsome. Do you believe in love at first sight?'

'I—' Abby remembered Dolph's presence within the doorway on Wimpole Street. 'I believe that a single moment can make one feel changed,' she said.

'Lord Ayeburn makes my stomach feel quivery, which sounds unpleasant but isn't, if you know what I mean.'

'Yes,' Abby said. 'Actually, I do.'

Before they could talk further, Lady Stanhope entered. Her appearance made even her daughter stiffen and Abby felt her own shoulders pull back and her chin lift.

Lady Stanhope was not a beautiful woman but she had a stylish perfection which instantly made Abby aware that her ankles were too visible, the dress too tight and, despite Maria's best efforts, the clumps of clustered curls and blue ribbons did not suit.

'You really must learn to school your expressions, Miss Carstens,' Lady Stanhope said. 'You appear uneasy. This is likely a natural enough sentiment. However, we aim to hide such weakness. We do not wear our heart on our sleeve. You should aim for the enigmatic.'

'Like the *Mona Lisa*,' Abby suggested equably.

'I have always thought her sly,' Lady Stanhope said. 'Lady Moffatt might be a better model. Her features never give her away.'

'I have not had the good fortune to meet Lady Moffatt, but if I do I will take note of her countenance.'

'Pert. I thought as much,' Lady Stanhope said, frowning repressively. 'I hope you will restrain yourself during dinner. Lord Ayeburn will be there. It was arranged prior to your dash here and I do not wish to cancel. However, as far as Lord Ayeburn is concerned, this visit was planned weeks in advance. You are purchasing a few items and are from a good family if impoverished. Your father was a vicar, I believe?'

'Yes,' Abby said.

'And on your mother's side? There is family in France?'

'*Was* might be the better word. They are largely deceased.'

'Well, dead relatives with social standing are still an asset.'

'A comfort, I am sure, for their families.'

Lady Stanhope frowned even more severely, her rather formidable eyebrows drawing together to form a solid, dark caterpillar. 'Has my great-aunt arrived at Lansdowne yet?'

'No, she was expected tomorrow,' Abby said.

'That is well. I hope that Miss Harrington is able to acquire the necessary polish. Indeed, if my dear Susan gets an offer, I may be willing to sponsor Miss Harrington. She is a pleasant girl, gauche, of course, but that can be improved. Certainly, Susan has made great strides, haven't you, dear?

'Yes, Mama.'

'I hear that you hold Miss Harrington in high esteem,' Lady Stanhope said. 'Therefore, I would assume that you behave in accordance with these sentiments.'

'I will endeavour not to do anything likely to shock Lord Ayeburn. It would be wonderful if you could sponsor Miss Harrington. She is very desirous of a debut,' Abby said.

Lady Stanhope made a tiny sniff but before she could further comment, Lord Lansdowne and Lord Ayeburn entered. Abby had not seen Dolph in full evening dress since the soirée and felt herself a little breathless.

Indeed, her stomach felt quite quivery, as Lady Susan had described, quite like a flip-flopping blancmange.

It was perhaps the perfect fit of his jacket, the cravat which was folded in a manner which was intricate but not foppish, that air of understated elegance and something in his gaze. It made her feel noticed as though he could come into a room filled with people and *see* her.

'It is lovely to make your acquaintance, Miss Carstens,' Lord Ayeburn was saying.

He was shorter and had a more colourful waistcoat but was pleasant enough and still far from a dandy. Both gentlemen bowed. With introductions over, Abby scoured her mind for conversation but found herself unusually tongue-tied.

She was keenly conscious that she must be less 'pert', for Lucy's sake, and the need to censor her conversation made her feel less able to participate as though needing to edit her words before committing them to speech.

There was also an awkwardness as they sat grouped in the elegant room about the elegant marble fireplace. It was as though she had a smudge on her nose or two left feet. The feeling was both familiar and unfamiliar. It reminded her of that time prior to her mother's illness and death, when she had been more bound to convention, and hadn't yet acquired the freedom afforded by her father's laissez-faire attitude to child rearing.

The butler came and they rose, going to the dining room. This, like the rest of the house, had a glittering elegance. Two chandeliers hung over the long table. They were not like the huge medieval lights at Lansdowne. These were intricate, beautiful creations, each lit with seemingly hundreds of candles, their light reflected and refracted in crystals which hung like icicles.

A huge mirror was above the mantelpiece, thus multiplying the flickering flames. Paintings on the walls featured hounds, horses, dead deer and men in breeches and wigs. Silverware and glasses were set against white damask cloth and glinted in the blazing firelight and candles.

Everything about this house suggested that she had walked into the wrong life: its size, its elegance, the huge portraits, the silent footmen, the dress she wore with its short sleeves, low neck and itchy lace.

Even the curls clustering about her forehead and neck felt wrong and irritated.

She supposed Lord Lansdowne's London house would be like this. A showplace but not a home. If she were his wife, she would be the mistress of such a house. They would have such a dining room. She tried to imagine herself sitting with Lord Lansdowne night after night, overlooked by stiff servants, dead relatives and horses while staring at each other from opposing ends of the huge table.

What would they even talk about?

And how would she entertain? She did not know the right way to greet a duchess, whether a viscount should sit below a duke or how to curtsey. Lucy had at least tried to learn this whereas Abby had instead applied herself to Mary Wollstonecraft's writing about education and women's rights.

This stuff about curtsies had all seemed so very foolish, this emphasis on such minuscule details, while children were starving and ships traded people as though they were nothing more than commodities.

But to mention such a thing within this environment would be like stripping naked or swinging from the chandeliers.

'You are very quiet,' Lady Stanhope said. 'I hope you are feeling well.'

'Oh, yes, absolutely, right as rain,' she said.

'Providing appropriate social discourse is not easy but an invaluable skill,' Lady Stanhope stated.

'Indeed,' Abby said, searching her brain for an additional comment which would not be construed as pert.

'I heard something interesting about clichés,' Lord Lansdowne said.

'What would that be?' his sister asked.

'I can't quite remember,' he said, with that half smile that showed his dimple and made her stomach wobble.

She glanced hurriedly away. Thankfully, Lord Ayeburn, Lady Stanhope and Lady Susan were all quite talkative. Lord Ayeburn seemed particularly interested in a recent acquisition to the Royal Menagerie and, surprisingly, Lady Susan had a similar interest.

'A giraffe, I believe,' Lord Ayeburn said.

'Indeed,' Lady Susan added. 'I knew so little about the menagerie until talking to the dressmaker. Apparently, there are all manner of creatures. At the menagerie, not the dressmakers. You see, other countries give animals to our royal family: lions and tigers and monkeys. I am quite certain that Ignatius would find it fascinating.'

Having just rescued the boy from a gambling hell, Abby was uncertain if she now wanted to introduce him to wild animals but held her tongue. She caught

Dolph's humorous glance and knew he was thinking the same thing.

She looked hurriedly away.

Fortunately, Lady Stanhope decided to curb the notion. 'I think that would be unwise,' she said. 'I just heard that a monkey attacked a little boy and Ignatius seems entirely the sort of boy who might aggravate even the calmest monkey.'

'Well, perhaps we should avoid monkeys,' Lord Ayeburn suggested.

'I think we should avoid the entire menagerie, at least as far as Ignatius is concerned,' Dolph said.

Dolph had accepted the dinner invitation with a confused mix of curiosity, anticipation and apprehension. He did not know quite what to expect. Abby was such a strong-minded individual that he wasn't certain how she would respond to close proximity with his opinionated sister.

His hope had merely been a dinner without overt discord. Indeed, if that was his goal, he should now feel most content. Abby had said nothing controversial. His niece was apparently happy to talk about monkeys and his sister seemed uncharacteristically pleasant.

And yet he felt no relief.

He sipped his wine. Analysis of his feelings did not come naturally. Indeed, he preferred to pretend that they did not exist, were an aberration or indigestion caused by underdone potato. However, the truth was while nothing appeared wrong, something felt wrong.

He glanced at Abby. She looked good. Indeed, she looked better than good. She looked beautiful. The dress brought out the blue of her eyes, the creaminess of her skin and the rosy flush along her cheekbones. The firelight added chestnut glints to her thick hair, making her eyes luminescent while the curls framed her heart-shaped face, softening the high forehead.

Her dress, her hair, her expression were all pleasant and yet there was a wrongness. He felt it. Nothing was wrong and yet something was missing, like a painting without red. And her expression was almost…bland…or decorous.

'I hope that the weather will be pleasant tomorrow when we return to Lansdowne,' she was saying.

The words were both innocuous and discordant, not because they were in any way shocking but because they weren't.

Talking about the weather? Abigail Carstens did not talk about the weather. The descriptors *bland* and *decorous* were words he would never have used to describe her—instead, she was serious, passionate, curious, angry, eager, worried, irritated, excited.

Not bland.

Or decorous.

'It is a pleasant day today. Mild for the time of year,' Abby said.

'Yes,' he said. 'I had a morning ride. It was quite pleasant.'

'How delightful.'

They had never experienced this awkwardness. They'd always had things to talk about, Basil, exploding chicken coops, modern invention, schools. They were never mired in this awful vanilla limbo of chit-chat

He could not imagine this woman wrestling Basil, rescuing Iggy or riding Catch Me Who Can.

She seemed like an edited version of herself. Her expression was not unpleasant. She was not frowning but there was also little joy or exhilaration.

What had she said to him? That one needed to feel the sad in order to feel the joy.

And it seemed to him as he sat within the decorous splendour of his sister's salon that wrestling Basil, espousing political opinion and flooding dairies were activities of vital import. For the first time in years, he had felt a connection to someone. He had felt that he could be himself or a close facsimile thereof. He had felt seen.

And that was gone.

She was obscured, hidden behind translucent glass.

* * *

The dinner drew to its conclusion. Abby felt a relief incongruent with the event.

This was, she supposed, a microcosm for what her life could be.

She would be with the man who excited her and made each moment the more precious. Even sitting at the table, she could feel him. There was his physical presence but there was also that shared connection and humour.

Conversely, there was a sense of isolation or knowing that she did not belong.

Lady Stanhope rose, suggesting that the gentlemen enjoy their port while she led the ladies into the salon. Abby and Lady Susan followed. The men would discuss politics. The ladies would discuss fashion or weather. Lud, she'd already discussed the weather. She'd be discussing cumulus nimbus next.

Thankfully, Susan took her place at the pianoforte, labouring through a music selection. Abby felt sympathy. Her mother had tried to teach her, but she had been a poor student. Her fingers always struck the wrong note and she had lacked the patience to practise.

'You know, as a wife, it will be important that you can play piano and sew and that you are able to make polite conversation and social chit-chat,' her mother had said. 'I know you enjoy Miss Brownlee's lessons but learning about Greek and numbers is really not an important aspect of being a wife.'

'Then perhaps I don't want to be a wife,' she had said.

Her mother had smiled, already tired. 'You'll change your mind,' she'd said.

Except she hadn't. Not really.

Lady Stanhope had just brought out the cards, when the gentlemen reappeared. Lady Stanhope put the pack down, for once seeming a little flustered as she stood, more abruptly than necessary,

'Randolph, dear, I must show you a delightful letter from a distant cousin that I received. Indeed, I will go immediately. I am certain that you would love to peruse it,' she announced, hurrying out.

Dolph stood, glancing at Abby and smiling in an almost conspiratorial manner. 'Indeed, I found an interesting book which you might enjoy on our return journey. Perhaps we could go the library.'

Abby complied and they walked out into the passageway.

'I thank you for your consideration. However, I don't read when travelling as the motion of the carriage tends to make me nauseous.'

He laughed, leaning into her, and his warm breath tickled her ear. 'It was a ruse. I rather I think that Lord Ayeburn might have something to say to Lady

Susan and I wanted to provide the requisite opportunity.'

They walked into the library. She had always liked libraries. They were full of books yet unpretentious. He stood a few feet from her. She felt herself taking in his features as though memorizing them. There was the straight, firm line of his chin, his well-shaped nose, his lips, his eyes, a dark grey with flecks of green. He was tall, his broad shoulders outlined by the dark jacket. He was so handsome, it hurt.

'I don't want to be a duchess,' she said.

She stared at him with her clear, direct gaze.

'The thing is I don't know anything about society or being a wife,' she said.

'I don't know a lot about being a duke. We'd learn.'

She inhaled. He watched the movement of her hands and she clasped them together.

'I know that I can learn rules about place settings, where to seat a duke or a count or a viscount and how to curtsey. But that is not my life. It would be like wearing someone else's life, just as I am wearing someone else's dress. I can't...do that,' she said.

The words hurt in a way he had not even anticipated. It was both a sharp pain and an awful aching sadness.

He had wanted the marriage. He felt surprised about how much he had wanted it. He had told himself that his proposal had been based on practicality, that she would help him and he would save her from what would be a gruelling life as schoolmistress, governess or wife to an elderly widower with a score of children.

But he knew this was not true.

He loved her.

He looked at her as she stood in the borrowed gown which made her eyes bluer, the pretty clustered curls which he knew she'd disliked and her serious expression which could transform into joy.

Her cheeks had flushed. She checked her lip, perhaps in nervousness. He wished he could kiss her and feel her lips open under his own. He wished he could touch the soft smooth skin of her neck and her cheek, loosen her hair so that it hung down her back and push away the gown.

But he couldn't.

He loved her and they could not and should not marry. Marriage would make her different. It already had. At dinner, she had been less…less vibrant, less blunt, less open. If she married him that would be her life. She would be the edited version.

He didn't want that.

'I understand,' he said, conscious of a deep heavy emptiness, even as he spoke the words. 'Truly, I do. I understand. I saw Barnaby being less, being diminished. I saw him trying to be someone he wasn't, trying to be the perfect son and heir. I don't want that for you.'

He stepped closer so that only a few feet separated them. He took her hands between his own. They rested in his palm. They were small. He could feel the bones oddly fragile like a bird. And yet she was not fragile. She was strong.

He traced the lines on her palm as a fortune-teller might. 'You are so many things. You are a reformer, a scientist, a dog wrestler, a teacher. You never presented yourself as anything else. You never worried about how people might perceive you. And today you did.'

He saw the tears shimmering in her eyes and hanging on her eyelashes until one fell, trickling down her cheek. He took out his handkerchief, very gently touching her cheek.

'I wanted to have what you have but I never, ever wanted to take it from you.'

'What do I have?'

'Hope,' he said. 'You gave me hope but tonight you seemed less hopeful.'

'What is that you hope for?'

'To be the landlord Barnaby would have been,' he said.

'You will be. You are a good man. You will be a good landlord.'

'I couldn't see it until I met you.' He paused, still holding her hand. 'I thank you for that.'

'And you are not like the other landlords, like Lord Ashleigh.'

He smiled. 'That is a relief. The man does not know how to tie a cravat.'

She laughed in that moment of shared humour. 'There will be someone who will fit into your world, into your life.'

He nodded. 'What will you do?'

'Look after Iggy until he doesn't need me and then find another post,' she said. 'Write about women's equality, poverty and even the abolition of the slave trade.'

'And you might teach the next Wilberforce.'

'Or make it so that in the future, women might sit in that parliament. That is my hope.'

Dolph's London house was huge, empty and cold. He hadn't wanted to stay with Madeleine. Her house, the portraits, tapestries typified everything he did not like. Everything Abby wasn't. Everything she rejected.

A servant had come over and made up a fire. It burned now in the hearth and Dolph bent over, rubbing his hands over the flames. He put some additional coals on the fire, thrusting in the poker so that sparks chased up the chimney with a crackling of flames.

As boys, he and Barnaby had believed that sparks took their wishes up into the night sky.

Dolph put down the poker and sat back in his chair. He watched the crazy movement of the sparks as they swirled and twirled and disappeared. If he were to make a wish, what would he wish for?

His brother back.

The answer was simple. He'd wished that Barnaby had never followed Lord Stanley into the mud and cannon fire. He stared at the crackling flames, glowing coals, the white ash at its base. He looked at the colours, the flicker of light, the smoke and sparks.

The cannon fire of battle had been so loud that, even now, he woke with his ears ringing and the stench of smoke in his nostrils. Yet later, afterwards, the battlefield was weirdly, eerily quiet. The silence seemed magnified by the low mist, like a shroud, damp and chill. And all around he saw bodies, twisted in unnatural angles, bleeding and broken. And then there were the cries of the wounded, becoming more silent in time.

It took strength, to peer into the memories, to hold them and feel them and remember them.

He usually didn't.

He glanced towards the cognac on the side table close to the fire. It was in a cut-glass decanter. At its side was his usual glass. It was made of a heavy lead crystal and would feel heavy in his hand. Heavy and comforting. Through its glass, he could see the flicker of flames, distorted by the thick glass and crystal.

The chamber was dark now. He had not lit candles or a lamp. The only light came from the mobile amber glow from the fire. He could almost imagine ghosts within the room dark corners, not lightened by the flickering flame.

This was a place peopled with memories. Was this the only room without cupids? His mother had put them everywhere as though their proliferation would be a balm for her own loveless marriage.

He remembered his conversation with his father before he had followed Barnaby into battle.

The boy has lost all sense. Gone off like an imbecile. Causing gossip. I won't have it. I won't have him causing gossip. Bring him back.

On the mantel, above the fire, he could see Barnaby's snuffbox. It was an ornamental thing—the jewels glinted. Barnaby had never liked snuff. It made him sneeze. Dolph guessed he only used it because others did.

The need to belong, to be what was typical, had threaded through the lives of his mother, his brother, his father and even his grandfather, he supposed. His grandfather had used his money to get his daughter a peerage. Not that it had made her any happier.

Abby had rejected that. She had rejected the luxury, the jewels, the trappings of wealth that others would consider vital—the gilded cage.

He could not wish her otherwise.

He stood, reaching for the snuffbox. He opened it. The tiny, exquisite hinges moved easily. It was engraved. He rubbed his finger across the roughness of the lettering: To Barnaby from Stanley.

This tiny thing had survived the hell of battle. And he had survived.

Barnaby and Stanley had died.

But he had lived. He had not asked for life. He still felt the heavy guilt of survival. He still remembered his father's anger and his mother's pain.

'He was my heir,' his father had said.

His father's health had declined soon after, a stroke robbing him of his words and movement.

If he'd had his voice, would he have said *You are my heir?* Did Dolph even want him to? Why did he need benediction from a man he did not like?

Dolph stood. He went to the window. Outside, he could see the night sky, the stars occasionally obliterated by the moving boughs. He could feel the fire's warmth at his back and smell of the smoke from the crackling fire.

I cannot be your conscience. I don't want to be

anyone's conscience. Abby had said those words. *And no one can make another person whole.*

There was truth in them. Briefly, Abby had seemed like a saviour, his saviour. He had wanted her to set the course, steer his ship and make him worthy.

But she couldn't do that for him.

And nothing would bring his brother back, not guilt or wishing.

Tentatively, Dolph went to his desk. He lit a candle and a lamp, setting them down with care before going to the bookcase. On its third shelf, there was a box of papers. It had been sent from the estate after his father's death. He hadn't even opened them.

Now he took down the box. It was made of wood and heavier than expected. He placed it on his desk and carefully opened the lid with a creak of unoiled hinges. It smelled musty. He inhaled the dusty scent.

Slowly, he took out the pages. The vellum felt dry. He put each sheet carefully on the desk, running his fingers over the surface to smooth out any wrinkles. Each sheet was filled with the neat script from the previous manager.

For a few moments, he had to force himself to perform the task, like a child who must do his sums or complete a homework assignment. Then, as he read, he found himself less aware of the passage of time, or of the need to complete and accomplish. Instead, he was drawn in, interested.

Each page had so much information. There were details about fish stocks in the lake, maps of the farms, the waterways, wells, location of buildings and fences. There were notes about the number of livestock, costs and profits.

As he read each line, ideas populated his mind, so quickly he could not grasp hold of them. He took out a pen, dipping it into the ink well. Then, still feeling like a schoolboy, he started to write. His pen scratched, the noise mixing with the clock's tick and the fire's crackle.

He completed two sheets. One itemized those things which needed to be done immediately, while the second explored those which he could do at a later date. There was a calming peace to his work, a sense of order which soothed. Occasionally a crackle from the fire interrupted the scratch of his pen. Sometimes, he'd hear the scrape of a tree branch on the pane or the drumming of his own fingers as he paused to review his notes.

He would find a good manager, he decided. That was a priority. Then he would mend the fences, ensure the wells were operating and that the cows had sufficient food. There were also buildings in need of repair. Much of the straw had got wet. Even the stables had lost a part of the roof in a winter storm.

These were immediate concerns.

But Barnaby had often talked about other, more long-term projects. He'd wanted to make the estate more efficient. Dolph wished now he'd listened more. As he recalled, some crops restored nutrients to the soil, while others removed them.

He made a note on another sheet labelled Research.

Of course, there were established researchers. He'd talk to them. But he could also conduct his own research. If he had a complete listing of all the crops planted at each farm, he could cross reference to determine which were most profitable, the type of crops grown, the proximity to water and other amenities.

Then there was, of course, the thorny issue of enclosure. Dolph would do research on that too. He frowned, again wishing he had listened more intently to Barnaby. As he recalled, his brother had said that it made good business sense. However, it resulted in the tenants having less control over the land. This was therefore unfair and unpopular.

Dolph paused, drumming his fingers again. He could understand how enclosure made sense from a business perspective; larger holdings run by landlords could yield more crops with greater efficiency. Such estates would permit the scheduled, organized rotation of different crops, the provision of more fodder for animals and the utilization of new tools.

He got up, walking across the room, needing to stretch his stiff limbs and gain some warmth from the fire. But surely individual ownership did not necessarily mean that cooperation could not occur? Indeed, with teamwork it should be possible. Granted, it might be more complex but not impossible. The most important thing would be the development of a process to ensure cooperation and that the smaller holdings worked together as an entity.

Dolph bent to throw another lump of coal on the fire. And there was no reason why he should not be involved. He could take on the role of business manager. Or gain greater scientific or agricultural knowledge. His father had seen only one way of being a landlord but that did not mean that only one way existed.

He paced faster. He heard the floorboards creak with his movement. Yes, he would first hire an individual with knowledge about scientific methods and crops. He would tell his man of business to advertise for such a person tomorrow.

Turning, he went to the desk and picked up the pen, adding this note to his list of more-immediate tasks. This time he would ensure that they hired someone competent. He could write questions and ensure that references were checked.

With this note completed, he sat back in the chair as the energy seeped from him. He stared at the notes about him in his own neat hand. He felt tired but also satisfied. For the first time, he felt that he was no longer an imposter. He was not pretending to be a landlord. Not a duke wearing someone else's boots.

He leaned forward, poking the fire again and watching the sparks.

Wishes.

Yes, he had wishes.

He wished for a society which could accept love in all its forms.

He wished for a society which did not cling, like a drowning man, to feudal privilege, but tried to make the world better.

He wished for a society where all people could vote, where education was a right and the concept of one person being sold to another was abhorrent.

He wished for Abby.

He wished he could offer her a life which would not limit her, not lessen her, not edit her but instead support her.

He drew back the curtains, pushing open the windows and inhaling the fresh predawn air. He had stayed up all night. More astounding, he had stayed up all night and was not drunk. Early-morning birdsong filled the air. He looked out into the darkness.

There was no ribbon of light or even the hint of sunrise and yet they sang. He heard their trills within the darkness. He supposed that was hope or trust.

Abby woke up the next morning. They were going back to the estate the next day. Dolph was sending his carriage. She peered blearily at the ceiling, aware that her head ached. Lady Susan and Lord Ayeburn had announced their engagement last night and she had drunk champagne. She had not drunk champagne before.

She remembered holding the glass. It had felt cold against her fingertips. She remembered noticing the chill wetness of condensation as though by identifying such minutiae this weird, numb feeling would lessen and her thoughts would become her own. Instead, they'd remained mired in mud, moving slowly like thick treacle.

Lady Stanhope was thrilled with the upcoming nuptials. Her elation even led to the generous promise that she would sponsor Lucy in her debut.

'We'll let her stay at Lansdowne for a couple of weeks. I am certain that Great-Aunt's tutelage will be invaluable but then she'll come here. Indeed, with my support she may yet get an offer.'

'I am certain Mrs Harrington and Miss Harrington will be very grateful,' Abby had said.

Lady Stanhope had nodded, waving a bejewelled

hand, generous in her happiness. 'I have no doubt. I am certain she will make a creditable match.'

After a moment of silence, Lady Stanhope had turned her intelligent and rather piecing glance towards Abby. 'And for yourself, Miss Carstens?'

'I would prefer to tutor Ignatius while he needs me and find another position when he does not.'

Lady Stanhope had shrugged. 'I'm certain that will be arranged. You do realize that you have missed out on what could have been a golden opportunity.'

'I am aware.'

Chapter Twelve

Abby stared at the ceiling. Like the rest of the house, it was too full of Greek or Roman gods. She wasn't sure which. She really must improve on her mythology.

There was also a tiny, minuscule crack, like the boot of Italy. She knew that she felt happy for Lucy. Or rather she knew that she should be feel happy for Lucy. Instead, she was without sensation and her thoughts were still stuck in treacle.

Miss Brownlee had once said that, in severe accidents, the injured feel nothing. When the wounds are too severe or the blood loss too great, victims report no pain…even moments before death.

This wasn't pain, exactly.

But a part of her had died.

Abby knew she had made the right decision. She knew it like she knew addition, subtraction, multiplication and Latin declensions.

She could have written an essay on the logic of

her conclusion. She could have presented the evidence and the reasoning behind her decision, as Miss Brownlee had so often asked her to do.

It was an undeniable, irrefutable fact that she was ill fitted for the life of a lady within England's upper classes. It was also undeniable that a wife was the property of her husband and that this opposed her every belief.

How could she be true to her principles if she let sentiment, lust and need influence her?

How could she have the freedom to teach and to write when she was entrenched within the very society that she opposed?

Abby rubbed her eyes almost roughly. Her throat felt sore, and it ached as though clogged. She had never been one for tears. When her mother had become ill, she'd assumed additional duties, squashing emotion with work.

Emotions did little. Sensible action did more.

Besides, she had no doubts. She had done the right thing.

And yet it did not feel right. Instead there was a huge, gaping hole of emptiness growing within her chest, extending into her stomach and down, leaden, into the very soles of her feet. And whenever she thought about Dolph it grew bigger and more barren.

The memory of his lips, the movement of his muscles under her fingertips, the hard leanness of his body, the warmth in his gaze, the way his lips curved into a smile and the flicker of that single dimple…

But physical attraction was not love.

And even it if it was love it would not be enough to bridge the differences between them.

She could not fit into his world. She could not abandon her beliefs. Nor could she be his conscience.

Eventually they would resent each other. She would resent her lack of freedom and lack of self.

He would resent her lack of gracious words, of fashion and style. Controversial letters to the editor or tracts about women's rights would embarrass him and ostracize them both.

She had made a decision. It was the right decision.

She would leave London.

But first, for one last time, there was something she must do. She got up and, pulling on her dress and cloak and taking her reticule, slipped out of the house and hurried down the street until she could summon a hansom cab.

'Torrington Square,' she said.

This time there was no queue. No carriages waited outside. The ticket booth was shuttered and the square deserted.

The hansom cab pulled to a stop.

'You sure you want to come here, Miss?' the driver asked.

Abby nodded. Even as she got out, she was aware of the absence of the noise and hubbub that had been omnipresent on the previous occasion. There were no voices from the other side of the tall fencing, no rattle along the tracks or hissing of steam.

Truthfully, she didn't feel particularly disappointed. It wasn't so much that she had desperately wanted to see the machine but rather that she needed to be here. She needed to touch the future. She needed to believe that the future could be better than the present. She needed to find her hope.

More than anything, Miss Brownlee had wanted to see change, to see women with freedom, poor children with education and people from foreign lands no longer ripped from their community and placed into slavery.

A man was working at ticket counter. He was doing maintenance, sanding the wood with big hams of hands.

'Not running today, I'm afraid, Miss. Maintenance issues.' He spoke in a rhythmic cadence, still sanding, the words matching the regular movement of his hands.

'May I go in and look?'

'No law against it but not much to see.'

'Thank you.' She stepped between the two fences and into the enclosure. The circular track was much as it had been but without spectators. The carriages had been disconnected and several workers studied the mechanism while two others examined the track. She supposed such breakdowns were a natural part of any experiment.

She sat on a bench, watching as the men worked.

Change. Socrates had said that one should not fight the old but create the new. Lord Lansdowne had said something similar. She stared at the track and the machine, trying to imagine it working, saving horses, bringing people together.

When Miss Brownlee had died, Abby had promised to keep working towards improving the lives of those without power, and mechanical inventions, no matter how ingenious, did not guarantee a more equitable society.

Other people could do that. But it was a place to start. Surely if people could build such a marvel, they could also develop a better society.

'Abby?'

She recognized the voice. 'Dolph!' She felt a surge of joy, quick, immediate, impulsive.

Her breath quickened. He strode towards her, tall, immaculate, achingly handsome with that lock of dark hair falling into his face. She shouldn't feel this joy, this burst of happiness, like bubbles of last night's champagne.

She shouldn't feel as though she had been going through the motions of living and now she was alive.

She shouldn't feel any of this because nothing had changed.

'Are we leaving now? I didn't mean to cause a delay. How did you know I would be here?' she asked.

'This is the future.' He smiled and that single dimple flickered across his cheek.

She nodded, consciously trying to imprint on her mind the dark grey-green of his eyes, the strong jaw and sculpted lips. She wished she could slow time, still it and hold on to this minute so that she could relive it in later years.

'And that is what I needed to tell you. Abby, we are also the future.'

'We? What?'

'I love you.' The words blasted from him as though no longer able to be contained.'

'But—'

'Last night, I didn't know that I did. I didn't believe in love. But now I do. This feeling has to be love. It is huge and wonderful and joyful and painful and overpowering and all encompassing. I want to be with you. I want to share my life with you.'

He stepped very close and she smelled the tangy, smoky scent of his jacket. He took her hands. She felt the firmness in his grip and, looking up, saw the intensity and the heat in his eyes. She felt a hesitant unfurling of hope. Yet there was also apprehension as if standing at a precipice.

'Abigail Carstens, I love you. I love your differences, your bluntness, your common sense and your good heart. I love that I can be myself with you. I am not looking for a conscience or a saviour or a duchess. I want a lover, a friend, a wife, a partner. I want you.'

'I think… I know I love you too.' She whispered the words, half-afraid to say them out loud. It was not that she doubted her feeling but they felt so precious, so amazing that words seemed insufficient.

'But will love be enough?' she asked.

'Yes, it is everything.'

'I always thought that to make the world better, I would have to walk alone.'

'You don't,' he said. 'We will choose our own path together. I don't care about the rules, the curtsies, the seating arrangements or the pretence. We can live where you want…country or city. Teach or write or protest in parliament or do none of the above. I love you. I love that you wrestle with dogs, take on danger and that you want to make this world better.'

'But other people, they care about that other stuff. They will talk.'

Her long lashes swept like fans against her flushed cheeks. They stood very close. He could feel the soft, uneven inhalation of her breath, and see the hopes, questions and uncertainty flicker across her mobile features.

'Yes, they will,' he said. 'And sometimes we may be hurt. And sometimes we will argue because we are both strong and independent. But that doesn't matter because we have the same dream. I realized that last night.'

'Tell me.' She raised her intense blue gaze to him.

They went to the bench, sitting with their fingers still intertwined.

'Sometimes people break,' he said. 'After Barnaby and my mother died, I broke. Or maybe I broke before. I didn't want you to live and to be less than yourself, but this is our marriage. We can't change society, at least not all at once, but we can make small changes. And our marriage can be our sanctuary. A place where we can be ourselves.'

'No hiding or pretence,' she said, reaching up to brush that lock of hair back and to let her finger trail across his cheek and chin.

'Abigail Carstens, will you marry me?

Chapter Thirteen

'I will marry you.' She drew out the words, savouring them as she cupped his face with her hands. 'I love you, Dolph. When you are away, I think of you. When you are present, I look at you. I want to be near you.'

Bending forward, he brushed his lips against hers. She felt the kiss and its promise through her body and into the core of her being. Apprehension had morphed into anticipation. She had taken flight and was indeed soaring through the heavens.

His kiss deepened. He pulled her closer. She felt his need. She felt her own need but also her strength and her power.

'We are giving the workers a show,' he murmured, teasing her lips.

'Good thing I care so little about my reputation.'

He kissed her again and she felt passion, wonder and a joyous contentment.

'And you have helped me see a future. Have a future,' he said. 'To have hope.'

She let her head rest on his shoulder.

'Your sister will not be happy,' she said.

'Yet another benefit.'

She heard the wry chuckle in his voice.

'You know I will likely cause her considerable distress. I want to open a school on the estate and write to politicians and talk and debate,' she said.

'That will likely plunge her in the depths of despair.'

'But seriously.' Abby straightened, gripping his hands more tightly. 'We will have to be prepared for a lot of criticism.'

'Yes, but it will be worthwhile. When Barnaby and I were little, we would talk about wishes. If he could wish now, he would not want to change his love but to change society. It will take a while. I don't know if this will happen in our lifetime, in a hundred years or two hundred years, but we can start the journey. Together, if you'll have me.'

'Yes,' she whispered.

'And our marriage will be the place where we can be ourselves.'

'No hiding or pretence,' she repeated. 'Which means I have to ask you something.'

'I'm ready,' he said, raising her hand and pressing a kiss against it.

I used to listen to my father when he was performing weddings and I thought the vows could be improved.'

'Naturally,' he said with that wry tone lacing his voice.

'For me, it would be better if the wife did not "obey". I am not very good at obeying. So I fear I might be able to keep that vow.'

He laughed. 'You astound me.'

'Do you mind?'

He shook his head. 'My father will rotate in his grave but no, I do not mind. I want a partner. Partners do not obey.'

'Will a vicar agree?'

'I have known Mr Walther for some time. He likes you very much, by the way. He will agree.'

'Good. And I really don't want to get married in London.'

'We will marry wherever you want. We are the future. We will rise above the ideas of our time. Together.'

They sat together on the bench within the surprising solitude of Torrington Square. The sun's orb could be seen through the clouds and there was a slight but cool breeze.

'We should leave,' he said. 'I don't want you to catch a chill.'

'I don't want to. I want to enjoy this moment, this

happiness. I want to keep it to ourselves and keep out the world for a little longer.'

'We will have to brave my sister eventually,' he said.

'Eventually,' she said, drawing out the word as though by doing so she could slow down time.

'But couldn't we go to your house?'

He shook his head. 'Only the bedchamber is open. The rest is shut up. There are no servants.'

'Really?' she said, leaning into him and pressing a kiss to his chin. 'That sounds perfect.'

'Abby?'

She laughed. She had a musical laugh. He would be happy if he could hear that laugh every day of his life.

'Don't look so shocked,' she said. 'Why should we wait? Banns and orange blossom will not make me love you more. It will only mean that I am more exhausted from saying all the right things at some wedding breakfast that your sister is bound to organize. And I want the magic of this day to continue and to be just ours.'

'Abigail Carstens, you still surprise me.'

'I was hoping for shock at least,' she said.

'We should wait.'

'That sounds so conventional. And didn't you say that shoulds are like a dose of castor oil?'

He laughed. 'Castor oil? How can you talk about castor oil and be so appealing?'

'A gift.'

He stood. She looked up at him, her expression humorous, shy, but with passion shimmering below the surface of the blue depths of her eyes.

He offered her his arm. 'Abigail Carstens, may I invite you to my home?'

'Why, yes, I would be delighted, my lord.'

Dolph held her hand as they descended from the carriage and approached his London home. He felt a joy but also a fragility, as though half fearing to breathe lest he lose this moment, this happiness, this whole new world that was unfurling and opening up for him.

Even the familiar sights and sounds of London were different. The colours had brightened. The birdsong from the morning was louder as though every sparrow and robin had braved the London streets to sing in celebration. Small patches of blue sky had opened, sly sunbeams slid between clouds and early snowdrops were peeking through the earth.

An empty house has a stillness. Dust sheets shrouded the furniture. There was an isolation but almost in a good way as if shielding them from the world's intrusion. Abby's cheeks were flushed, her eyes huge and her lips still pink and swollen from his kisses. Yet there was also a delightful primness about her that made him hesitate.

'You're certain?

'Indeed, my lord.'

'I can pull off a dust sheet in the parlour.'

'That wouldn't be very sensible,' she said.

'Sensible?'

'Because we would be more comfortable in your bedchamber.'

His heart squeezed and opened and he was cognizant of both the excitement of an adolescent but something deeper.

'I love being sensible,' he said.

They went upstairs to his familiar bedchamber with its massive bed, fireplace and bay window The maid had laid a fire in the grate but the air felt chill. He lit it. The flame flickered along the kindling with an eager, crackling sound, casting a warming glow.

Abby stood close. The fire cast a golden light, highlighting her flushed features, making her eyelashes form long delicate shadows, her chestnut hair glint and her moist lips gleam.

'You are so beautiful,' he whispered.

'I am not,' she retorted, in firm, blunt, Abby-like tones. 'You must not bamboozle me because you love me.'

He cupped her face. 'I do love you. I love every prosaic, unique part of you. And you are beautiful.

You are all the more beautiful because you do not realize it. You equate beauty with fashion, but you are so much more.'

Very slowly, he brushed back the tendrils which had escaped her neat bun. Then, with gentle care, he pulled out her hairpins so that her hair fell, cascading about her shoulders. It was thick, long, lustrous and just a little wild, as he had known it would be. He lifted his hand and ran his fingers down its length so that it shimmered in the firelight.

He'd waited so long to see her like this, with her hair unrestrained by pins or clips and the primness falling away, cast aside, morphing into a passion all the greater because of her natural restraint. His hand moved to her back, not quickly but with deliberation. He undid the neat buttons of her grey dress, pushing it over her shoulders so that it circled her waist, puddling in a pool of cloth on the floor.

She inhaled. He saw the movement through the white cloth of her chemise. The chill air made her nipples visible, straining against the cotton. He touched her chin, tipping her jaw upwards. Slowly and tenderly, he kissed her. Her lips parted.

He ran his fingers across her shoulders. He felt the satin smoothness of her neck as he kissed her nape, running his fingers down her spine, pressing her to him, cupping her bottom so that she could feel his need.

He heard her gasp and he felt the eager quickness of her hands as they slipped under his jacket, her fingertips warm through the linen of his shirt. There was an innocent exploration in the touch.

His cravat was undone. He pulled it away, stripping off his jacket and shirt so that he was naked to the waist. Her fingers traced his muscles, igniting sparks with her touch. She pressed her palms to his chest, tangling her fingers into the fine hairs and moving closer to him so that he could feel the swell of her breasts through her cotton shift.

He liked, even more, her growing confidence, the eagerness as her body pressed closer to him, her touch emboldened.

'Do you know what you're doing to me?' he muttered.

'I have an idea.' She ran her fingers down his chest, and abdomen, slipping them under his waistband, intuitively teasing.

He groaned. Scooping her up in a quick, fluid motion, he laid her on the massive four-poster bed. He stretched out beside her. His hands roamed her satin skin, feeling the swell of her breasts as he untied her chemise. Her nipples puckered against his palm as he kissed each rosy tip.

With increased urgency, he kissed her lips, the

slim column of her neck, her soft satiny skin, as he felt the curves of her thighs and buttocks before removing her drawers.

Dolph pulled off his pantaloons, pressing her close to him. She loved the heat of his skin, the feel of his muscles and the weight of the lean length of him. His fingers touched her, igniting this searing, needful heat from deep within her body.

She hadn't known that she could feel like this… this need, this wanting. It overwhelmed thought. Control slipped. Passion surpassed cognition. She was driven by a single urge, a single need. She wanted only to be with this man, to feel him.

'I love you,' he whispered as he lowered himself into her.

'I love you too.'

Later they curled against each other, sated, content, joyful.

'I should get up and add more coal to the fire,' he whispered.

She groaned in protest. 'You keep me warm.'

He held her tighter. 'And when we're married can we do this all time?' she said.

'All the time.'

'After the wedding, we should we go to the estate

and we can banish everyone and stay by the fire,'
she said.

'All day.'

'And make love.'

'And make love,' he agreed.

'You seem a very agreeable husband,' she said.

'Indubitably.'

'I like the idea of just being together, just being
us.'

They were silent for a while. She would hold on
to this moment for ever, she thought

'What are you thinking?' he asked softly.

'That I belong. I have never belonged before. And
you?'

'Socrates.'

She laughed, raising herself onto one arm so
that she could look at him. He smiled that crooked
smile, she loved, with that one dimple. 'What about
Socrates?'

'Didn't he say something about embracing
change?' he asked as he kissed her, flipping her so
that she was on her back. 'I think we need to do
some more embracing.'

'I would never argue with Socrates.'

Chapter Fourteen

One month. Thirty days. Seven hundred and twenty hours. Forty-three thousand two hundred and twenty minutes.

Abby felt as though each second was too long but then again, there was something wonderful in the anticipation. Time moved too slowly. And time moved too fast.

They had announced their news to Lady Stanhope first, before returning to Lansdowne. Madeleine had been rendered quite speechless and had, initially, accused Dolph of making fun of her. She then suggested his continued insanity before retiring to bed.

They had left the premises before she rose again, with her powers of speech fully restored.

Mrs Harrington and Lucy were similarly dumbfounded although both swiftly pivoted from shock to elation. Indeed, Mrs Fred was the only one not astounded and appeared downright smug as though she had foretold this outcome.

Iggy shifted between disappointment that Abby would no longer be his tutor and hope that His Lordship might take him to London's foundries upon their return to the metropolis.

They chose not to stay long in Lansdowne. Mrs Harrington was very eager to shop for Lucy's debut and Abby's nuptials. Great-Aunt Edith had provided limited instruction but seemed satisfied with Lucy's progress. Besides, Mr Trollope had been writing every day and both Lucy and Mrs Harrington were hopeful that he might make an offer.

Therefore, after three days, the carriages were again loaded as the party returned to London.

Lady Stanhope visited promptly after their arrival. It was teatime and they had been sitting rather comfortably in Dolph's London house when they heard the arrival of a guest, followed by Benton's somewhat lugubrious tones announcing her presence.

Always the height of fashion, she had swept into the chamber.

Mrs Harrington was attempting a piece of needlework but hurriedly thrust this away. Handicrafts had never been her forte, and the item in question appeared to be tangled and rather more blob than pattern.

Abby was reading a book while Dolph stretched his feet towards the fire. Abby glanced at him with apprehension, but he smiled reassuringly, mouthing the word *together*. Lucy made an audible gulp, straightening as though anticipating a military review, while Ignatius was eating a large piece of sponge, an occupation he continued without pause.

'It is nice to see you. I will get a fresh pot of tea,' Abby said, nodding to Benton.

'A cup of tea, perhaps, but no sponge. I am going out later,' Madeleine said, seating herself near to the fire. 'Another debutante event, although they are less strenuous now that dear Susan is engaged. Did you see the announcement in *The Times*? Likely you noted that Susan will be married at St George's Chapel. I feel it is the very best place. Dolph and Abigail, it occurs to me that it would be much better if you were married there. It would be a more advantageous start to your married life. Indeed, all the best people are married there. I will see what I can arrange.'

'Thank you,' Abby said. 'But that won't be necessary. I have already spoken to the vicar at Lansdowne, Mr Walther.'

'Good heavens, no one will come to Lansdowne.'

'Then that will be quite perfect,' Abby said.

Madeleine frowned. 'Likely you intend to be amusing but your meaning could be misconstrued. I hope you will be more careful with your words.'

'And I hope that Abby will continue to be as blunt and honest as she has always been,' Dolph said.

If Abby had been looking for Madeleine to have a set-down she might have felt some satisfaction. She saw the older woman frown, then blink as though needing to reformulate her thoughts or find her direction in a landscape suddenly changed.

'We thank you for your offer but we only want people that we know and care about as well as the villagers and tenants to be involved,' Abby said.

'That is very unfashionable,' Madeleine said, with a slight purse of her lips.

'We know but Susan's wedding will make up for it. I hear it will be quite magnificent,' Dolph said.

'Yes, well, it will,' Madeleine said. 'One has a certain standard one must maintain.'

'Indeed, and we know you can be counted on to maintain such standards.'

'Yes,' Madeleine said, pursing her lips with a slight tsk. 'Well, as for you and Abigail, the engagement has been announced in *The Times*, so the die is cast so to speak. I will, of course, do my duty and support you both as much as possible.'

Abby glanced at Dolph, and humour flickered between. 'Thank you,' she said gravely.

'However, I don't think we will require extremely strenuous support. We are not exploring unknown lands. Or climbing mountains,' Dolph added.

'I should think not. Such activities would not be the thing at all. On a brighter note,' Madeleine continued, 'Jason does not seem disappointed that he may be less likely to inherit Lansdowne. Indeed, he said that Stanhope is quite sufficient to his needs.'

'That is a relief,' Dolph said. 'As it is my fervent hope to keep on living for some time. I am finding it rather enjoyable.'

'Yes, Jason seemed to think he could learn something from you. I find his behaviour more settled, and he quite likes you, Abigail.'

Madeleine's tone and the raising of her eyebrows suggested that she found his sentiment somewhat contradictory to common sense.

'Called you a "good egg",' Iggy suddenly announced, his mouth still full of sponge. 'I hadn't heard the term before but it is complimentary.'

'I am relieved,' Abby said. 'And please try not to talk with your mouth full. Where is Basil, by the way?'

'Mr Fred took him out for a walk. Martin says as how he is very good at training dogs.'

'Martin has just become my hero,' Abby said.

'I believe it will take more than Martin to train that animal,' Madeleine said fervently as she placed down her teacup.

'He is much improved. He hasn't eaten any roses,' his owner averred.

'We think he will fare better in the country,' Abby explained.

'How fortunate for the country. However, I did not wish to talk about that beast. I wanted to mention that Susan and I will be going shopping tomorrow. I would suggest that you might attend also. It is important that you have sufficient gowns. There will be numerous social engagements, of course.'

'Thank you. I am certain Lucy and Mrs Harrington would love to go,' Abby said, her words quickly endorsed by nods from both individuals. 'However, I will stay home. I must determine the best curriculum for the small school that I will open at Lansdowne.'

'A school—you will have more important things to do than running a school once you are Duchess.'

'Surely the education of one's youth is the most important thing that one can do.'

Madeleine frowned, as though again trying to readjust to the changing landscape. 'Well, your own children perhaps. But not village children. Not peasants. Indeed, it is absolutely vital that you develop a positive social presence in London. I really must insist that you accept my advice. I have superior knowledge in these matters.'

'Except,' Dolph said easily, 'our aim is not to do things as they have always been done but to do things differently.'

Madeleine sniffed. 'Differently? How?'

'We're working that out together. We will spend

more time in Lansdowne and less time at social events in London. Or perhaps we will go to meetings which support things like education.'

'Of the abolition of slavery,' Abby said.

'Or votes for women.'

Madeleine stared, quiet for a long moment. 'I am quite certain Father would not approve.'

'Indeed, I am counting on it,' Dolph said and then added, more gently, 'but I think Mother would have and Barnaby.'

'I have never quite understood Barnaby or you. However, those ideas are not sensible. Good heavens, they would never pass in parliament or gain any sort of support.'

'Maybe not today or tomorrow but some day,' Dolph said.

Madeleine stood. 'You are my brother and I will do what I can to protect our family name. However, I hope that you both come to your senses. You are certain you do not wish to shop tomorrow, Abigail?'

'Quite certain.'

'Very well, I will come in my carriage after lunch and pick you both up,' Madeleine said, nodding towards Lucy and her mother.

Then she stood, exiting the room with a rustle of her fashionable gown.

Lucy giggled. Iggy ate another piece of cake while everyone exhaled with some relief.

'I think she means well,' Abby said. 'She could likely run the world very effectively and it must be hard to be limited to the drawing room.'

'Are you going shopping?' Iggy asked Dolph.

'No, shopping with my sister is not one of my most favoured occupations.'

'Good,' Ignatius said. 'Then likely you will have time to show me around a foundry. Miss Carstens, you may come also, if you would like.'

'You are very generous,' Abby said.

'Do you think you will get dull and boring, like most ladies, once you are married?'

'I hope not.'

'Never,' Dolph said. 'Not while there are foundries to expand the mind.'

Dolph looked across the pews of the pint-sized country church. He recognized their faces from the last few weeks and also from childhood. He felt their warmth. He felt their approbation and a deep, satisfying, wonderful sense of belonging.

The organ's volume rose, played by Miss Robson, a nervous spinsterish woman who had played the organ at Lansdowne for ever.

Sunlight filtered through the single stained-glass window, splashing blobs of colour onto the pews and upturned faces. Grass, flowers and the mustiness of an old building scented the air.

Family and friends sat in the front row. He saw Mrs Harrington, already clutching her handkerchief and dabbing her eyes. She wore a new bonnet, which was an improvement but had a very large brim so that he quite feared for Mrs Fred. Lucy Harrington held a vial of smelling salts but seemed unlikely to require it as her expression was one of singular joy.

Ignatius sat beside his mother and he noted her restraining hand already on his knee. The Freds sat together, holding hands, and across the aisle he saw Susan, Lord Ayeburn, Madeleine, Benton, Martin and other familiar faces.

Jason stood at his side. Indeed, he had not stopped smiling, except for the occasional flicker of worry, when he felt for the ring. Mr Walther stood in front, elderly, but with an expression of such kind wisdom.

And then he heard the creak of hinges as the door opened. The murmur of voices hushed and the wooden pews creaked as the parishioners turned, angling their bodies towards the rear of the church.

She had come.

The back doors were swung wide. Sunlight splashed in, dappling the floor gold. The music grew louder and more jubilant as though competing with the fast, rhythmic beat of his heart.

His bride stood silhouetted briefly against the brightness outside. Her body swayed as she stepped forward and the doors shut behind her.

She walked steadily, not fast exactly, but with a businesslike determination which was so typical.

And she looked beautiful—no, nothing as bland as beautiful. She looked resplendent. The ivory dress clung to her slim form. The cream veil did not fall in front of her face but behind, softening her chestnut hair and framing her heart-shaped face.

The music ended. A thick silence filled the church. Dolph heard the quickened intake of her breath and the rustling movement of the veil. Their eyes met and she smiled. Her serious expression transforming into joy.

Dolph wore a dark coat and breeches and looked handsome, unbearably handsome. When he smiled, she loved him so much that it was almost painful, even as a heady joy pulsed through her.

The vicar cleared his throat. A fly buzzed. Someone coughed and a child whispered, his voice quickly shushed. She wanted to remember every detail, like pearls on a necklace, every one precious, even the most mundane. Even the fly.

Dolph took her hand, holding it as he removed the glove. She watched their fingers entwine as the vicar said their timeless vows.

And then they walked down the aisle while Miss Robson pounded on the organ with sudden confidence. Bells pealed. They emerged, blinking in the sunshine. Villagers gathered, throwing rice and flowers so that petals rained, tickling her face, sticking to her hair and splattering against the silk.

She looked at her husband. He looked at her.

'Together,' he said, lifting her hand to his lips.

'For ever.'

Epilogue

Abby sat at the desk in the small cottage close to the rectory that she and Dolph had converted into a schoolroom.

From outside, she could hear Albert, whistling rather tunelessly as he brought in more firewood for tomorrow's class. There was the nip of fall in the air, and the deciduous trees around Lansdowne had dressed the world in shades of orange and red.

Albert came in with his arms full of kindling. His hair was still wild and tufted but he had shoes and clothes. Abby quite thought Albert might learn sufficient to be a clerk or accountant.

She rose to put away the slates, ready for the morning's class. Attendance was still sporadic but increasing each day. Just then, with a series of barks, Basil, ran into the room, taking advantage of the door Albert had left open.

'Basil!' she said, trying to capture the animal but in his usual wild euphoria, he raced around the schoolroom, completing three circuits before heading back outside.

Iggy was likely coming down from the house. He had a tutor, but often visited in the afternoon.

'You head off,' she said to Albert. 'No need to build up the fire. I'm going home soon.'

Home—what a wonderful word. She had tried to create a home with her father but Lansdowne was so much more. It was a sanctuary, a place of love, belonging and discourse. Sometimes she still felt a disbelief, followed by quick spurt of joy.

She stood, picking up her cloak. Dolph had been away in London but would be home later. She always missed him but the anticipation of his return was compensation. Mrs Harrington, Lucy and George Trollope were coming also. She hadn't seen them since Susan's wedding, an extravagant affair with sufficient orange blossoms and lace to please even the most romantic soul.

Lucy had been married a month earlier than Susan and had chosen a much quieter affair at the Trollope estate.

Getting up, Abby went to the door to look for Iggy. She stepped onto the porch. The leaves rustled under her feet as she stepped into the October breeze. With that immediate surge of happiness, she saw that Dolph was coming also. He strode down the path, tall, broad shouldered and with an easy limber movement.

That quick surge of happiness pulsed through her as she hurried out, waving. Then, seconds later, Dolph's arms were around her, lifting her off her feet and swinging her around as he kissed her, the caress restrained but promising later passion.

'Ugh,' Iggy groaned. 'He's only been away three days.'

'You made it home earlier than I hoped,' she said, laying her head on his shoulder, feeling the solid, reassuring strength of him. 'I missed you.'

'I missed you so much we left early. Benton was astounded by my new-found love of early mornings,' Dolph said.

'And he got these.' Iggy waved two books at her but so fast that she could not read the titles. 'And some other books. Where should I put them?'

'Slow down. Let me take a look,' she said.

'Two new volumes of Virgil, some primers and a copy of Mary Wollstonecraft's work,' Dolph explained.

Basil had, of course, run into the schoolroom and now seemed intent on removing a piece of kindling.

'It is not a stick,' Abby said. 'I thought Martin was proficient in dog training.'

'Apparently, Madeleine may have been right in

this regard and Martin has met with a force beyond even his ability,' Dolph said.

'So what should I do with the books?' Iggy asked as he grabbed Basil, removing the kindling from his mouth.

'Virgil and the primers can stay here, but I am eager to read *The Vindication of the Rights of Women*. I read it with Miss Brownlee but that was some time ago. I hope it will inspire my own writing. I will start tonight.'

'I might have other plans for you tonight,' Dolph whispered, tickling her ear and keeping his voice low so Iggy could not hear.

Iggy was, however, somewhat occupied with an ongoing battle over kindling.

Abby laughed. 'You have brought in some heady competition in Mary.'

'I promise I am up to the challenge.'

'I know.'

Together they closed the small school and, with Basil bounding ahead, walked towards Lansdowne, its tall turret peeking out from above the multihued trees.

Abby sighed, tucking her hand into Dolph's elbow.

'Happy?' he asked.

'So happy.'

Iggy walked on Dolph's other side, as always talking and moving his hands as though explaining some new apparatus. Abby listened with half an ear. She loved the way Dolph listened, bending forward to give Iggy attention, that one dark lock of hair falling forward.

The courtyard had less moss now, the broken window had been repaired and the ivy trimmed back. The employment had helped many of the families and during the spring and summer, seeds had been sewn and crops harvested.

The Great Hall was still imposingly medieval, but Abby felt she had made peace with its history. There had been laughter here, as well as tears. Good times and bad, which she supposed was true of any house or life.

'Master Ignatius.' Mrs Fred bustled forward. 'That dog looks filthy.'

'I think he was chasing a rabbit and ended up in the mud.'

'And I am thinking he needs a bath and you might as well, before Mr and Mrs Trollope arrive.'

'I don't think I need a bath for Lucy. She is my sister,' Iggy complained.

'That's as maybe. Come on. Upstairs with you,' Mrs Fred said. 'I am not having Mrs Harrington thinking we can't keep you clean while she is away.'

'Being clean isn't really very important,' Iggy started to say but was chased upstairs by Mrs Fred while Basil was removed, presumably for a bath in the servants' quarters.

'It would appear that things are not too much changed in my absence,' Dolph said as they walked upstairs.

'I doubt Iggy will ever change. He definitely believes that growing up is optional.'

'I am glad he is not going to Eton. The village school and his tutor will be sufficient until he goes to Oxford.'

'I am glad also. I know that you didn't enjoy it.'

'Madeleine did not approve, of course,' Dolph said. 'She worries he will more closely resemble the monkeys at the menagerie than a boy.'

'How is she?'

'Still worries for my sanity and social standing. I am uncertain which is the greater concern. However, Jason is doing so well that she is quite mellow.'

Abby raised a brow.

'Well, mellow for Madeleine. I think she is happy. I have never seen her in a better humour.'

'Susan's wedding was wonderful.'

'And Jason is looking after the estate so well and no gambling at all.'

'Happiness is a wonderful antidote to bad temper,' Abby said. 'Did George and Lucy say what time they meant to arrive?'

'In a couple of hours. Lucy said that she needs frequent breaks—otherwise the nausea returns. By the by, did you ask Mrs Lamprey or Mrs Fred to make cream puffs? Apparently she craves them all the time now when she is not feeling nauseous.'

They opened the door, stepping into the bedchamber they shared.

'Welcome back,' she said, lifting her arms and pressing her lips to his.

'I have missed you,' he muttered.

'Show me,' she whispered.

'I thought you'd never ask.'

Later, she lay in the bed with her head resting on his chest, content to hear the steady thump of his heart and to feel that sated happy contentment.

'I never asked you. Were you able to talk to Mr Wilberforce?' she asked, stroking his chest with her fingers.

'I was. I also have some ideas for ensuring that the students at Lansdowne get more than just their basic letters. I believe I could convince the Philanthropic Society to support us, and wouldn't it be wonderful if we could provide schooling for more than just our own tenants?'

'Absolutely and I am so glad you brought me Wollstonecraft's work. I plan to write something similar, but I would broaden it to perhaps discuss the rights of other ethnicities.'

'Lucy and George won't be here for a while. You can start now,' he said.

Abby giggled, raising herself so that she could press a kiss on his lips. 'Maybe not now. I might have other plans.'

* * * * *

COMING SOON!

We really hope you enjoyed reading this book. If you're looking for more romance be sure to head to the shops when new books are available on

Thursday 26th October

MILLS & BOON

MILLS & BOON®

Coming next month

MISS ROSE AND THE VEXING VISCOUNT
Catherine Tinley

'It is not the custom…' Lord Ashbourne offered, his voice sounding strange, 'for young ladies to kiss bachelors in a darkened garden.'

'Lord! I am sorry! I ought not to have done it!'

'Do not—' he bit off. 'Do not apologise, Rose. Not for that. Never for that.'

His hand reached out, tracing her face as if learning it by touch, and she caught her breath. His hand was warm, and gentle, the fingers firm and smooth, and where they trailed they left a line of sensation—rather like pins and needles, only a thousand times stronger, a thousand times more pleasurable. Now his thumb was on her lower lip, gently sliding across from one side to the other, and causing some sort of havoc to unleash itself throughout Rose's body.

'Rose.' It was half speech, half groan, and it proved to be her undoing.

'Kiss me.' Rose's tone was low, but in that instant she knew she had never wanted anything more in her entire life than she wanted his kiss.

He needed no second invitation. His arms slid around her back leaving a trail of tingling fire in their wake, and he pulled her close.

Closer.

Closer yet.

So close their bodies were touching—pressing—from chest to thigh. The feel of him—warmth, strength, his heart thudding against her—set fiery desire scorching through her. At the same time his cheek brushed hers and he turned his head, trailing his warm lips over her face. Closer, ever closer to her lips.

Rose was in heaven. The sensations generated by his lips on her skin, by their bodies tightly bound together, by his strong hands on her back, seemed almost too much, so potent were they. And his lips had yet to join with hers!

He pulled her even tighter, pressing his hips to hers and moving them in circular motions which made her knees suddenly weak. Desperately she clung to him, knowing she could not possibly stand upright without him.

Now he parted his lips a little, kissing first her lower lip, then her upper one. Now the corner of her mouth, now the middle. And now...*Lord!* Now his tongue was touching her lips—just a little, now and then, but where it touched, she burned.

Continue reading
MISS ROSE AND THE VEXING VISCOUNT
Catherine Tinley

Available next month
www.millsandboon.co.uk

LET'S TALK

Romance

For exclusive extracts, competitions and special offers, find us online:

- **f** MillsandBoon
- **🐦** @MillsandBoon
- **📷** @MillsandBoonUK
- **♪** @MillsandBoonUK

Get in touch on 01413 063 232

MILLS & BOON

THE HEART OF ROMANCE

A ROMANCE FOR EVERY READER

MODERN

Prepare to be swept off your feet by sophisticated, sexy and seductive heroes, in some of the world's most glamourous and romantic locations, where power and passion collide.

HISTORICAL

Escape with historical heroes from time gone by. Whether your passion is for wicked Regency Rakes, muscled Vikings or rugged Highlanders, awaken the romance of the past.

MEDICAL

Set your pulse racing with dedicated, delectable doctors in the high-pressure world of medicine, where emotions run high and passion, comfort and love are the best medicine.

True Love

Celebrate true love with tender stories of heartfelt romance, from the rush of falling in love to the joy a new baby can bring, and a focus on the emotional heart of a relationship.

Desire

Indulge in secrets and scandal, intense drama and sizzling hot action with heroes who have it all: wealth, status, good looks...everything but the right woman.

HEROES

The excitement of a gripping thriller, with intense romance at its heart. Resourceful, true-to-life women and strong, fearless men face danger and desire - a killer combination!

To see which titles are coming soon, please visit

millsandboon.co.uk/nextmonth